HEARTBREAKS & HALF-TRUTHS

22 STORIES OF MYSTERY & SUSPENSE

Edited by
JUDY PENZ SHELUK

Superior Shores Press

PRAISE FOR HEARTBREAKS & HALF-TRUTHS

22 STORIES OF MYSTERY & SUSPENSE

"This book is a real orthopedic workout. There are stories that will shiver your spine, tickle your funny bone, and, in a few cases, drop your jaw."—*Robert Lopresti, author of* SHANKS ON CRIME *and winner of the Derringer and Black Orchid Novella Awards.*

"A stellar collection of short stories where the reader is in constant quandary. Insofar as you wish to linger on the ending of one delightful gem of a tale there is also the urge to dive into the next and to stay up into the small hours. I stayed up."—*Kevin Thornton, seven-time Arthur Ellis Awards finalist*

"A memorable collection. If you like short crime fiction with the impact of a shiv's thrust or the attention-grab of a loaded .38, this collection is right up your (very dark) alley. Yes, there's heartbreak, but those half-truths will get you every time."—CRIME FICTION LOVER

"Who hasn't had their heart broken at some point? And wasn't there always an element of deception involved? Here 22 writers explore the theme and deliver 22 strikingly different viewpoints. Prepare yourself for an entertaining journey. A satisfying literary adventure awaits."—*J. R. Lindermuth, author of* THE BARTERED BODY.

"Heartaches come in all shapes and sizes with truths, half-truths, or no truths at all, but are they filled with good intentions or mired in felonious revenge? However it is served, these 22 stories are always entertaining."—*Kathleen Costa,* KINGS RIVER LIFE MAGAZINE

PRAISE FOR THE BEST LAID PLANS
21 STORIES OF MYSTERY & SUSPENSE

"An entertaining collection of tales that deliver in all aspects. Much like buying a lottery ticket, these characters are dreaming up ways to permanently solve problems."—*Kevin Tipple, KEVIN'S CORNER*

"Sometimes the best laid plans just don't go quite as expected. And sometimes, they go exactly as hoped for. A dazzling collection of twenty-one short tales of mayhem, leaving both the reader and the corpses breathless. A five-star read that you will never forget."—*Kate Thornton, DERRINGER-nominated short story author*

"Even the best laid plans can go awry, and with these well-thought out mysteries and 'I didn't see that coming!' short stories, you get to enjoy it twenty-one times. Different styles, different settings, different murderous intentions, but all are entertaining, intriguing, and just plain fun."—*Kathleen Costa, KINGS RIVER LIFE MAGAZINE*

"Crime doesn't pay, especially for criminals who think they've found a loophole...*The Best Laid Plans* should be read by anyone who loves this genre." —*LONG AND SHORT REVIEWS*

"Delicious! That word best describes the yummy bites of well written, crafty crime stories. Murder for hire, money, sibling rivalry, envy, infidelity. Murder of the wrong person. Killer acting and get-rich schemes...the clever twists are endless. A feast of delicious short bites that adds up to a very satisfying literary meal."—*Catherine Astolfo, bestselling author and two-time winner of the ARTHUR ELLIS AWARD for Best Crime Short Story*

Heartbreaks & Half-truths: 22 Stories of Mystery & Suspense

*'Checkmate Charlie' by Gustavo Bondoni was originally published in *Robotica* (2015).

*'In the Halls of Mercy' by Rhonda Eikamp was originally published in *Fictionvale Magazine, Episode 5 (Of Magic And Mayhem).*

*'Blackjack Road' by John M. Floyd was originally published in *The Strand Magazine (June-September 2012)* and reprinted in *Deception* (Dogwood Press, October 2013).

*'Goulaigans' by Judy Penz Sheluk was originally published in *The Whole She-Bang 3* (Sisters in Crime Toronto, 2016).

*'The Short Answer' by James Lincoln Warren was originally published in *Ellery Queen Mystery Magazine* (July/August 2017)

Excerpt from 'Hard Song' by Barry Dempster (*Love Outlandish*, Brick Books, 2009) used with permission.

Excerpt from 'Cleopatra Slippers' by Judy Penz Sheluk (*THEMA*, Spring 2005; *Unhappy Endings*, 2016) used with permission.

Compiled and Edited by Judy Penz Sheluk, www.judypenzsheluk.com

Proofreading and editorial assistance by Victoria Gladwish, Gladwish on Demand Editing, www.vickigladwish.com

Cover Design by Hunter Martin

Cover Illustration by S.A. Hadi hasan

Published by Superior Shores Press

ISBN Trade Paperback: 978-1-989495-22-3

ISBN Kindle: 978-1-989495-23-0

ISBN ePub: 978-1-989495-24-7

ISBN Kobo: 978-1-989495-25-4

First Edition: June 2020

It's the crack in his heart
    where the melody lingers, the hiss
    of an old 45. How can I help
    but sing along, hard, hard song,
    unconditional illusion.

— BARRY DEMPSTER, 'HARD SONG'

INTRODUCTION

I was fifteen the first time a boy broke my heart. With shoulder-length hair, the bottom of his blue jeans frayed to perfection, and a history of changing schools, albeit not entirely by choice, he was the bad boy to my good girl.

And, of course, I fell madly, passionately in love with him.

Years later, he would get an honorable mention in my first published short story, *Cleopatra Slippers*:

> *My boyfriend of the moment had dropped me off at the corner. I wasn't allowed in his car, an ancient blue Volkswagen bug. But there was no way that I'd make curfew walking the mile home from school. It was embarrassing, the early curfews and the no-car rules, but he was pretty good-natured about it. We wouldn't last, not many relationships do at that age, but I didn't know that then.*

What I didn't mention in *Cleopatra Slippers* was the way the boy dumped me without warning.

By phone.

On Valentine's Day.

For a blonde-haired, blue-eyed girl he'd been seeing behind my back. A girl with "experience."

I wonder, sometimes, if the boy even remembers my name, let alone the lies he told me. My guess is, probably not.

And that got me thinking about the theme for the second anthology under the Superior Shores Press umbrella: heartbreaks and half-truths. Would the theme resonate with writers? I didn't know, but I was willing to give it a try.

As was the case with *The Best Laid Plans*, once again, I need not have worried. In all, 105 submissions were received, representing authors from Argentina, Australia, France, Germany, Scotland, the UK, US, and Canada. Their interpretations of the theme, from settings to solutions, went far beyond anything I could have imagined.

Culling those down to a manageable number was a daunting task, but the end result is a diverse collection of mystery fiction in which one common thread emerges: Behind every broken heart lies a half-truth.

And behind every half-truth lies a secret.

Judy Penz Sheluk

KM ROCKWOOD

KM Rockwood draws on a diverse background for her stories, including working as a laborer in a steel fabrication factory and supervising an inmate work crew in a large state prison. Since she retired from working as a special education teacher in correctional facilities, inner city schools, and alternative schools, she has devoted her time to writing and caring for her family and pets. Her published works include the Jesse Damon Crime Novel series (Wildside Press) and numerous short stories. A repeat offender, KM's short story, 'Frozen Daiquiris,' appears in *The Best Laid Plans: 21 Stories of Mystery & Suspense*. KM is a member of Sisters in Crime National, Chesapeake, and Guppy Chapters.

Find her at kmrockwood.com.

BURNING DESIRE

KM ROCKWOOD

My cousin Sophia leaned in close, her boozy breath assailing my nostrils. "Such a lovely party, Roger. Aunt Regina thought you might be pretty much down in the dumps right now, what with the wedding called off and all. She thought a party for your fiftieth birthday would be just the thing to cheer you up."

Champagne glass in hand, I maintained my plastic smile. "Kind of her."

Sophia giggled. "And she asked all of us to contribute to your gift."

"How very generous."

Annoying as Sophia was, I couldn't afford to alienate anyone in my family just now. The cancelled nuptials meant I would not be marrying Daphne Hillard Jenkins, heiress to the Jenkins pet supplies fortune.

Which meant I had lost the opportunity to access the Jenkins pet supplies fortune.

Which meant I would have difficulty paying my outstanding debts.

The syndicate that had loaned me money found that out, and decided they could wait no longer for me to begin making payments on what I owed. They demanded a payment of ten thousand dollars by midnight tonight. Or else.

I didn't have ten thousand dollars. Truth be told, I didn't have ten dollars.

When Aunt Regina proposed the party, my first reaction was horror. The entire family? In my house?

This mansion was the old family home, but I was the one who had inherited it. The costly upkeep was one of the reasons I was always short of money. Of course, the gambling had something to do with that, too. And once I began borrowing from the syndicate, I realized I was in way over my head. Marriage to Daphne was the best way I saw to resolve my financial problems.

It was not to be.

But I reflected that many members of my extended family had the means to bail me out. I had to be careful about how I approached them. If there was an extravagant birthday party, could they be persuaded to come up with gifts of cash? Possibly.

So instead of replying in the negative, I said, "A party sounds lovely, Aunt Regina. And I appreciate the gesture. But I have to confess that I'm in the midst of—how shall I say this—a temporary embarrassment. I could not fund a party right now."

"Oh?" Aunt Regina had raised her eyebrows.

"Yes. You saw Daphne's engagement ring. I overspent on it, as well as the matching wedding ring. She has not returned it. I have no way of knowing if she will. And I certainly will not stoop to asking for it."

In reality, the ring sported a huge cubic zirconium. I intended to have it replaced with a diamond when I could afford it, and the poor girl would never be the wiser. I should have realized her father would insist she take it to a jeweler to be appraised for insurance purposes.

Was that the reason she had called off the wedding?

Or had she found someone new, someone closer to her own age? I couldn't imagine that. Daphne was only in her early twenties, but she was homely and shrill. I'd assured her I found her mismatched eyes and crooked chin endearing, that my vast worldly experience had led me to the conclusion outward appearances were of minimal importance compared to inner beauty. I could blather on like that all day.

I did have some concerns about how long I could endure her nasal, high-pitched screeching day in and day out. She spoke that way even when she was happy. Especially when she was happy. Then she'd add that irritating giggle to everything she said.

"Roger?" Aunt Regina had evidently still been talking.

"I'm sorry." I shook my head. "I find, with the shock, that my mind wanders and I have trouble concentrating."

"I said I'd take care of all the arrangements. You shouldn't have to shoulder the cost of your own fiftieth birthday party."

That meant she'd need access to the house. I grimaced inwardly at the invasion of my privacy.

She added, "I'm sure, if I put the word out, people will want to help you address this 'temporary embarrassment' and your quite understandable disappointment."

With financial gifts, I hoped. "Thank you, Aunt Regina. So thoughtful of you. I would like that very much."

THE PARTY EBBED and flowed around me.

So far, no one had offered any gifts, monetary or otherwise.

Aunt Regina had pointed out an odd party decoration in the den. Sitting on my desk (oh, the violation...why had she felt it necessary to invade my most private area, the den?) was a huge eyesore of a flower arrangement.

Except they weren't actually flowers, but rather an assortment of origami nestled in greenery. Golden cranes, stubby silver stars, odd little green flowers. And folded slips of paper on picks.

It took up almost the entire surface of the desk. The phone was crowded into a corner. Heaven only knows where my pen set and pictures were.

As Aunt Regina showed it to me, I turned to face the flickering fireplace to hide my grimace and rolling eyes. When I got my facial features back under control, I forced a smile, turned to look at it, and professed admiration for the monstrosity.

"I've recently taken up origami as a hobby." Aunt Regina gave a self-satisfied nod. "And this struck me as the perfect opportunity to exercise my new skills."

"You made all those? Very impressive."

She gave me a withering look. "Several of us spent the entire afternoon yesterday creating this masterpiece. It's your fiftieth birthday, so there are fifty of each."

Reaching into the midst of the display, she pulled out one of the slips of paper. "These are affirmations. You will want to take your time and read them thoughtfully. This one says, 'We can always depend upon Roger to mediate family squabbles diplomatically and unemotionally.' How true."

I raised my eyebrows. What nonsense. The vast majority of family squabbles had to do with inheritances and trust funds. All one had to do was read the relevant paperwork to clarify facts. Which I did, and explained the terms to all parties involved.

Emotions had nothing to do with any of it.

She refolded the paper and inserted it back among the greenery. "The cranes are for health. The stars are for luck. And the flowers, of course, for prosperity."

Prosperity, yes. I could use some prosperity right now.

As the evening wore on, some of the guests began to depart.

My stomach tightened in alarm. Surely "affirmations" and folded paper doodads were not the entirety of the gifts I could expect.

Was Aunt Regina planning to call everyone together and announce a gift-giving? She liked that kind of dramatic gesture.

It would, of course, be unforgivably rude for me to bring it up. But I needed that ten thousand by midnight. Several unsympathetic and very large men would be showing up then, seeking the money. I was hoping for cash gifts, but if I could show them checks that added up to ten thousand, they would probably be willing to settle in for the night and accompany me to the bank in the morning. Not ideal, but it would do.

The caterers began to pack up. Guests left in droves.

I stood hopefully by the front door, bidding people good-bye. No one offered so much as a greeting card.

Unnerved, I went to fill my glass one more time.

When I returned, Aunt Regina herself had left.

Soon I was alone. I thought about locking and double locking the front door. But that would never keep the men from the syndicate out. They would merely break the expensive and hard-to-replace door down, leaving me with yet another bill I couldn't pay.

If, by then, I was in any shape to worry about it.

Whiskey in hand, I went into the den and stared at the origami travesty.

What was I to do? The men from the syndicate didn't fool around.

I took another gulp of my whiskey. The intricate arrangement was apparently the only gift I was to receive.

A ridiculous image of me handing the absurd composition over to the collectors when they arrived ran through my mind.

Rage and despair in a wave washed over me. I picked it up and heaved it into the fireplace. Flames flared up.

The phone rang. I answered it.

"Roger." It was Aunt Regina. "I'm so sorry I didn't get to say goodbye. My ride was leaving and I didn't see you. Did you enjoy the party?"

No point in making things worse. If I were lucky, I would be needing help with medical bills. If I were unlucky, it would be funeral expenses. Not that I would care at that point.

"Yes, Aunt Regina. Thank you."

She laughed. "I hope you enjoyed your gift! We had such trouble finding enough crisp hundred-dollar bills to fold into flowers for the arrangement. It takes three for each flower, and we had to make fifty of them. The teller at the bank was scrambling to find them for us."

Alarmed, I swung around to stare at the fireplace.

Flames were licking over the remains of the arrangement. I dropped the phone and reached for the fire tongs. I managed to extract a small portion including one of the little green flowers. I smothered the flames with my bare hands.

The edges of the flower were singed, but I ripped the petals apart. Each was a bill, with a "100" in the corners.

I heard the front door open. Heavy footsteps crossed the living room and approached the den.

PEGGY ROTHSCHILD

Peggy Rothschild grew up in Los Angeles. Always a mystery-lover, she embraced the tales of Nancy Drew and the Hardy Boys before graduating to the adult section of the library. An English major in high school, she switched to art—her other passion—in college. A repeat offender, Peggy's short story, 'The Cookie Crumbles,' appears in *The Best Laid Plans: 21 Stories of Mystery & Suspense*. Peggy has also authored two adult mysteries, *Clementine's Shadow* and *Erasing Ramona*, and one Young Adult adventure, *Punishment Summer*. Peggy is a member of Sisters in Crime National.

Find her at peggyrothschild.net.

THE DEVIL'S CLUB

PEGGY ROTHSCHILD

THERE WERE two things Jessie Mayhew hated: visitors and talking about the past. The man standing on her front stoop was a problem on both counts. Unwelcome, unshaven and underdressed for the weather, he stood in that familiar cocky way, gloved hands on hips.

"Jesus, Jess. Thought I was gonna break my fist pounding on the door. Living out here at the ass-end of the world makes me think you're trying to avoid me. That true?" Frost clung to this knit cap, mustache, and wool peacoat. A shiver shook his tall frame.

"What do you want?"

"No 'Great to see you?' No 'How you been, Al?'"

Jessie ground her teeth and gazed past him at the charcoal sky. "What do you want?"

"It's snowing out here. Why don't you ask me in?"

"It's sleet, not snow."

"Sleet, snow. Who the hell cares? Whatever it is, it's damn cold. You gonna let me in?"

Dampness darkened his jeans all the way to his knees. His feet must be halfway to frozen. Surprising he wasn't shivering more violently. But Al had always acted the tough guy. Too bad she'd figured out too late he hadn't been playing. "You walk here?"

"Neither your damn drive or the road are plowed. Had to find a turnout and leave my car up on the highway."

She knew the spot. Al had trekked at least a quarter-mile to her narrow road and another ten minutes to reach her door. Fists clenched, Jessie stepped aside and waited for him to enter.

"Not much of an invite, but I'll take it." He stamped his black high-tops against the worn linoleum, leaving clumps of snow to melt and puddle. Rubbing his stubbly jaw, he studied the knotty pine ceiling and walls. "You're a hard woman to find. Gotta say, I never expected you to wind up living someplace like this."

She closed the front door and glared at the man who, four years ago, had stomped the life from her already bruised and broken heart. "What do you want?"

"Give a man a chance to settle in. Maybe ask him to sit down or something."

"If you want to sit, sit." Jessie moved to the wood stove. Though the fire was still going, she opened the front and peered inside. It gave her an excuse to look away from him. She knew why he was here. The question was: What was she going to do about it?

The orange and gold flames reminded her of sunsets they'd once shared on the beach. Shoving away the memory, she added a couple pieces of kindling, then straightened.

She wouldn't let him hurt her again.

Behind her, a kitchen chair scraped across the linoleum. The creak of wood told her Al had sat.

"You've changed." His voice sounded both gruff and surprised.

She set the kettle on top of the stove, then retrieved a mug from the cupboard. "What? You expected me to still be the starry-eyed idiot you once knew? That girl's long gone. Thanks to you."

"Whoa. Don't go pointing any fingers at me. Running away was your choice."

Jessie moved to the shallow pantry and opened two jars, then packed a mix of leaves and berries into a stainless steel diffuser. Dropping the diffuser into the mug, she turned and walked to the stove. "What do you want?"

"Money. Of course." Al grinned and scanned the narrow kitchen again. "Doesn't look like you've spent much of your share."

"My share? I wasn't your partner. You…" She shook her head, then stared at the kettle, willing the water to boil.

"Doesn't matter. I still got the videos of us in bed. I guarantee those'll set the cops' heads spinning. Give them the final piece of the puzzle—show the reason why you hired someone to kill Tyler."

"You bas-"

"Don't know why you're so fussed. Tyler was coiled tighter than a rattlesnake on a cold night and twice as mean. How many times did that S.O.B. send you to the hospital?"

"That's not the point. And you know it. I'd already filed for divorce."

"Right. And you and I were gonna ride off into the sunset to live happily ever after. Wasn't I always telling you to take off those damn rose-colored glasses?"

"Yeah. But I didn't realize you were the one I wasn't seeing clearly."

"Hey, your husband's dead. You got the insurance money. Far as I'm concerned, I did you a favor."

She held her palm a quarter inch from the kettle. Hot enough. "I never asked you to do it." Tyler had been an abusive jerk, but the plan had been to leave, not kill him.

Steam billowed as she poured, obscuring the muddy-looking water and carrying the calming scent of mint. She cradled the mug and closed her eyes, focusing on the heat radiating through her palms as the tea steeped. Finally, she set it on the counter and faced Al again. "How much do you want this time?"

His eyes narrowed. "How much you got?" He chuckled then broke into the brilliant smile that had lured her in once upon a time. "I'm just funning. Forty grand oughta tide me over."

"You're not getting a cent until you give me the videos."

"Don't have them on me."

"I already gave you half of what the insurance company paid out. How do I know you won't come back for more?"

"If you can't trust the guy who killed your bastard husband, who can you trust?" He pointed at the mug in her hand. "You gonna offer me some coffee? I'm half-froze here."

"Don't have any."

"What the hell's that, then?"

"Tea."

"It'll do in a pinch. Maybe you got a little something to liven it up?"

"Like?"

"Geez, you really have changed. How about some bourbon? Or scotch? Anything to make it taste less like boiled leaves?"

"I don't keep alcohol in my home."

Al snorted. "You call this a home?"

Jessie cocked her head and studied the man she'd once thought was her future. Married at eighteen, disillusioned by nineteen, she'd met Al when she was twenty-one, just two days after her husband put her in the hospital for the third time. Al had been charming and funny. He'd spun a cocoon of lies she'd mistaken for a safe harbor.

He'd played her then. This time it was her turn.

"You haven't changed at bit, have you Al? You still want what someone else has." She crossed the small kitchen and handed him her mug, then returned to the cupboard and removed another. While her back was to him, she scrubbed out the diffuser, rinsed it in the sink and toweled it dry before re-opening the jar of dried leaves. After pouring the water and dunking the tea leaves, she breathed in mint again. When she faced Al, he was already gulping the hot brew.

He screwed up his face. "What is this? Tastes like crap."

"A mix of herbs and berries. Maybe you got a bad leaf. Or berry."

"Least it's warm." He tipped the mug and drained it. "Forgot you hated coffee, but even you gotta admit coffee tastes better than this stuff." He wiped a trickle of tea from his chin with his sleeve. "Anyway, about that forty grand."

"I don't have that kind of money here."

"What do you have?"

"Fifty bucks. Maybe."

"You're lying."

Jessie sighed. "Out here, I don't need much in the way of cash."

"So, we make a run to the bank."

"Closest one's in Fairbanks. That's a two-hour drive. If the weather holds." She moved to the window and pulled back the curtain. "Sleet's turning to snow. Make that a three-hour drive."

Al jumped to his feet. "Don't try to bullshit me. You can get cash at the grocery store."

"Not forty grand. Besides, the closest grocery's in Fairbanks, too. And without those videos, I'm not paying you again."

"I'll say this, you've toughened up since I saw you last. Back then you didn't know how to change a spark plug or hammer a nail. How the hell are you surviving here in the middle of nowhere?"

"Like you said, I've changed."

Al chewed his mustache. "The closest grocery's two hours away? How do you keep yourself fed?"

"I drive into town every six weeks or so. For dry goods. Got a greenhouse out back and grow and can my own vegetables."

Al looked up at the lone antler hanging on the wall. "Looks like you hunt, too."

"I mostly fish."

"That didn't come from a damn fish. What is it?"

"Moose antler."

"You killed Bullwinkle?" He chuckled. "Rocky the Squirrel must be pissed."

Jessie had always disliked the way Al laughed at his own jokes—especially when they weren't funny. But this time his laughter probably had a different cause. His pupils already looked huge. "I'm on the roadkill list."

"The what?"

"Roadkill list."

"Tell me that isn't what it sounds like."

Jessie shrugged.

"Okay, I'll bite. What happens when you're on the roadkill list?"

"If someone hits a moose or caribou near a mile marker close to here, I get called to collect the animal and clean the road. As long as it's my turn. If I can't come right out, they call the next person on the list."

Al frowned. "You eat roadkill?"

"Just because someone killed a game animal with their car is no reason for it to go to waste."

He eyed the moose antler again. "Damn, Jess. You really have changed."

"Yeah, I have."

One of Al's knees sagged. He lurched to the right. The mug landed on its side on the table. A thin brown line trickled across the oilcloth. Al managed to plant one hand on the tabletop. "Whoa. I… I'm feeling kinda funky."

Jessie studied him as he lifted his other hand and held it front of his face. His eyes appeared unfocused and his mouth hung open. He waved his fingers back and forth, nearly poking himself in the eye. The arm supporting him gave out and his elbow cracked against the table. Unable to regain his balance, he landed on his butt.

Laughing, he looked up at her. "I heard people talk about the Northern Lights. Is this what they look like?" He appeared mesmerized by his wiggling fingers.

"You're not seeing the Northern Lights, Al. You're high."

"Not so high." He laughed again. "Think the gas station att… atten… The guy at the station said something 'bout the town being thirteen-hundred feet in alti-something. You know, feet high."

Jessie walked past him and lifted her snow gear off the hook behind the door. After pulling on waterproof boots, heavy gloves, a wool hat, and sub-zero jacket, she grabbed Al's arm. His gaze stayed focused on his hand.

"Come on."

Her words seemed to break the spell his moving fingers had cast. Pupils huge, he looked at her. "Where we going?"

"Outside. You can see the Northern Lights better there." She hauled him to his feet and led him out the front door.

He staggered behind her, sneakers plunging into the crunchy snow covering her drive. Delicate flakes spun down around them. Al tried to catch one in his hand, but missed and fell. He remained sprawled in the snow bank, laughing, until she hauled him to his feet again.

"Come on."

"I don't see the lights."

"You will soon. Sun's already on the way down. Keep moving."

Ten yards later, he stumbled again. "I don't feel so good."

"You'll feel better once we get you to the road."

"Why'm I going to the road?"

"You wanted to see the Northern Lights, remember?"

"Right." He struggled to his feet and trudged on finally making it to the road. Six yards later he dropped to his knees.

Jessie stared back at her driveway, then out toward the highway. He would never make it all the way to his car. She eyed the tall spruces lining the road. Along with the crescent-shaped bend, the trees hid her and Al from the highway—and from any passersby.

Still kneeling, Al swayed, then collapsed onto his side, sinking into the snow. He wrapped his arms across his chest. "I'm cold. Got more t-t-tea? Tasted like hell. B-b-but warm."

"You always were a greedy man, Al. Taking things that didn't belong to you." Like the tea he'd downed that she'd laced with Devil's Club berries and a pinch of magic mushrooms. His giddiness and lack of coordination were the result of that greed. Shaking her head, she retreated a step.

Jessie raised her face to the leaden sky. "Storm's coming. We're supposed to get another couple inches tonight."

Snow already spangled Al's shivering form. Soon it would erase his presence—something she'd been unable to do even by moving from San Diego to Alaska. When next spring arrived, his death would be chalked up to another poorly equipped visitor succumbing to the harsh Alaskan winter. More sparkling flakes landed on top of his body.

Four years ago, Al had destroyed her life. Then he'd turned bad to worse by taunting her with the threat of framing her for her husband's murder. Threatening to release videos of them together in bed if she didn't pay up. Videos she'd been too love-stupid to realize Al was shooting.

With her husband's history of beating her bloody and breaking her bones, Jessie was the cops' number one suspect as soon as his lifeless body was found. Al knew releasing those videos would almost certainly land her in prison.

Still…for a fraction of time—when she'd felt cornered and lost and before he'd shown his true self—Jessie had thought she loved him. To her surprise, a tear ran down her cheek. She wiped it away with a gloved hand.

"Guess this is goodbye, Al. You weren't a good man. You weren't an honest man either. But you did give me hope. False hope, sure… but hope nonetheless."

With a final nod, she turned and hiked back to her cabin.

Before the next thaw, at least another thirty inches of snow would carpet the landscape. If some animal didn't get lucky and eat him first, Al's body would turn up then. There was a good chance the sheriff would knock on her door and say they found a guy frozen to death on the side of the road. He might even know there'd been a man of similar size and age asking about her around town during the winter. If that happened, Jessie wouldn't shy away from identifying Al. She might even manage another tear as she told the sheriff he'd never made it to her door.

Jessie stepped into the warmth of her small cabin and pulled off her outerwear. Now she didn't need to worry about the past any more.

Or about visitors.

JOHN M. FLOYD

John M. Floyd's short stories have appeared in *Alfred Hitchcock Mystery Magazine, Ellery Queen Mystery Magazine, The Strand Magazine, Mississippi Noir, The Saturday Evening Post,* two editions of *The Best American Mystery Stories,* and many other publications. A former Air Force captain and IBM systems engineer, John is also an Edgar nominee, a three-time Derringer Award winner, a three-time Pushcart Prize nominee, and the recipient of the Edward D. Hoch Memorial Golden Derringer Award for lifetime achievement. His seventh book, *The Barrens,* was released in late 2018. John is a member of the Mystery Writers of America and Short Mystery Fiction Society.

Find him at johnmfloyd.com.

BLACKJACK ROAD

JOHN M. FLOYD

DAVE COTTEN SAT on his back porch with a .38 revolver in his lap, staring at nothing in particular. Under other circumstances, it would have been a fine day: sunny and humid but not quite steamy, with the kind of fresh, crisp clarity that comes only after a recent storm. Squirrels chased each other in chattering zigzags across his lawn, and a light breeze stirred the leaves of the mossy oaks behind the house.

It was in the twisted shade of those oak branches that his son Christopher had taken his first steps, had staggered the eighteen inches from Victoria's outstretched arms to Dave's, all three of them laughing and clapping. Twenty-four years ago.

Dave felt a lump form in his throat. Losing Victoria had been almost more than he could bear. Now he'd lost Christopher too.

A faint, faraway sound interrupted his thoughts—the lonesome cry of a marsh bird, maybe, or the whine of a piece of farm machinery. He couldn't tell. Whatever it was, it sounded sad and tormented, and just spooky enough to send a chill down his spine and raise the hair on his forearms. He was somehow reminded (his memories had been roaming all over the place lately anyhow) of the bright, vibrant days of his youth, and of hunting trips with a weathered and soft-spoken black man named Homer Sartin. Homer, who had lost part of his right arm in a sawmill accident, had once told him, dead serious, that if you hear the scream of a panther in the fall of the year it means you'll have a good winter. He hadn't bothered to define what "good" meant, and Dave hadn't bothered to point out how foolish he thought that kind of prediction was. Not that it mattered. Whatever it was that he'd just heard, sitting here on the porch, it wasn't a panther—he figured there hadn't been a panther in these parts for twenty years—and for once Dave Cotten didn't care if the coming winter would be a good one or not.

He looked down at the gun in his hand, and for the third time checked the load. One bullet, shiny and new, taken from the box in his bedroom closet and chambered such that when the trigger was pulled it would be next under the hammer. One was all he would need.

But not yet. It was a pleasant afternoon, not as hot as usual for September, and now that he'd made up his mind he was in no particular hurry. He tucked the gun underneath the light blanket that covered his thighs and swiveled his wheelchair to face the rows of cotton that stretched away in arrow-straight lines almost all the way to the southern horizon. The fields blazed white and soft in the four-o'clock sun, almost ready for harvesting, and water stood shining in the middles from this morning's thunderstorms. A few hours from now, the rainfrogs would be in full chorus.

Not a single house was in sight from this angle, and only a couple of barns and outbuildings. Dave's only neighbor within shouting distance lived a hundred yards west, just behind him and to his right. Madeleine Fairhope, the lady Christopher had always called Aunt Maddie, even though they weren't related at all and even though Maddie Fairhope was old enough to be his *great*-aunt if they had been. At the moment she was gone into town to shop and make a mail run. It was only three miles to the post office, and she and Dave were the only two residents on Blackjack Road who'd chosen not to install curbside mailboxes. The rent for a keyed box inside the P.O. building was money they could certainly have used elsewhere, but they were both stubborn, he and Maddie, and she liked the routine of making the daily trip downtown and visiting with whomever she cornered once she arrived there. The fact that she always picked up his mail too worked out especially well for Dave. His wheelchair wasn't built for gravel driveways.

As he sat there thinking about Maddie and the fact that he wouldn't be hearing the rainfrogs' song tonight, he heard another sound, this one close at hand. He turned to his left—

And saw a man standing there in the side yard, ten feet from the edge of the porch. Looking at him.

"Good day to you, sir," the man said. He was fortysomething, wore an Atlanta Braves baseball cap, and had what Dave's late wife Victoria would have called a "hard" face, lined and pale and humorless. The sleeves and legs of his expensive-looking sweatsuit seemed too short for him.

"I've had better," Dave replied, but smiled anyway. Why be rude to the last person he might ever see?

"Name's Anderson," the man said. "I was walking by, happened to notice your faucet there. You mind?"

"Help yourself."

The stranger got down on one knee in the grass, turned the water on, and gulped from his cupped hand. When he was done he stood and wiped his mouth with a sleeve. "Strange name, Blackjack," he said, nodding—Dave assumed—toward the street sign in front of the house. "There a casino around here someplace?"

Dave smiled again. "No casinos. But I'm told there used to be an old blackjack oak, biggest one anybody ever saw, beside the Baptist church down the road a piece. It fell one night years ago and squashed the preacher's Cadillac flat as a pancake, with him and one of his lady parishioners in the back seat at the time. That must've stuck in someone's memory, when the county roads got named."

The man in the yard chuckled and rubbed his face with his wet hands. "Don't the Lord work in mysterious ways."

"Indeed he does."

"Case you're wondering"—Anderson jerked a thumb over his

shoulder—"I've had some car trouble of my own, just east of here. Left me afoot."

Dave nodded slowly. "You sure that's the only kind of trouble you've had?"

"What do you mean?"

"I mean the biggest thing just east of here's the state prison. And most folks there are afoot."

A silence passed. Each man was studying the other.

Finally Anderson cleared his throat. "You saying you think I'm on the run?"

"I'm saying I saw your picture on TV today." Dave Cotten was a little surprised at how calm he felt. He had shifted the wheelchair so they were facing each other. "You really do all those things they say you did?"

A look of something like pride flashed across Anderson's face. "You bet. And I plan on doing more of 'em, if they don't catch me and send me back."

Another silence. "I believe they said your name was Bentley."

"Bennett."

"What exactly do you want from me, Mr. Bennett?"

Anderson Bennett stepped closer to the edge of the porch. "I want you to give me your car keys."

Dave shook his head. "Can't do that."

The stranger—he was taller than Dave had first thought, at least six three—moved closer still, and pulled a black pistol from inside the waistband of his sweats. "Do yourself a favor," he said, "and hand 'em over."

"Or what?"

"Or I'll kill you."

This time it was Dave who chuckled. *Who says there's no irony in life?*

"Go ahead," he said.

And he was serious. The only thing that had been bothering him, and had bothered him for several days now, was his life insurance policy. Last week, not long after he'd gotten the news about Christopher, Dave had phoned an old lawyer friend and had his will changed. Then he called the insurance company. Maddie Fairhope, although she didn't know it, was now set up as his sole heir and sole beneficiary. Suicide would of course negate the insurance payment—he hadn't thought of that at the time. But if someone *else* killed him…

The man called Bennett hesitated. "You actually mean that, don't you?"

"'Fraid so."

"You don't mind dyin'?"

Dave glanced again at the shade beneath the oaks, heard the happy, musical voices from years ago. His passing would affect the lives of no one except Maddie and his creditors, and Maddie would wind up better off than she was now. He looked back at Bennett. "You'd be doing *me* a favor."

"Let me put it this way, then. Give me your keys, or I'll kill you and your closest neighbor. How's that sound?" Bennett waved the gun in the direction of Maddie's house. "It won't take long, and it's not like I mind going to the extra trouble."

Dave Cotten's stomach muscles clenched. It was as if the man had plucked Maddie Fairhope right out of his thoughts.

"Don't matter how many folks live there, either. I got plenty of ammo."

For the first time Dave looked closely at the gun in Bennett's hand. An automatic, a big one. Just to be saying something, he said, "You steal that, or take it from a guard?"

"I took it from a redneck citizen, like you. He's dead now, and you will be too if you don't do as I say."

Dave shook his head, his mouth dry. "I told you, I can't give you my car keys."

"Why not?"

"Best reason in the world. I don't own a car."

"You what?"

Dave spread both hands, as if to emphasize the wheelchair. "Regular car's no use to me, and I can't afford a customized ride. As for my neighbor, she's not home."

"She?"

"A widow. Lives alone, like me."

Bennett gave him a long stare.

"What's the matter?" Dave said.

"I don't believe you."

"Which part don't you believe?"

"That she's not home. You're just trying to save her skin."

"Take a look, then." Dave leaned back so the convict could see past him. "That building with the window is her garage—you can see it's empty."

"Where is she?"

"Gone to town." But as soon as he uttered those words he knew he shouldn't have. "Not to our town. I mean to Vicksburg, to visit her daughter. She won't be back till tomorrow," he added quickly.

Too quickly.

Bennett sighed. "You ain't a good liar, my friend." He glanced down at his fancy wristwatch. *Stolen,* Dave thought. *Like the gun, and the cap, and the too-small clothes.* "I think I'll just wait for her."

Dave blinked, thinking hard. "You don't want to do that," he said.

"Why not?"

"Because I phoned the police already. I saw you in the distance, long before you got here. The news said to be on the lookout." He tapped the crystal of his own watch, doing it fast to hide the trembling of his hand. "They should be here in a few minutes."

"Let me get this straight. You phoned the police."

"Yep."

"And they're on their way."

"That's right."

"And your neighbor'll be gone until tomorrow."

"At least."

Bennett nodded at the wheelchair. "How'd you manage that?"

"Manage what?"

"How'd you call the cops? Roll inside to the phone, make the call, and roll outside again?"

"I used my cell phone."

"And where's your cell phone now?"

"In my bag." Dave pointed to a deep leather pouch hanging from the right arm of his wheelchair. "Want to see it? Check the call log?" *Make him come closer,* Dave thought. *Make him lean over to look...*

Bennett seemed to ponder that. "If you saw me and had time to call the cops before I saw *you,* why'd you stay out here on the porch? Why didn't you go inside and lock up, or get a gun to defend yourself with?"

"I didn't go inside because I'm not afraid of you. Did I not make that clear?"

"That's right, I forgot. The death-wish thing."

"The I-got-nothing-to-lose thing. As for a gun, I already had one."

"Oh, you did, huh?"

"I still do," Dave said. "It's in my bag, here."

"With the cell phone."

"That's right. Want to take a look?"

Bennett narrowed his eyes. "You normally sit out here on your porch with a gun in a pouch hanging from your wheelchair?"

"I've found it handy," Dave said. "Now and then a snake crawls into my yard."

For a moment neither of them spoke. Bennett was apparently smart enough to pick up the double meaning, and laughed aloud. "I think I like you, Mr.—I don't believe I caught your name."

"David Cotten."

"Cotton?"

"With an 'e.' Like Joseph. The actor." *Keep him talking,* Dave said to himself. *If he'll just move closer, and look away for more than a second or two—*

"You any kin to 'King' Cotten?"

"Kingston. He was my grandfather."

"I heard of him." Bennett raised one eyebrow, then glanced up and around, taking in the once-grand house and grounds. "Don't look like you came out too well, inheritancewise."

Dave shrugged. "My daddy ran into hard times." He thought a moment and said, "Both of us did."

"Haven't we all. What do you do now? Anything?"

"Research, for private clients. Historical stuff, mostly. Internet searches."

A wide grin. "What you're saying is, you're not only crippled, you're worthless."

"Not as worthless as you."

Bennett barked another laugh. "As I said, David Cotten, I believe I like you. Even though you're crazy as a treeful of owls." He paused. "But I don't need your company while I wait on your neighbor to come home. And I got a feeling she won't be gone long."

Because of his height, and standing as he was, on the ground beside the raised porch, the escaped inmate's head was almost on a level with Dave's, and about six feet away. Bennett took two steps closer and raised the stolen gun.

Dave realized he'd waited too long. He tensed, ready to reach for the revolver under his blanket. He wouldn't be fast enough—he knew that—but he had to try. Not for himself but for Maddie.

"Nice meeting you," Bennett said, and aimed the big pistol straight at Dave Cotten's forehead.

Then they both heard a voice, from the side yard.

"Davey," a woman called. "You back there?"

Both men turned to see Maddie Fairhope march around the corner and up the steps to the porch. Clutched in her hands were a colorful wad of mail and a washbucket half full of peaches. Bennett, with an expression somewhere between amusement and annoyance, had taken off his baseball cap and placed it over the gun. Dave knew it was still pointed at him.

"Well," Maddie said. "Who's this?"

Bennett nodded to her, his shaved head gleaming in the sun. "My name's George Anderson, ma'am. Just stopped to chat."

"Glad you did—it's a good day for visiting. Rain's cleaned everything off. How you feeling today, Davey?"

Dave swallowed. "We're kinda busy here, Aunt Maddie. Why don't you—"

"I'll put these peaches in the kitchen for you, and get out of you menfolks' way." She opened the screen door and disappeared inside.

Dave leaned forward, the hidden revolver heavy in his lap. "She's just a kind old lady," he said. "And she doesn't recognize you. Don't hurt her, okay?"

Before he could say more, Maddie Fairhope appeared again. "Left your mail on the table. Mostly advertisements, except for this." She handed him an official-looking envelope.

She stomped back inside—"I'll just wash up these lunch things"—but Dave had stopped seeing or hearing her. He was staring at the envelope's return address. For the moment, even the stranger and his gun and his threats were forgotten.

Dave Cotten ripped open the envelope, unfolded the letter inside, read the first paragraph—

And felt his heart turn over. His body went rigid; hot tears blurred his vision.

Bennett, who was staring past Dave to watch the screen door, didn't seem to notice. He replaced his cap on his head and hefted the gun in his hand. "After I shoot you both," he said, as if commenting on the soybean crop, "I'll be relieving you of whatever cash you got in the house. Care to tell me where it is?"

Dave pulled himself together, looked Bennett in the eye—the man was standing barely four feet away now, and half-smiling—and said, "You won't have time."

Bennett frowned. "I what?"

"Don't you hear that noise?"

"Hear what noise?"

With the letter still clutched in his left hand Dave Cotten pointed north, toward Blackjack Road, and when Bennett turned to look, Dave reached underneath his blanket with his other hand, took out the pistol, and shot Bennett square in the left temple.

For several long seconds the tall man stood there expressionless, like an unplugged robot. Then everything went slack—forehead, jaw, shoulders, arms, legs—and he fell face-first into the mud.

From the kitchen Maddie called, "Davey? What was that?"

Dave looked over his shoulder and saw her standing at the door, holding a spoon and a drying cloth. Bennett's body was hidden from her view by the porch's edge.

"What are you doing—shootin' at rabbits from the house?"

He turned again and cleared his throat, afraid to trust his voice. He backed the wheelchair away from the edge of the porch, set the smoking revolver on the floor beside him, and looked down at his gun hand. It was shaking. His left hand still held the letter. He drew a long breath and said, "Could you come here a minute? We need to talk."

He heard the screen door slap shut, heard her footsteps approaching.

"Where'd that Mr. Anderson go? Is everything all ri—"

"They found him," Dave said, looking up at her. He held up the letter and swallowed hard. "They found Christopher. He's alive."

She stopped in her tracks. "Christopher?" she said. She still hadn't seen Bennett's body.

He could feel the tears again, stinging his eyes.

"But…his whole unit," she whispered. "They said everyone in his patrol was—"

"He survived. They found him yesterday, in the rubble. He's hurt, and dehydrated, but he'll live. Aunt Maddie, my boy's coming *home*."

She dropped the spoon and dishcloth and ran to him, knelt beside the wheelchair, squeezed him in her arms. Both of them were sobbing.

Finally Dave pulled away, still sniffling, far enough to look her straight in the eye.

"There's one more thing," he said. And pointed toward the edge of the porch.

DAVE COTTEN HAD NEVER OWNED a cell phone. Until now, he'd never seen the need for one. Maddie made the call to the police from the wall phone in his kitchen while he waited on the porch. The precious letter was folded carefully in his shirt pocket. The county sheriff arrived twenty minutes later, followed by a small army of granite-faced state policemen and prison honchos.

When the questioning was finished and the body had been ID'ed and photographed and carted away, Sheriff Wingate handed Dave back his revolver. It was clear to everyone that the shooting was self-defense: Bennett's stolen gun had been out and underneath his body, and there were no wheelchair marks or anyone else's footprints on the muddy ground near the corpse. The case was closed before it was ever opened. Though no one said so, the prison officials looked relieved that Bennett was dead and the state cops looked irked that they hadn't been the ones to shoot him. The sheriff just looked tired.

"Something I been wondering about," he said. "Why was there only one round in your pistol?"

Dave thought about that for a moment. "One was all I needed."

After the law-enforcement parade finally left, he and Maddie Fairhope sat side-by-side, wheelchair-by-rocker, in the spot where he'd been sitting before all this started. The wind had died with the approach of dusk, and tendrils of Spanish moss hung as straight and still as gray icicles from the lowest branches of the oaks. After a while Maddie said, "You saved me, you know." She looked at him. "He would've shot us both."

"You saved me first. If I ever accuse you of butting in…well, just remind me of that."

"I will."

They both fell silent. It would be dark soon, and September or not, cooler than usual or not, Dave could still feel the last of the heat baking off the wet yard. Out in front of the house, on Blackjack Road, he heard a heavy truck rumble past.

He figured Maddie had probably overheard the sheriff's comment about there being only one bullet in the revolver, and that she might have figured out—or at least suspected—the reason. Maddie Fairhope didn't miss much. And if she'd figured that out she might also have realized that not only had they saved each other, but that Bennett might have wound up saving Dave. If not for the escapee's arrival on the scene and the delay that it had caused, Dave Cotten might've ended up using that bullet as planned, before Maddie returned from town with the mail.

Maybe everything *did* happen for a reason...

Dave found himself gazing once more at the distant fields, at the land his grandfather had worked, and his father too until most of it had to be sold to pay gambling debts. Jeremy Cotten had crawled into a whiskey bottle shortly afterward and had never come out; Dave could scarcely remember him. The rest of the land Dave had been forced to sell two years ago, to pay funeral expenses and medical bills after the car accident that had taken away his wife and both his legs below the knee. Dave wondered idly if old man Tollison would consider selling part of the property back to him, now that Dave's only son was coming home.

"You think he'll stay?" Maddie asked him.

"What?"

"Christopher," she said, reading his thoughts as she always did. "Aren't you wondering, when he gets back and gets well, whether he'll stay?"

Dave felt himself grin. "It's nice just to be able to wonder, about something like that."

She didn't reply, but he knew she was smiling too. After a long moment she heaved herself out of the rocker. "How about I fix you some supper?"

"I'm not that hungry, Aunt Maddie."

"How about a peach?"

"I'd love a peach."

And he sat there listening to her bustle about in the kitchen, sat there smelling the damp grass and dirt and leaves, feeling the warmth of the dying sun on the right side of his face and the warmth of the letter against his chest.

All of a sudden he heard that sound again—louder this time. And this wasn't the screech of a night bird or the metallic scream of a distant combine; he would recognize those. This was the sound of a woman shrieking, a woman dying, somewhere in the darkening bottomland west of Maddie's house, near the river—a piercing wail that set his already frayed nerves on edge and froze his mind. It seemed to last half a minute or more.

Behind him the screen door opened, and Maddie Fairhope stuck her head out. He swiveled his chair and saw that her eyes were wide and surprised but not frightened.

"Panther," she said.

Dave Cotton blinked, his heart still hammering. "What?"

She just nodded, as if to herself. "We'll have a good winter." She smiled at him, then turned and vanished again into the house.

He leaned back in his chair, his fingers easing their deathgrip on the armrests, his breathing returning to normal. He sat there and watched the last of the light drain from the day, and thought about Victoria and escaped convicts and big cats gliding silently through the swamp, and the simple joy of being alive and hopeful. Most of all, he thought about his son the soldier, resurrected and on his way home.

Off to the west, in the bottoms, rainfrogs began to sing.

JAMES BLAKEY

James Blakey's fiction has appeared in *Mystery Weekly*, *Crimson Streets*, and *Over My Dead Body*. His story 'The Bicycle Thief' won a 2019 Derringer Award. He lives in suburban Philadelphia where he works as a network engineer for a software consulting company. When James isn't working or writing, he can be found on the hiking trail (he's climbed thirty-eight of the fifty US state high points) or bike-camping his way up and down the East Coast. James is a member of the Short Mystery Fiction Society.

Find him at JamesBlakeyWrites.com.

THE GREATEST SECRET

JAMES BLAKEY

AUGUST 1962

My Fairlane backfires, drawing glares from the foursome of old-timers lining up putts on the ninth green. I return shaking fists with a friendly wave and continue up the looping driveway to the valet station.

A blond surfer-type in a red vest looks like he'd rather be out on the water. He raises an eyebrow at my car: unpainted front-left quarter-panel, missing hubcaps, crack in the windshield. The engine continues to sputter, black smoke rising from the tailpipe.

"Don't go drag-racing my ride." I slip a buck into his palm.

He glances at the bill like I handed him a dead rat. I bet he's thinking of abandoning my car at the boneyard.

I climb the set of stone steps to the clubhouse and am met at the entrance by a slender redhead.

"Can I help you?" She frowns at me like I'm crabgrass on the fairway.

I squint at the name embroidered on her blazer. "Hi, Linda. Phil Zlotnick. Here as a guest of Mr. DiMeglio."

She consults her list. "Yes, Mr. DiMeglio is expecting you on the terrace."

"Great. Let's go meet him." I take one step forward.

She slides in front of me, holding up her hand. No ring. Long red nails. "The Club Rules require gentlemen to wear a jacket and tie." *THE CLUB RULES.* The capitalization is clear in her voice.

I shrug. "I don't have a tie, Linda. But we both know Mr. DiMeglio isn't the sort of gentleman who likes to be kept waiting."

She ignores that. "I guess your jacket will do." She gives me a look like she ate a bug. "And we can lend you a tie." From beneath her station she produces a selection.

I grab a solid blue one, slip it around my neck, and fumble a knot. Linda leads me to the terrace that overlooks the lawn tennis courts. On the nearest court, two ladies swat the ball like it's an annoying mosquito.

Johnny DiMeglio sits at his table under a giant umbrella. I recognize from him the papers. Big trial last year. Not guilty on all counts. Salt-and-pepper hair. Roman nose. He's reading *The Racing Form.* Open collar and no jacket. Some animals are more equal than others.

Linda says, "Mr. DiMeglio? Your guest, Mr. Zlotnick has arrived."

DiMeglio doesn't stand or offer his hand. "Have a seat, Phil."

I comply. "Pleased to meet you, Mr. DiMeglio." He doesn't suggest I call him Johnny.

I have no idea *why* DiMeglio wants to see me, but it's not a mystery why we're meeting here. My office is little bigger than a shoebox and on the wrong side of the tracks, squeezed between a takeout rib joint and a pawn shop.

The real question is why I'm here at all. I'm a one-man operation. I do missing persons, cheating spouses, insurance investigations. DiMeglio's our city's number one crime lord. His organization is plenty capable of doing anything I can, and plenty I can't or won't. If he needs to go legit, he could hire one of the big firms like Waterbury. I say a silent prayer that I haven't run afoul of DiMeglio's business interests.

DiMeglio says, "I suppose we should get down to business. Are you married, Phil?"

I hold up my hand, showing no ring. "I was lucky to escape."

He doesn't seem to think that's funny. "I'm married. Wonderful lady. No children yet, but I am already rich in my blessings."

"Marital bliss. Glad someone's enjoying it."

"However, it has come to my attention that my beloved wife is having an affair. While this pains me deeply, I am a forgiving man. Plus, the church frowns upon divorce."

I fake-frown in mock sympathy. Does the church say anything about having one of your goons throw acid in a reporter's face?

His voice takes on a hard edge. "But the man who seduced her into adultery, this I cannot forgive. He must be made to pay for his sins. And he will pay here on Earth. Justice and vengeance cannot wait until the next world."

I ask, "And who is this unfortunate man?"

"That's what I'm hiring you to find out."

Now I understand. An unfaithful wife is quite an insult to a guy like DiMeglio. If the other syndicates, or some of his own people, found out, they could take it as a sign of weakness and be tempted to act.

He says, "Ten thousand, total. That's to cover everything. I don't want to be nickel-and-dimed on expenses. Five thousand up front. The rest when you give me the name."

I lie to myself that DiMeglio's just going to scare this guy off, but even I don't buy my own BS. At a minimum, Mrs. DiMeglio's paramour is going to have several body parts broken. Worst case: He'll never be seen again. As long as DiMeglio doesn't tell me his plans, I'm in the clear, legally. Ethically is another matter. But I could use the money: Fix up my beater, get current on the rent, maybe take a vacation. And if it's not me, some other PI will be happy to puzzle it out for the fee. Lover boy's fate is already sealed, no matter what I do. Plus, any fool who sleeps with Johnny DiMeglio's wife should know better.

I say, "Ten sounds fair."

"And I must also have your complete discretion." DiMeglio stares at me with eyes blacker than ink. "If this was to become public, if you was ever to discuss this matter with another living soul, I would be...quite disappointed."

That doesn't sound healthy. "I understand you completely, Mr. DiMeglio."

"Johnny!" A tall blonde in tennis whites leans over, touches DiMeglio on the shoulder, and kisses him on the cheek. Sweat glistens on her tanned skin. I can't decide which is more impossible, her short skirt or her long legs.

"How'd you do today, Darling?" asks DiMeglio.

"I won! Beat Julia Davenport in straight sets."

"Julia's good. Now, I know who I'm betting on in the Club Championship."

"Oh, you!" The blonde playfully hits his chest with her fist.

DiMeglio notices my amusement at the scene. "Amanda, this is my associate, Phil Zlotnick."

"Hi, Phil," She flashes me a dazzling white smile.

"Hi Amanda!" I reflexively grin back.

"Anyway, Johnny, I've got to run. Need to shower up. I'm having lunch with Patty and Violet. Bye, Phil. Nice meeting you. Toodles." She waves goodbye and glides away on those long legs.

"Amanda's a friend," DiMeglio explains.

"She does seem friendly."

He resumes his dour demeanor. "Here's the first half of the money, a photo of my wife, and her schedule." He passes a bulky manila envelope across the table. "I'll explain to my people not to bother you if they spot you near my home."

"Okay." I open the envelope, see the green inside, slip out the photo, and gasp.

"Quite a looker. Isn't she, Phil?"

Glossy brown hair down to her shoulders, not a strand out of place. Gray eyes the color of winter clouds. Cheekbones so sharp they could slice a pizza. And a smile like she knew the greatest secret in the world. And if you were nice enough, good enough to her, she just might share it with you.

I know this face.

And the rest of her.

Intimately.

I'm the one sleeping with Johnny DiMeglio's wife.

THE DRIVE back from the club is nothing more than a blur. I'm lucky I don't wrap the car around a telephone pole. I stagger into my office, lock the door, and pull down the shades. With shaking hands, I retrieve my revolver and an ankle holster from the filing cabinet. I slide up my pant leg, strap on the holster, and slip the gun in. Not going anywhere, even the shower, unarmed.

I sit at my desk and grab the bottle of Limestone Cave from the bottom drawer. I miss the glass and spill whisky all over the blotter. I give up and drink straight from the bottle.

Does *he* know?

Johnny doesn't have a reputation for subtlety. He's not a cat playing with a mouse. If Johnny DiMeglio is after you, you'll know it.

Unless sleeping with his wife is a whole new level of game playing for Johnny.

What if he's not sure? He suspects and wants to see what I'll do? And a bunch of his goons are watching, ready to drop me if I hightail it out of town?

No. If Johnny has suspicions, he'd take the direct approach and beat the truth out of me.

What if I go back and say I'm too busy? Here's your five thou back?

Nope. You don't turn down a guy like Johnny DiMeglio.

The door rattles.

I put down the bottle and grab my gun. I wobble across the floor and lean against the wall. The door jiggles again. So, Johnny does know and sent one of his boys for me. The action plays out in my head: I flip the latch, grab the knob, open the door, shove the pistol in his face, ready to fire.

Here goes.... One.... Two....

A mess of envelopes tumble through the mail slot to the floor.

The freaking mailman!

I wipe the sweat from my brow, pick up the mail, return to the desk. I take another swig from the bottle. The whisky burns as it trickles down my throat.

What if I go back to Johnny in a week and say I can't find anything? Maybe it's over. Tell him, "Mr. DiMeglio, I followed your wife everywhere. I can assure you whatever happened in the past, she's not having an affair now."

That might work. Unless he isn't satisfied and gives the job to someone else. I didn't cover my trail, didn't think I needed to. Even a PI who's in the bag and half-blind could dope out that I'm the guy.

Could I convince Johnny that it's all a big mistake? That there is no affair and Susan is completely loyal.

I don't think you can convince a guy like DiMeglio. Once he gets an idea into his head, it stays there.

The smart thing is to play it straight. Johnny hired me to come up with a name. That's what I need to do. But how am I g—

The phone rings.

It's Mike O'Malley. Asking how the skip trace is going on Angel Ramirez. The bottle is half empty; I slur my words into the phone. I assure Mike that I've got a hot tip and should have Ramirez any time now.

Mike is insistent that I track him down yesterday.

I continue to spin lies and tell Mike I'm close. But the last thing in the world I'm worried about is tracking down some random deadbeat.

I hang up and focus on the problem at hand.

Susan.

Smart, lovely, funny Susan. With her inquisitive eyes and a scent like peach blossoms. And that smile. How I want to, need to, hold her in my arms right now. And protect her from Johnny. I don't trust him on the matter of forgiveness.

Could Susan run away? Could we run away? How far does Johnny's reach extend? Florida? Argentina? Australia? I always wanted to see a kangaroo.

What could I do there? I'm a decent PI, but I have no connections. Hire on to a big security outfit? Or maybe it doesn't matter what I do. I'm not afraid of hard work, never have been. I imagine the life Susan and I could have down under.

I take another swig from the bottle. And my fantasies of life in Australia turn to resentment.

Susan didn't tell me. Sure, she said she was married. And maybe I should have been a better guy and not have gotten involved with her, but I did.

But if she told me when we first met, when I first saw her eyes, those legs, and that smile that she was married to Johnny DiMeglio what would I have done?

Walking away would've been the smart play.

But I never was too smart. Doesn't matter now. What's done is done. But I would like an explanation from the lovely Susan as to what she was thinking, now that my life's on the line.

And a plan. I need a plan. And I need to talk to Susan about the plan. But I can't approach her, because DiMeglio's goons could be tailing her. Or me. Or both of us. Not likely. It makes sense Johnny wants to keep this quiet, but I can't run the risk.

This Thursday afternoon, Susan and I have a rendezvous scheduled at the Jack and the Beanstalk Motel. I need to come up with a plan by then, one that saves both our lives.

I lift the bottle and drain the last of the whisky as I consider all the different ways Johnny DiMeglio has of killing me.

MONDAY MORNING and I'm pretending to tail Susan. No, I'm really tailing her. I park down the hill from her house, slouched in the driver's seat of a green Dodge. I swapped rides with Scooter McDuffy. Wouldn't be good if Susan spotted my Fairlane following her.

She cruises right past me in her blue MG, hair dancing in the wind. I want to hold her, slap her, kiss her, and shout at her. My stomach feels like it's doing the bop. I'm medicating with whisky. I don't dare approach her. I don't think Johnny's goons are watching, but they might be.

After three days of following Susan to the country club, the hair salon, the library, lunch with friends at El Dorado, and the Junior League, I'm convinced no one else is following her.

Thursday, day four, and it's time for our rendezvous. Jack and the Beanstalk Motel is south of the city. Caters to families on vacations and couples who need a place. I get there thirty minutes early, check-in with a phony name, and pay cash. I use a different name each week. The clerk doesn't care. I have my car back from Scooter and park in front of number eleven.

While I wait, I work on another bottle of Limestone Cave. I'm four shots in when there's a knock. As I toddle to the door, I consider that it's Johnny or one of his boys. That Susan spilled the beans, or he beat it out of her.

I look through the peephole. It's Susan. She looks marvelous in a sleeveless lime green dress, a string of pearls around her lovely tanned neck.

I swing open the door. Susan launches herself at me. Embraces me. Hands slide down my back. Her tongue explores my mouth. I'm a statue. My arms at my side. I don't kiss back. I want to.

She breaks the embrace. "What's going on?" A look of concern on her face.

"Your husband. H—"

"You're drunk." She cops an attitude. Face hard. Smile gone. "I told you I was married when we began this."

"Yeah, but you didn't tell me *who* you're married to?"

"You found out?" She glares at me, sits on the corner of the bed, takes out a cigarette, and lights up. "Did you follow me?"

I laugh.

"What's so funny?"

"Johnny hired me to follow you."

"Johnny?" The blood drains from her face.

"Yep, Johnny knows that you're stepping out on him."

"How?" She's shaking like a Mexican hairless in a blizzard.

"Don't know. Didn't ask."

"You talked to Johnny?" She puffs harder on her cigarette.

"Yep. Your dear sweet husband brought me out to your fancy country club. Told me the whole story. He's paying me ten grand to find the guy."

"He doesn't know it's you?" Her face is incredulous. "But why did he hire you?"

I shrug. "Can't do it with his guys. Wouldn't trust a big firm."

"Yeah, makes sense." She blows a smoke ring. "But you took the job?"

"What am I going to do? I'm not in a position to say 'No' to your husband."

She stubs out her cigarette in the ashtray. "What are you going to tell him?"

"I'm thinking I'd rather emigrate. I hear Buenos Aires is nice. Always wanted to learn to tango. Maybe the other side of the world is beyond Johnny's reach."

"You'd leave? But what about me?" Her lips form a tiny pout.

"You're fine. Johnny forgives you. He made that plain."

She shakes her head. "You don't know Johnny. You run. He'll put it all together. Then I'm the one who's going to pay the price."

"So, what do you think?"

She smiles that smile, and my knees go wobbly. "Come sit with me. I think we both run, together. We head to Reno. I establish residency and file for divorce."

I'm next to her on the bed. Her hair smells like summer air after a thunderstorm. "Reno? We'll be sitting ducks."

"You hide out. I'll get a divorce lawyer. He'll let Johnny know that if anything happens to me, a letter detailing all of his crimes will be delivered to the police. I know enough to send him to the gas chamber."

"Then what?"

She fiddles with my collar. "In the divorce settlement, I get enough to go far away." She leans close. Her breath hot on my neck. Her lips brush my ear. She whispers, "What about Australia? I always wanted to see a panda bear."

"Koalas. Pandas live in China." I grab Susan and hold her tight. She kisses me. This time I kiss back.

We break the embrace, only when we need to come up for air.

"Are you in?" She's unbuttoning my shirt. "Ready to start our lives over?"

"When?"

"Just wait for my call."

It's a dangerous plan, but the only one we've got. I unzip her dress, and we go from sitting to horizontal.

BEFORE SHE LEAVES THE MOTEL, I give Susan my gun. Insurance in case Johnny becomes a little less forgiving. While I wait for her call, I tie up the loose ends of my life: sell my television to the pawn shop, settle up accounts with Bobby G., give General McArthur, my orange tabby, away to a neighbor.

Johnny phones once, asks about my progress. I tell him Susan hasn't seen anyone. And suggest that the guy might have gone out of town on business or that he's a family man and he's taking the wife and kids on a final summer vacation before Labor Day.

Johnny grunts. "Keep watching."

Wednesday afternoon Susan calls me from a payphone. "It's tonight. Johnny's going bowling with the guys. He always stays out late. Come by about seven. We'll have a few hours head start, and he won't know what direction to look."

"Your place? Can't we meet somewhere else?" Last thing I want is running into Johnny by accident.

"You got to help me with my bags. Just come over. It will be fine."

At 7:05, I arrive at the DiMeglio's place, my nerves as tight as piano wire.

When I was pretending to follow Susan, I always picked up her car down the street, never got a good look at the house. DiMeglio's place is like a mansion transported from Italy—marble columns, statues, and bubbling fountains everywhere.

I ring the bell. It's really happening. Susan and I are going to drive through the desert and start our new lives together. I'm giddy like a teenager on his first date.

Johnny answers, and my heart stops.

"Hey there, Mr. Shoe Leather. You okay? You look pale."

I shake off my disbelief. "Just something I ate."

"So, I'm assuming that you're here to give me the name."

"Yes," I lie. Where is Susan? Is this a setup? Did DiMeglio figure it out? My mind reels as I try to concoct a story I can sell.

"In that case, come on in." DiMeglio's wearing a lavender dress shirt, black slacks and pointy shoes.

"Honey, who is it?" Susan enters the room. She's wearing a red-and-white checked top and tan capri pants.

Johnny says, "This is an associate of mine, Phil Zlotnick. Phil, this is my wife, Susan."

I nod. "A pleasure to meet you, Mrs. DiMeglio."

Her face is tight, the smile forced. I try to read her eyes. Is that fear?

"Likewise, Mr. Zlotnick."

"Susan, can you get Ernie to fix us a couple of drinks? I'll take a gin and tonic. And what about you, Phil?"

"How about a beer?"

Susan says, "I gave Ernie the night off. I'll get the drinks."

Johnny growls. "Why'd you do that?" He starts to raise his hand, but stops. "Fine. Phil and I will be in my office."

DiMeglio escorts me down a hallway to his office, closes the door, and takes a seat behind a massive desk. There's a bay window that looks out over a pool. Bookshelves line two walls. Dickens, Austen, Dumas, Dostoyevsky. Johnny doesn't strike me as a reader.

He sees me glancing at the shelves. "Yeah, I can't get into the high-brow stuff. Susan picked them all out. Just give me a good Mickey Spillane."

"Mike Hammer's a little too violent for my tastes," I say.

Johnny grins. "Violence, and the threat of its use, are a great tool in the proper hands."

I nod.

Johnny asks, "So you got the name?"

"I do." I've been thinking about this since he opened the door, trying to come up with a tale that won't have any holes.

"Photographs?"

I shake my head. "Didn't take any. Didn't think you wanted to take the risk of anything turning up. No notes either. It's all up here." I tap the side of my head.

Johnny nods. "Smart thinking. What's the name? If you're thinking I'm paying the other five before you give it to me, it doesn't work that way."

"Of course." Here goes nothing. "His name is Angel Ramirez."

A blank look on Johnny's face. "Who the hell is Angel Ramirez?"

"Small-time alley rat."

Johnny shakes his head. "Susan with a Goddamn Mexican third-rater."

"He's from the Dominican Republic."

"Same thing." Johnny waves his hand dismissively. "And where is he now?"

"Gone," I say.

"Gone?" Anger in his eyes.

"From what I've pieced together he went home to the island. The word is he won't be back in the country until March at the earliest."

"The Dominican Republic? That's in the Caribbean?"

I nod. "Yeah."

Johnny frowns. "Maybe I can call Davey Four Cats in Miami, and he can get me a line on this guy." He drums his fingers on the desktop. "I would have appreciated this information a little faster."

"I wanted to be sure."

"And you're sure?" He glares at me. "I'll pay when *I'm* sure."

"Fine." The money is the least of my worries. Looks like I've saved the plan for now.

A knock.

"Come in, Susan." Johnny's lips twist into a malevolent grin.

The door squeaks open.

I think Susan is safe. He won't do anything to her, yet. Johnny wants confirmation it's Ramirez. For now, I ju—

A gunshot explodes to my left. A second and another.

Johnny's lavender shirt erupts in red. He slumps in his chair. Eyes open but lifeless.

Susan rushes behind the desk, ignoring Johnny's body.

It takes a few seconds for the shock to wear off. "Wha—what are you doing?"

"Change of plans." She puts down the gun. My gun. She's rifling his desk.

"No, no, no. We need to think about this. The cops. Johnny's guys. The other mobs."

"I've got it all thought out." From one of the drawers, Susan pulls a pistol and points it at me. "The hotheaded lover and the jealous husband kill each other in a gunfight."

The woman I risked everything for, the woman I loved, still love, flashes her smile at me. And now I know the greatest secret in the world. Her secret.

"How long did you have this planned? From the beginning?"

She shrugs. "Does it matter?" She pulls back the hammer.

"I guess not."

No place to run. Nowhere to hide. Doesn't matter. A gut shot couldn't hurt worse than my broken heart.

EDWARD LODI

Edward Lodi, whose felonious career began at an early age, is the perp behind the six novels in the Cranberry Country Mystery series. A repeat offender, Lodi's short story 'Oubliette' is included in *The Best Laid Plans: 21 Stories of Mystery & Suspense*. Other offenses include short stories in magazines, journals, and anthologies. Under the guise of legitimacy, he has written a series of books on seventeenth-century New England history, beginning with *Ghosts from King Philip's War*.

Find him on Facebook as Rock Village Publishing.

SO LONG

EDWARD LODI

SUNDAY

3:17 p.m.: Hey Sarah, Doc here. Not asleep I hope? The sedative should've worn off by now. I wouldn't want to disturb you. You'll need all the rest you can get to build up strength for what's to come. Anyhoo…bet you didn't know I was a computer whiz besides all my other talents. I've programmed your voicemail to remain on permanent speakerphone, you won't have to lift a finger to listen to your messages. How cool is that? I think I got the volume right, not too soft, not too loud. We wouldn't want to disturb your neighbors, though as I recall the walls to your apartment are as thick as the Great Wall of China. I also fixed it so your messages aren't being recorded. You'll hear them once, as they come in, then poof—off into the ether. This way your mailbox won't get cluttered. Added bonus, there'll be no record of my calls. Patient confidentially and all that. I know it's difficult for you to concentrate at times, but please try to listen carefully to each message so you don't miss anything important. That's about it. Oh, one other thing. I'm making arrangements to look in on you now and then. In the meantime, get plenty of rest. You're going to need your strength in the days to come. So long.

8:22 p.m.: Sarah, it's Sis. If you're home could you please pick up? Okay, so I guess you're out. Damn. I'd hoped we could talk. But I suppose if you're able to go out that's a sign your health is improving. *[pause]* I know it's a sensitive subject and maybe I said some things the other day I shouldn't have, but…are you sure you're doing the right thing about Charlie? You two were an item, for what, almost three years? I was so sure you'd marry him. But Sis, to ditch him like that. I know it's none of my business, but what do you see in that doctor friend of yours? Doctor…what's his name? Doctor Alberti. There's something about him…I don't know. Whereas Charlie's so nice. Anyway, Sis, the main reason I called was to remind you that Joey's birthday is Wednesday. I know you'd never forget, you haven't the past nine years. But you're his favorite aunt and he looks forward to seeing you. Oh, and as before, no presents. Just your presence. Little play on words there. And of course the cake. Joey loves seeing his name written in icing. Oh, I hate leaving messages on voicemail. Call me first chance and we'll discuss Joey's party and cake and all that. Bye now.

MONDAY

9:03 a.m.: This message is for Ms. Saunders. This is Doctor Jaffee's office reminding you of your one o'clock dental appointment Thursday. If for some reason you cannot keep this appointment, please inform us at least twenty-four hours in advance. Failure to keep your appointment without advance notification could result in a fifty dollar cancellation fee. Thank you.

10:07 a.m.: Hey Sarah, Doc again. How's my little chickadee today? Did you sleep well? Look, I'm sorry about the paralysis, but I assure you it's necessary. You'll understand better once I explain the full details of my little experiment. You aren't able to move, though unfortunately you can still feel pain. Not hunger or thirst I hope— it's not my intention to make you suffer needlessly. So long.

4:30 p.m.: Sarah, it's Charlie. I know you asked me not to phone, but when I heard you haven't been feeling well and took time off from work…I guess in your heart of hearts you know I still care.

Yeah, yeah. You don't want to hear it. But I'm still your friend. Please give me a call, let me know how you're doing or if there's anything I can do. Unless you've gone back to work? I hope so. Anyway, give me a buzz and I promise I won't bother you again.

4:51 p.m.: Hello, Sarah. This is Kristen from the office. The boss wanted me to check in case there's something you need or something we can do. We all miss you. Don't hesitate to phone if there's any way we can be of help. Get well soon. *[chuckle]* There'll be a ton of work waiting for you when you get back. Bye-bye.

8:23 p.m.: Sarah, guess who? Doc of course. Comfy? Of course not. How could you be, spread out like that and unable to move. Joke in poor taste—my apologies. You must be bored stiff just lying there. Second joke in poor taste. I guess I missed my calling. I should've been a comedian. Okay, down to brass tacks. The paralysis will persist, I'm afraid. You'll never be able to move any part of your body again, just an eyelid perhaps, if that. Remember yesterday I mentioned I was making arrangements to look in on you from time to time? Arrangements completed. I've appropriated an apartment across the way—don't ask me how. Hint: there's an old lady and two cats that won't be heard from again. No matter. The arrangement is purely temporary, just for the duration of the experiment. The point is, I have a clear view down into your apartment. With binoculars I can watch your...forgive me, I was about to say every move...let us say I can watch your progress. Rather, the progress of my little experiment. Little...I do myself an injustice. If this proves a success it will be the crowning achievement of my career. Heh heh. A somewhat checkered career, some might say. But I ramble on. Oh, one other thing, FYI, something you may not have noticed because of your inability to move. You're naked as a jaybird. I removed all your clothes while you were unconscious, not for prurient reasons, though I will admit I enjoyed our lovemaking while it lasted, but that's all in the past. Where was I? Oh yes, not for prurient reasons but to monitor the progress of my experiment. You probably haven't felt cold because I jacked the heat up in your apartment. Don't flatter yourself, though. I did it, not so much for your comfort, as for the success of my experiment. This will all become clear soon enough. I'll sign off now. Just remember that from my vantage point across the way I'll be looking in on you. So long.

TUESDAY

9:48 a.m.: Miss Saunders, this is Mrs. Rosenbaum from Jane's Bakery. The birthday cake you ordered last week is ready for pickup anytime today. We close at five. Thank you.

1:01 p.m.: Sarah dear, the Doctor is watching you. So long.

4:37 p.m.: Miss Saunders, this is Mrs. Rosenbaum from Jane's Bakery again. We'll be closing in about twenty minutes. If for some reason you can't pick your cake up today I can assure you it will still be nice and fresh tomorrow. We open at seven sharp. Thank you.

6:03 p.m.: It's Sis. Sarah, I'm getting concerned. Joey keeps asking what time you expect to get here tomorrow. I know you've never missed his birthday and I can count on you for the cake, but you'd ease my mind if you'd only give me a call. I know you haven't been feeling well of late. Can't that...can't Doctor Alberti diagnose what's wrong? Carl sends his love by the way. The party's at two as usual. You're not angry with me for the things I said the other day? I was only thinking of your best interests. Please get in touch to put my mind at ease. It's not like you not to phone.

8:21 p.m.: Doc again, Sarah. I don't want you to feel neglected. Rest assured—sorry, bad choice of words—perhaps be mindful is the better phrase. Anyhoo...just letting you know that beginning tomorrow morning I'll be keeping you under steady observation from my little perch across the way. Tomorrow morning is when things should start happening. You might even feel some slight stirrings before then, though I doubt it. I'll explain all of this tomorrow. No sense in unduly alarming you prematurely. So long.

WEDNESDAY

8:49 a.m.: It's Charlie again, Sarah, in case you've forgotten what my voice sounds like. Scratch that. I'm sorry for the sarcasm. *[pause]*

Look, I don't give a damn if you're pissed off at me for phoning again but there's something you should know. About your new heartthrob, Doctor Damon Alberti. The man's a quack, pure and simple. Did a quick internet search…it was like turning a rotten log over and exposing what's underneath. For starters, as a grad student he was kicked out of Tuft's School of Medicine for unethical experiments. There's nothing to indicate that he has a degree in medicine anywhere. He's been in trouble with the law numerous times, and even served time for his cruel experiments on animals. What you see in this creep is beyond me. That's it, Sarah. You won't be hearing from me again. *[long pause]* But if you ever need anything, anything at all, I'll be here for you.

11:22 a.m.: Howdee, Sarah. Anything stirring? If not, there soon will be. It's time, I think, to explain what's going on, though admittedly I'm keeping you informed strictly for my own vanity. After all, you're the only person in the world I can talk to about my experiment. I'm keeping meticulous records of course, but it will be years—decades—before I dare reveal the results to the scientific world. After my death, preferably. By then I will have achieved the acclaim my genius deserves. Ever hear of the ichneumons? Hint: they're found everywhere, in rural areas but in cities, too. Boston Commons, Boston Gardens, everyone's backyard. Give up? The Ichneumons are a family of wasps. Parasitic wasps. The females seek out and sting appropriate hosts in which to deposit their eggs, usually a fat caterpillar. The venom from the sting paralyzes the caterpillar but doesn't kill it. It remains alive—for a while at least. After stinging the insect, the female deposits one or more eggs into the living body. The rest is simple. The eggs hatch into larvae, the larvae feed on the living host until they're fully grown, and then emerge as wasps. By that time the caterpillar has died, of course, having been devoured alive, little by little. By now you must have an inkling as to the nature of my experiment. Over the years I've genetically altered a species known as the Giant Ichneumon. Altered it so now that it's truly a giant. I mean humongous. You should see them. Unfortunately that won't be possible. I'm sure you've already guessed it. You, Sarah, are the big fat caterpillar. Last Saturday I injected you with wasp venom, hence the paralysis. Then I did a little operation on your tummy and inserted—not, as you might expect, eggs, but mature larvae. I did this to speed things up. So you see the wriggly vermin have been feeding on you ever since. But you must've realized something terrible was happening to you. I can't imagine the agony you must be experiencing as they eat away at your gut. But don't despair. It's all for a good cause—the advancement of science. So long.

5:36 p.m.: What's going on with you, Sarah? I can't believe you deliberately missed Joey's party. I know you wouldn't hurt him like that. There's gotta be some explanation… Luckily I was able to get a cake at the last minute so everything went off okay but…Sarah, I'm really worried now. I told Carl if I don't hear from you soon I'm going to phone the Boston Police Department. Something's wrong, I know it. We love you, Sarah.

6:06 p.m.: Ho ho, Sarah. Now for the moment of truth. Here they come, the little buggers. Oh, I hope, I hope you're still alive and conscious to share in my triumph. They're wriggling through. Look at the size of them suckers. I know you're dead Sarah, I know you're dead, but I can't contain myself. This is the culmination of all my efforts. They're alive and kicking. As soon as they dry off they'll take wing and buzz around until someone unlocks the door or breaks it down. Just think, a part of you is in each one of them. And Sarah, I want you to know, if by some remote possibility you can still hear me…I want you to know that in honor of your sacrifice I intend to name this newly created species of ichneumonidae "Sarah."

KATE FLORA

Kate Flora's fascination with people's criminal tendencies began in the Maine Attorney General's office. Her true crime novel, *Finding Amy*, co-written with Portland, Maine's Deputy Chief of Police Joseph Loughlin, was an Edgar finalist. *Death Dealer*, an Anthony and Agatha finalist, won the Public Safety Writers Association 2015 award. Her star-reviewed Joe Burgess books have twice won the Maine Literary Award. Flora has also written nine Thea Kozak mysteries, *Careful What You Wish For*, a collection of short stories, as well as memoir and nonfiction. She is a member of Sisters in Crime National, Mystery Writers of America, the Short Mystery Fiction Society, and the Maine Writers and Publishers Alliance.

Find her at kateclarkflora.com.

AFTERLIFE

KATE FLORA

SINCE HAL DIED, Ida has had too much time on her hands. While he was with her, she never noticed how much of her day was spent taking care of his needs. Now, she never cooked breakfast or lunch, and was content with a bowl of soup or a quick sandwich for dinner, instead of the meat, starch, and vegetables she'd cooked daily for fifty years. She needed far fewer groceries and wasn't always going to the store to pick up donuts or chocolate milk or some fancy juice drink. Ida was happy with water, coffee, or tea. Her kitchen counters weren't cluttered with returnable cans and bottles. She wore clothes that didn't need to be ironed. She slept until after eight because there was no one to accuse her of getting lazy.

Not that she didn't miss him. The bed was too cold. She hated taking care of the car herself. There was no one to talk to. She even missed his pleasure when he sat down to a hot meal. But Hal had gone to the afterlife, and Ida was trying to make the best of it.

One bright aspect of being allowed to be lazy, what another person might have called "relaxing," was sitting at their big picture window and watching the world go by. Now that she was an old lady —and at eight-four, she *was* an old lady—she could watch the world with impunity, ignoring her mother's ingrained admonition to mind her own business. Her life was dull. She liked minding other people's business.

Her favorite kind of business was watching the lobstermen coming in with their catches on the lobster dock across the road. When Ida was young, men were generally covered up. Sure, on an occasional hot summer day, a working man would take his shirt off, but it was not common. Of course, there were shirtless men at the beach. Maybe men were different back then, because she couldn't recall seeing a single man without a shirt who was really worth looking at. Her Hal might have been the exception. But these young lobstermen? Striding unselfconsciously around with no shirts and their pants slung low on their hips? They were a sight for aging eyes.

She supposed there were people who would accuse her of being a dirty old lady, but Ida thought, like paintings in a museum, they were made to be admired, and she was a dedicated admirer.

The season for shirtless lobstermen in Maine was short, so Ida put in all the time she could sitting at the window, watching the display of male pulchritude. She had two she especially liked to watch, taking pleasure in what she called her "silent movie." She called them the Red and the Black, which she was pretty sure was the title of something she'd read in French class a thousand years ago. Red wasn't really red. His hair was a rich red-brown that got lighter, with almost blond streaks during a summer in the sun. He was made just like a man should be made. A big man. Strong shoulders and chest with visible muscles, and the narrow, almost sinuous hips of a swimmer. His chest and arms were furred with lighter red, enough that, had he not been so lovely, he would have been simian. When the sun lit him up and his red hair glowed, Ida imagined a Scotsman on some long ago battlefield, hips wrapped in a kilt and girded with a sword.

From her window, Ida couldn't tell what color his eyes were. They might have been green, but she imagined them the deep blue of a summer sea. He seemed to have some kind of authority over the others. When he spoke, the rest of them nodded and deferred. Maybe because his dad owned the company that bought everyone's catch? She thought that was the case.

Ida liked to watch him, but only as a voyeur, as an object, not someone to be cared about. Even without hearing him speak a word, she knew she didn't like him. Ida believed that how you treated people showed who you really were, and he didn't treat people well. He threw his authority and his strength around. Hal used to say that a true leader lead by example. Led quietly. Led with respect. He'd been that kind of man. The man she called Red wasn't. He bullied the smaller men and was disrespectful to the older ones, men who'd been doing this job since Red was in diapers.

The one she called Black was quietly and certainly his own man. He was a smaller man. Compact, lithe and wiry, with a way of moving that suggested at any moment he might spring into violent action. He carried a kind of suppressed anger that never left him. He didn't try to interfere with Red's treatment of others, but he never nodded or deferred to Red, something that clearly made Red fume. Ida admired his independence even as it concerned her.

Ida favored him for two reasons. First, his hair. All her life, Ida had been a sucker for men's hair. Their eyes, of course, but more so their hair. Black had black hair. Truly black hair, the kind that was almost blue. He must have been vain about it because he kept it ridiculously long, tied back with an elastic, the springy curls bouncing down his back. Any woman would have been jealous of that hair. Many women must long to run their fingers through it.

The second reason she favored him was that he was kind. When they were sitting here together talking, after Ida had confessed her fondness for watching them, her friend Mabel had wanted to know how on earth, from way over here, Ida could possibly know that a man was kind.

The truth was she just knew. The evidence was the many times she'd seen him take a moment to help someone who needed a hand. Lifting the other end of something heavy or laying a comforting hand on the shoulder of someone Red had just chewed out. She'd seen him give his sweatshirt to the kid who was just starting out. Maybe sixteen or seventeen, not yet filled out, on a day when it had suddenly turned cold. She'd seen him give money to someone who'd had a bad week.

Ida had spent over fifty years with a kind man. Hal had been like Black. He had seen when people needed help and offered it without being asked. Known who was down on their luck and might need a hand. He'd dropped off wood for people's stoves and vegetables when the garden was in season. Never asked for thanks. He just believed that's how people ought to be. So even though physically, Black was nothing like Hal, who'd been a big man, hefty, with big hands and a big voice, Black reminded her of Hal.

Even though folks would likely label her a silly old lady for thinking this, Ida found watching Black made her feel closer to Hal. Sometimes she indulged in the lonely old woman's habit of talking to herself, or at least setting out a second plate and cup for her now departed Hal, and then talking as though he was still sitting there.

"There's something going on between Red and Black, Hal. Something that isn't good."

Hal would have watched for a while and then said, "I see what you mean."

All those years together, it didn't take much talk for there to be communication.

"I'm worried about him. About Black. The way Red is looking when Black's back is turned makes me uneasy."

Hal would have leaned back in his chair. She could almost see him do it. He'd hook his thumbs behind the bib of his faded denim overalls. He'd watch. He'd rock a bit. Then he'd tell her what he was thinking. Now that he was gone, she had to supply both sides of the conversation. But she knew how he thought, how he saw the world, so she could speak for him. What he'd say was, "That lad, Black, had better watch himself. Something is brewing there with Red, and that Red isn't a man to restrain himself if someone comes between him and anything he wants. I haven't heard any rumors, but my guess would be there's a girl involved."

There was a girl involved. One as lovely in her way as Red and Black were in theirs. She was a smallish girl with long honey-brown hair. Ida especially liked her because she wore dresses. The day Ida first saw her, it was a flowery delphinium blue dress that looked like something a girl in a French movie would wear. On the girl, it was sweet. It swayed in the wind and was so graceful and feminine. These days, most girls didn't seem to care about being feminine. Sexy, yes, but not graceful and demure and womanly.

Hal had thought that she, Ida, was demure and graceful. He said that was why he first asked her to dance. Because she wasn't just pretty, she had "something." He hadn't quite been able to describe it, but he'd used the words demure and feminine. Hal would have liked this girl.

The girl stopped her little silver car right in front of Ida's house and walked down to the dock, looking like she was there to pick someone up. She had dainty little black shoes with straps across them. The ones Ida had always called Mary Janes. Ida looked over at Hal's chair and said, "I wonder who she's come for?"

Hal would have said whoever it was he was a lucky guy.

Because she favored him, Ida hoped the girl had come for Black. They would have been lovely together, both with their long flowing hair. Like the cover on those fantasy books her granddaughter read. As the girl started down the driveway to the dock, the wind off the sea caught her dress and she had to grab the skirt to keep it down. Ida remembered her skirt doing that. Hal had teased her about copying Marilyn Monroe.

Before the girl got to the bottom of the drive and Ida could see who she was meeting, Mabel drove in and honked her horn. Here to drive Ida to the library for their afternoon working on puzzles. Ida had to go into the hall to get her sweater and her tote bag. By the time she got out on the steps, the girl had disappeared into the building.

The girl was back again the next day. This time Ida had no reason to leave her window. She sat in her rocker, watching. Today the girl's dress was a pretty coral and the shoes were matching espadrilles that tied with ribbons around her ankles. Those bright little feet tripped down the driveway, slowing at the bottom and looking into the room where the men weighed and sorted their catch. A moment later Black appeared and the girl hurried toward him.

She linked her arm through his and they started back up the driveway to her car. Utterly lost in each other, as young lovers were.

Behind them, Ida saw Red appear in the doorway, watching them. He didn't speak but she didn't need words to know what was going on. It was in his look. In the set of his body. Red wanted the girl and was vowing to do some harm to his rival to make that happen.

Ida disliked conflict. It made her uneasy and raised her blood pressure. She could have saved herself some grief if she'd simply closed the curtain, or gone out on the back porch where she could look out over the garden. She had just a small garden this year. Her daughter had helped her put it in. She didn't need much because she didn't eat much, but the thought of going through a whole summer without lettuce and broccoli and beans and zucchini and carrots, and especially fresh tomatoes, was unbearable. She could have gone to the farmer's market. They were pleasant. But she'd had too many decades of nipping out the back door and picking what they needed. She wasn't ready to give that up.

Fresh vegetables and watching beautiful young men. That was Ida's summer, this first year without Hal.

On Wednesday, she'd seen Red gathering some of the other men around him. Their heads had come together like parties to a conspiracy, and then they'd broken apart and gone back to work. Black hadn't been around just then, he was down on the lower dock, helping another lobsterman unload his catch.

At the end of the day the girl had come as usual. Wearing the blue dress again. Once again Ida saw them walk up the drive arm in arm and drive away in the little silver car. Once again she saw Red in the doorway. This time there were other men with him and he was gesturing toward the silver car and then toward one of the boats and his gestures looked angry.

That night Ida set the table for two. She needed to talk to Hal about what she'd seen. Hal was always so sensible. He would counsel caution. He would agree that it looked suspicious but that Ida shouldn't jump to conclusions. He would urge her to be patient.

Most people were good at heart. She really didn't know Red or whether he was capable of wrongdoing.

Ida always listened to his counsel. He was wise. She admired that about her Hal. Other people used to come to him for advice both because he was wise and because he was sensible. Ida tended to be more emotional. Hal said that was okay. It was feminine. Besides, he'd said, feminine intuition also had a place in decision-making.

She wished he were here now. She had convinced herself that something terrible was going to happen. She was so agitated she couldn't watch her favorite TV shows. Around nine, she figured the next best thing to consulting Hal was to call his younger brother, Reggie. Reggie was twelve years younger, practically a spring chicken at seventy-one. Reggie was also a retired lawman.

Ida explained that she needed his advice and didn't want to wait for the morning. Reggie only lived a couple miles away. He said he'd be right over.

Like Hal, Reggie loved to eat, so Ida pulled an apple pie from the freezer and put it in the oven. Apple pie and ice cream were the least she could do for interrupting his evening, even though, like her, he had lost his spouse and probably spent his evenings watching television.

Reggie arrived in an agitated state, perhaps because he felt responsible for taking care of his brother's widow.

She got him seated in the living room, promised that there would be pie in fifteen minutes, and sat across from him to describe her dilemma. He listened with a cop's attention, asking her questions to clarify things, and never once made her feel nosy or ridiculous. Like Hal, Reggie was a kind man.

"Believe it or not, Ida, many times alert and attentive people like you were essential in helping us solve crimes. Regardless of what our mothers may have told us about minding our own business, being curious can be a good thing."

Ida imagined Reggie had been very good at calming distressed crime victims.

Over warm pie with ice cream, she asked, "Reggie, tell me honestly, am I overreacting? Making a mountain out of a molehill?"

"I'll be straight with you, Ida. When you started to tell me about this, I was skeptical. I...um...what I said about alert and attentive people, I meant that. But we'd get plenty of calls that didn't...um... that were making a lot out of nothing."

Reggie ducked his head, clearly embarrassed at saying this to his older brother's wife. Like most people, Reggie had looked up to Hal and that respect also attached to Ida.

Ida waited. Maybe he was telling her it was all her imagination, but there seemed to be something else Reggie wanted to say.

"But here's the thing. I'm pretty sure the men you describe are Red Schofield and Garrett Stetson, so I believe you're reading the situation right. Schofield is a bully, has been pretty much since he could walk, and his daddy believes he can do no wrong. Stetson is a good man, but he and Schofield rub each other the wrong way. No one owns Stetson and Schofield is used to being deferred to. Now the girl in the picture is Reverend Porter's daughter, Rebecca. There's not a sweeter girl to be found around here. I hear Schofield has been after her for the better part of a year and she's just not interested, where she's very interested in Garrett Stetson and he's head over heels for her. Schofield's mad as hell, and there's no telling what he might do."

Reggie patted Ida's hand. "Don't look so upset, Ida. The right people know what's going on. Nothing bad is going to happen." He looked longingly toward the kitchen. "I don't suppose there's more pie?"

She fed him another slice and sent the rest of the pie home with him. She could always make another, and she kind of missed feeding a hungry man.

Hoping Reggie was right, and that there really was nothing to worry about, she washed their few dishes and went up to bed.

It was the next day—she was sure it was Thursday because that was the day she went to the library to work on jigsaw puzzles with her friend Mabel—that Black, or rather Garrett Stetson, disappeared. She'd seen him around in the morning, heading down to his boat. Watched his boat go out and Red's boat go out a little later, at a time when Red didn't usually go out; he'd send a crew with his boat and stay behind.

She'd gotten wrapped up in gardening and then she'd seen Red's boat come back, the other boats come in, and all the other guys milling about, doing whatever it was they did with lobsters, but Black didn't come. She was so worried she didn't want to go with Mabel, but it was a regular thing they did. Mabel was a lonely widow, too, and she had no good reason to cancel.

She was a wreck the whole time they were at the library, so inattentive that Mabel asked if she was okay. She said the thing everyone always said, that she hadn't slept well. It was true, too. Eating pie so late in the evening meant the sugar always kept her up. But she hadn't wanted Reggie to feel uncomfortable about eating pie alone, so she's sacrificed her sleep. She couldn't tell Mabel about Red and Black and the lovely girl. Mabel already thought she was too caught up in watching half-naked young men and weaving her fantasies about them.

When Mabel dropped her off, she went straight to her window to watch. It was getting late. Maybe the girl had come and Ida had missed her. Still, she watched, worried about what was happening. All the other boats were back except Garrett's.

Then she saw the little silver car stopping out front. Today, the girl—Ida knew her name now, Rebecca Porter—was wearing a pink dress. A pretty pink dress to please the man who wasn't there. Hands knotted in distress, Ida watched those happy little feet trip down the driveway. Watched Red Schofield step out and speak to her. Watched the girl's anxious questioning. Saw Schofield shake his head, point to where Garrett's boat was usually moored, then shrug. Then say something and laugh. The girl didn't laugh with him.

Ida's heart went out to the girl as she turned and slowly climbed back up the drive. She stood a while beside the car, staring out to sea, as though her love could call Garrett Stetson back.

Out in the cove, a Marine Patrol boat was towing in Garrett's boat. They left it at Garrett Stetson's mooring, but there was no sign of Garrett, though the girl stood watching, her body rigid.

As the day grew cold and the sunlight began to fade into dusk, the girl finally gave up and got in her car. She was backing into Ida's driveway to turn around when two Sheriff's Patrol cars came around the bend and pulled into the lobster wharf's driveway.

The passenger door in the first one opened and Garrett Stetson sprang out. His clothes clung to his body as if he'd just been fished out of the sea. Neither wet nor cold held him back as he sprinted toward the little silver car. Just like in a romance movie, the girl leapt out and raced toward him, wrapping her arms around him, heedless of her pretty pink dress. They kissed like they were the first people in the world to discover kissing.

Ida liked that expression. Hal had taught it to her.

Officers from both cars continued down the driveway and disappeared inside. Moments later, they reappeared, a handcuffed Red Schofield between then. They placed him in the back seat of one of the cars, then both cars reversed and went back the way they came.

Reggie said that the right people knew what was going on. That was likely true. Still, she felt she'd had a part in it. Maybe made them more vigilant. It was a big ocean, and too easily bad things could be made to look like accidents. Before she fell asleep, she turned to Hal's side of the bed.

"Thanks for teaching what me a good person does, Hal."

BUZZ DIXON

Buzz Dixon is a longtime writer in television animation, films, graphic novels, comic books, video games, short stories, and soon, novels for the Young Adult market. His most notable credits in television include writer on the original *G.I. Joe* and *Transformers* animated programs. His short fiction has been published in *Mike Shayne's Mystery Magazine*, *National Lampoon*, the *Pan Book of Horror Stories*, *Analog Science Fiction and Fact*, and numerous anthologies.

Find him at BuzzDixon.com.

TONGOR OF THE ELEPHANTS

BUZZ DIXON

HERE, lemme show you something you've never seen before.

I've only shown this to maybe six other people in the last thirty years, but I'll be honest, I must've watched it dozens of times whenever I find myself in a bad mood, an ugly mood.

A mean mood.

Lemme thread it up on the ol' Moviola.

Now, I know you've seen all the footage in the Gemstone Studios archives if you're researching "lost" serials.

Most of 'em aren't actually lost—*Tongor of the Elephants* isn't, just abandoned. Studios announce projects all the time that get canceled without so much as a single frame of film getting exposed. Sometimes they get revived under different titles—the way Republic's *Superman* serial got reworked into *The Mysterious Dr. Satan* or Columbia's *Phantom* sequel became *Captain Africa*—but low-budget studios never really abandoned anything they started production on.

They couldn't afford it…with this one exception.

Here, watch.

See that?

You recognize him, of course: "J. Cecil Revell, the Million Dollar Profile."

"J. Cecil Revell, the thick slice of ham" is more like it.

That's Evalyn, Evalyn Baumann. Beautiful name for a gal who looks like a sack of potatoes, isn't it?

There she is helping him up on Old Jezebel…

Getting nervous? Yeah, you guessed what this is. Think you can take it?

Okay, on with the show.

Watch take one. Look at how Hambone—that's what the crew called Revell—look how he's kicking Old Jezebel behind the ears to get her to move forward.

Take one, no problem.

Take two, no problem—but look how he keeps kicking her.

Brace yourself. Take three—and *pow!*

No more J. Cecil Revell.

Let me show you that again, frame by frame.

Take three. Hambone kicks Old Jezebel behind the ears again, Old Jezebel gets her fill, reaches up behind her left ear with her trunk, grabs Hambone's left ankle.

Ten frames, that's all it takes, less than half a second.

Frame 237, she grabs him.

Frame 238, she yanks him off her neck.

Frames 239 to 247, she's swinging him like Joe DiMaggio aiming for the fence.

I don't think Hambone ever fully realized what was happening. I think he had just barely enough time to realize *something* went wrong, but not what lay in store for him, and if you ask me, that's a pity.

Sonuvabitch deserved at least a second of sheer terror to appreciate what was coming.

Frame 248—*pow!* Like dropping an overripe cantaloupe off the top of the Wiltern Theater.

Frame 247, he's still alive, he's still J. Cecil Revell, the Million Dollar Profile.

Frame 248, and J. Cecil Revell is gone, reduced to nothing but a spray of gray and pink goo as his head hits the boulder.

247, alive.

248, dead.

247, 248. One twenty-fourth of a second and everything that J. Cecil Revell ever was, everything he ever could have been…gone.

Good riddance to bad rubbish.

Let me show you the rest so I can explain what happened next.

Old Jezebel slams Hambone's headless corpse into the ground one—two—three—four—five times.

Completely superfluous, of course. Hambone's as dead as he's ever gonna be.

Now she stomps him flat into the dirt, now she yanks up his legs and hips, throws them a dozen yards away.

Here's where I bolted…and here's the end of the clip.

You know what happened next. Big inquiry by the coroner, sensational news story for two days, then something else happened —something else *always* happens—and people forgot.

Hambone made it easy to forget. Everybody enjoyed a good, bitter laugh over what happened to him, then got on with their lives.

Coroner's jury filed their report. Recommended Evalyn for prosecution, but by then she'd fled the state.

The DA saw little point in going after her for negligent homicide, but left the case open in the event she was dumb enough to return to California after he got voted out of office and replaced by somebody who couldn't care less what happened to an old has-been ham everybody hated.

Evalyn went back to Florida, helped look after the Ringling Brothers animals during the circus's winter break. Got involved in a wild animal park. Died six years ago, natural causes. Didn't find her body for three days and by then her cats—and by "cats" I mean ocelots, not damn kittens—fed off her.

So they got put down and I'm sure if Evalyn had known, she'd have felt bad about it.

Certainly a lot worse than she felt about J. Cecil Revell.

IN THIS TOWN, everybody gets typecast.

At twenty one, I got to be a camera operator on a B-Western second unit shoot. Shot a cattle stampede—really nothing but eight bored old cows. Following that, I shot a couple of shorts PRC did about a boy and his dog. The dog proved a lot easier to work with than the boy.

A couple of more Westerns, then I worked on *Six Gun Circus*, and all of a sudden I was shooting circus pictures as well.

And because I worked with lions and tigers and elephants in circus pics, I became a jungle movie expert, and by my fifth year, a director of photography.

Producers typecast me as "the animal guy."

No courtroom dramas, no romantic comedies, no horror films.

Just a steady diet of Westerns and jungle movies and dog pictures.

Okay, fine. I'm not complaining.

Maybe I never got nominated for an Oscar, but on the other hand I made enough to pay for a house, a wife, an ex-wife, and two sets of kids I put through college.

Not a bad life and better than most.

I met Evalyn on *Six Gun Circus*. An animal wrangler for one of the companies that rented exotic animals to the movies, she specialized in elephants and big cats.

She was in her mid-forties when I met her, a former circus animal trainer who got tired of touring but found zoo work too confining.

Like I said earlier, not much of a looker but animals don't care about your looks, only if you're treating 'em right.

Six Gun Circus is also where I met Daniel Drake and Old Jezebel.

Lemme tell you about Danny first. You recognize the name. Brief career playing sensitive young man parts, typically a soft teen who needed a strong, masculine mentor to set him straight—no pun intended.

Not one of those overly swishy types with exaggerated lisps and gestures, but clearly homosexual.

Some people wonder how straight gals can fall in love with gay guys, but the way I see it, it makes perfect sense.

They get a good, personal relationship with a member of the opposite sex and there's no romance or lovemaking to get in the way.

All the messy stuff is off the table, and you can get really close emotionally to somebody who isn't going to break your heart.

Evalyn fell in love with Danny in a big, big way; you could hear it in her voice when she spoke to him.

They found common ground over a love of animals. See, Danny grew up on a farm in Nebraska and was a helluva lot tougher than the characters he played.

Remember what I said about typecasting? Well, Danny got typecast as the weakling who became a man. In *Six Gun Circus*, he played a spoiled millionaire's kid who ran away from home, got taken under the wing of Tom Mix, and learned to be a rootin' tootin' cowboy.

Absolute nonsense, of course, but nonsense audiences ate up.

Anyway, he and Evalyn worked together because he appeared in several scenes with elephants and big cats. Evalyn always stood just off camera, guiding the animals through their paces.

As I said, she and Danny hit it off real well, and while I don't think Danny ever felt the exact same kinda feelings she felt for him, he liked her and they became friends.

You could see the love in her eyes whenever she looked at him, but Evalyn was also a realist, a practical gal. She knew she couldn't have him as a lover or a mate, so she didn't embarrass herself by pining for him hopelessly. She decided to be happy with what she had.

And as long as she felt happy and Danny felt happy, whose business was it?

They worked on a couple of pictures together. I shot both movies. After *Six Gun Circus* he made *Jungle Trial* about a weakling who gets shipped off to Africa—Africa! Ha! Griffith Park is more like it—and gets straightened out by a big game hunter.

The wife of some middle management sort over at Universal

started a charity to look after movie animals too old or too temperamental to perform. Both Evalyn and Danny joined, so they got to see each other outside of work.

All things considered, not as bad a relationship as many.

The turd in the punch bowl? Old Hambone himself, J. Cecil "Million Dollar Profile" Revell.

Some studio PR hack hung that nickname on him at MGM and it stuck like a cow pie to the sole of your boots.

The gimmick was every time Hambone appeared in a movie, the producers were supposed to insure his profile for a million bucks.

I don't know if anybody ever actually did that except for MGM and Herbert W. Ralston.

Ralston ran Gemstone Studios, and while a penny pincher, he could smell a good PR gimmick.

He contacted an insurance company and negotiated a "million dollar" policy for Hambone's profile. Of course, by the time the insurance brokers finished writing in all the clauses and exclusions and wherefores they wanted, the policy seemed about as useful as a square of wet toilet paper.

But good PR is good PR, and it cost only a hundred bucks or so, and Ralston got to write it off as a business expense.

Hambone started at MGM about seven or eight years before Danny drifted into town. He played basically the same kinda roles: Weakling who toughens up—or dies.

Hambone being Hambone, he was no pleasure to work with.

Bad enough if he just acted like your typical self-centered snobbish star, but Hambone proved worse than that.

A sneak and a snitch, Hambone supplemented his income—and eliminated more than one rival—by slipping dirt on them to the gossip rags.

You can't keep that sort of thing a secret in Hollywood, and word got passed around the campfire pretty quickly.

Hambone cost MGM two starlets Louis B. Mayer was personally grooming, so they let his contract lapse.

Being older than Danny, Hambone soon found that with the

roles he did audition for, half the time he'd be competing against Danny Drake.

Well, he dug around and he found some dirt on Danny, a batch of photos Danny posed for when just starting out. I don't think there's an actress in Hollywood—Shirley Temple excepted—who hasn't done the same thing.

Hell, if you've got time after this, I'll show you a stag reel I've got of Joan Crawford back when she was Lucille Le Sueur.

But this country being what it is, we can accept a gal taking her clothes off for a camera. That's *normal*, that's okay.

Let a *guy* do the exact same thing, and he's a pervert, a deviant.

He's gotta go.

Hambone found out about Danny Drake's plain brown envelope photos—"art studies" as we euphemistically refer to 'em—and acquired a set.

You'd think that would be enough, but old Hambone took no chances.

He knew from the grapevine that Danny was the kinda fella who took comfort in the company of like-minded fellas, if you catch my drift.

Now, I don't know if Hambone got wind of the hush-hush party Danny was invited to and tipped the police, or if the police learned about that very private affair on their own, but after Danny's arrest on a morals charge, he saw to it that every tabloid and gossip columnist in town got a copy of the "art studies" Danny posed for.

Maybe Danny could have weathered a simple arrest, gotten a lawyer to plea bargain it down, kept a low profile for a few months then resumed his career, but the photos guaranteed he wouldn't get any more work in this town.

Danny's agent dropped him, and all the acting gigs dried up, including one role he was up for: *Tongor of the Elephants*.

Tongor was a cheap pulp knock-off of *Tarzan* by way of *Chandu The Magician*: A wealthy English lord whose missionary parents took him to India where he studied under the mystic yogis and became master of the elephants.

Yeah, doesn't make one lick of sense, but serials don't need to make *sense*, they just need to make *dollars*.

Gemstone bought the rights to do a *Tongor* serial and originally cast Danny Drake as Tongor, but when Danny got arrested and Hambone shared the "art studies" with the Hollywood press, that was that.

Now, other guys—and gals—have gone through the same thing and survived. Their on-screen careers might end, but they find other jobs in and around Hollywood.

But Danny hailed from Nebraska, and he was a big deal back in his old hometown, so when he got busted, old Hambone also mailed a set of photos to the local paper.

Not only did his hometown fans turn on him, but they shunned his parents and sisters as well.

I think that's what drove Danny to suicide, a bottle of gin and a handful of pills being less painful to face than his disappointed family.

Evalyn took it hard, you could tell, but she acted like a pro and kept soldiering on.

Gemstone replaced Danny with Mr. Million Dollar Profile, even though people already started whispering about what he'd done to get it.

We began filming in the wilds of Chatsworth. If Evalyn knew that Hambone ratted out her beloved Danny, she never revealed it —which would've made her a better actress than most gals before the camera.

But she *had* to know—*everybody* knew. The only difference between a Hollywood secret and a Hollywood press release is that fewer people know about the press release.

RALSTON BUDGETED *Tongor of the Elephants* at $125,000—not a lot but enough to do the job.

Since he was supposed to be a "master of the elephants"— whatever the hell *that* means—we decided to film all of Hambone's elephant related footage over two days about midway through the shoot.

We set up near the Santa Susanna Pass in Chatsworth where they've got these big, dramatic looking rocks and boulders. Y'know, we use those rocks for everything: The Wild West, Africa, Egypt, the South Seas, even the Moon and Mars.

Evalyn, as the elephant wrangler, brought along three Indian elephants, including Old Jezebel.

Nobody in the know wanted to work with Old Jezebel. She acted moody and angry and just plain defiant after years of abuse in a circus, and if I got any say in the matter, we'd never use her, but hey, I'm just the director of photography, what do I know, right?

The one thing in Old Jezebel's favor was her size: She stood about three feet taller than most Indian elephants and size does matter, at least when it comes to putting elephants on a movie screen.

In *Six Gun Circus*, the director, G. R. Prince, told Doris Shubert, the actress playing the animal trainer, to guide Old Jezebel along by prodding her behind the ear with her staff.

Big mistake. Old Jezebel did *not* like that and trumpeted loudly, turning towards Doris, who screamed and ran off.

Fortunately, Evalyn stood just out of camera range. She managed to calm Old Jezebel down, but we lost at least an hour shooting time because of that.

Afterwards, nobody tried to get Old Jezebel to do anything on camera again other than just stand there and look impressive.

And after a few years, not even that. Evalyn and the company she worked for realized how hair-trigger Old Jezebel could be and just let her graze away while their other animals worked to earn their keep.

"She gonna be okay?" I asked Evalyn, and Evalyn nodded and said Old Jezebel seemed a lot mellower recently.

"Krunch" Keyser drove up from Fort Keyser, the movie cowboy ranch he owned and rented out to cheap productions. You know about Krunch: Real name Oscar Herkimer. They groomed him to be a B-Western star, but he realized he could make a lot more money buying a ranch and renting it out to studios, so he did—but he didn't exactly turn his back on performing.

When he learned how much Charlie Gemora made donning a monkey suit for the movies, crazy old Krunch ordered a custom-made suit for himself and played gorillas in movies.

They planned to make a big star out of him, and he turned his back on that to run around in a monkey suit. Sounds crazy, but it's the gospel truth. Only in Hollywood....

Anyway, Krunch came up because we cast him as a gorilla in our serial and we wanted to shoot some scenes with him and Hambone and the elephants the next day. Krunch wanted to judge the elephants' temperament so he wouldn't spook them when he played a gorilla.

Krunch mighta been crazy but he sure wasn't stupid.

Hambone didn't appear too thrilled about working with elephants, but when you're playing a character called Tongor of the Elephants, you just gotta expect an elephant or two in your life, right?

I guess he worried about his precious profile, though considering what happened that worry seems pretty legit.

Hambone showed up on time—I'll give him credit for that, he never missed a call—and got made up and in costume: Turban, safari jacket, puttees, and those silly little pointed Persian slippers.

Evalyn took Hambone aside to explain the basics of riding an elephant.

Everybody could tell he really didn't want to do it, and he didn't make things any easier with his condescending attitude.

Still, Evalyn acted graciously and carefully explained things to him.

I didn't hear everything she had to say—I was riding herd on my own crew—but I know I heard her say "...steer her by kicking her behind the ears."

Knowing what I did about Old Jezebel, I thought Evalyn was saying "*Don't* try to steer her by kicking her behind the ears."

Like I said, I didn't pay all that close attention.

We finally got Hambone up on Old Jezebel. Hambone was

getting cranky and eager to get it over with, director Bill Tillerson was getting cranky and eager to get it over with, and I'm sure Old Jezebel was getting cranky and eager to get it over with.

Bill told me to get a couple of medium shots of Hambone turning Old Jezebel left and right that we could intercut with the long shots of his stunt double.

Of course, Hambone couldn't do anything properly, and we needed to do extra takes, and that ticked Bill off.

They don't call him "One Take" Tillerson for nothing.

I was too busy making sure everything stayed in frame and in focus to watch what Hambone was or was not doing with his feet.

When everything went south, I bolted with the rest of the crew. Old Jezebel knocked our camera over and crushed it—a big, heavy duty 35mm designed to take a real beating so you can guess how badly she trampled it.

We all scattered seven ways from sundown as Old Jezebel tore through the craft services tent and overturned the honey wagon.

Bill Tillerson chose that as his hiding place, so you can imagine what he looked and smelled like when he crawled out.

Most of us climbed up high into the rocks where Old Jezebel couldn't follow, and after she finished flipping over the honey wagon, she took off down the road down to Fort Keyser.

Krunch jumped in his car and took off at the first sign of trouble—but give him his due, he took the script girl and two gaffers to safety with him.

Like most Western stars, Krunch owned a fair size gun collection and did some big game hunting.

He roared back to Fort Keyser, warned his workers about Old Jezebel, then went in his house and dragged out his elephant gun—yes, crazy old Krunch owned an elephant gun.

Of course he would.

When Old Jezebel came trumpeting down the road towards Fort Keyser, Krunch stood there, took careful aim, and planted a .470 round right between her eyes.

THE PAPERS PUBLISHED sensational stories for two or three days with Krunch as the hero who saved everybody—everybody except old Hambone.

The coroner's inquiry took about six weeks, and by then, most folks already forgot about it.

Evalyn swore she told Hambone not to kick Old Jezebel behind the ears. They never looked at the footage you just saw 'cause I lied to them, said the film magazine got smashed along with the camera.

It hadn't, but I paid for my house and my wife and my ex-wife and my two sets of kids by working regularly for Gemstone Studios, and I knew if I didn't protect the studio, the studio wouldn't protect me.

At first I believed Evalyn when she swore she warned Hambone about kicking Old Jezebel behind the ears.

But after I smuggled the footage of Hambone's death back home and developed it, I saw him repeatedly kicking her.

Now, as I said, I didn't notice it at the time because I was focused on other things.

But *Evalyn* stood right there watching everything, and she should've said something to Hambone after the first take.

But she said nothing for three takes and finally Old Jezebel got fed up and went berserk.

Did she plan for that to happen? Or did she just think Old Jezebel would give Hambone a scare?

She knew what Hambone did to Danny, so she certainly hated him, but enough to kill him?

And what about the rest of us? We could've been killed, too.

Did she think she could calm Old Jezebel down after she went berserk?

Did she consider us complicit in Danny's death?

Or maybe she hoped she'd get killed as well, that life just wasn't worth living without Danny Drake?

I dunno. Honestly don't.

The coroner's jury decided it was death by accidental negligent homicide and recommended charges against Evalyn, but not the studio.

They didn't need to punish Evalyn: Her career was o-v-e-r. You don't let an animal you're wrangling kill the star of your production and expect to get hired again.

She packed up and moved back to Florida the day before they announced the verdict.

I kept my mouth shut and kept working at Gemstone Studios with Bill Tillerson and Herbert Ralston, looking at the footage already shot and trying to figure out if we could craft it into a coherent enough story to make a short feature.

In the end Ralston decided there wasn't enough and just cancelled the serial.

Here's the funny thing: He got his money back on the production insurance guarantee 'cause the serial couldn't be finished, but since old Hambone didn't have any friends or family to leave his estate to, Ralston set up his "million dollar profile" insurance to pay out to Gemstone Studios.

The insurance company didn't want to honor the policy, but Ralston took them to court and proved Hambone's profile indeed got ruined when Old Jezebel smashed his head to bits against the boulder.

Gemstone got that million dollar payoff.

Kinda ironic, don't cha think? The serial Gemstone made the most money on was the one that never got completed.

J A HENDERSON

Jan-Andrew Henderson (**J A Henderson**) is the author of twenty-nine teen and adult thrillers and non-fiction books. Published in the UK, USA, Australia, Germany, and the Czech Republic, he has been shortlisted for thirteen literary awards and is the winner of the Doncaster Book Prize and Royal Mail Award. He owns Green Light Literary Consultants (Brisbane, Australia) offering advice, workshops and talks to budding writers. Jan-Andrew is a member of the Australian Society of Authors, UK Society of Authors, Springfield Writers Group, and the Scottish Book Trust.

Find him at janandrewhenderson.com.

THE GOD COMPLEX

J A HENDERSON

JENSEN AND MURPHY peered through the smoked glass partition. On the other side, a dumpy, middle-aged woman sat at her console. She had unusually dark hair, short and bobbed, with a purple butterfly clasp fastened to one side. It looked suspiciously like a wig.

"We call this part of the facility the God Complex," Jensen said dryly. "That's a pun."

Murphy sighed.

Of the pair, Jensen was taller and thinner. He had a clipboard under one arm and was wearing a white lab coat. He looked so much the typical scientist, Murphy wondered if the man had ever considered becoming anything else. Murphy, on the other hand, resembled an Irish bricklayer—short, squat and ginger—and the name didn't help.

Murphy squinted through the window at the woman. She was wearing a gold badge that said *Edith* in small black letters. With a handle like that, it was no surprise she was middle-aged. Edith had a small microphone on the desk in front of her and was talking into it. Two wires, one red and one white, wound from the back of her head into a bank of steel panels set in the roof.

"It's really quite fascinating." Jensen's voice was slow and emotionless, as if he mentally read over everything he thought before voicing it. "It's almost like you...plug yourself in. You...plug yourself in, yes. Plug yourself into the computer."

"And you can see what's going on in the past?" Murphy asked.

"Yes. No. Yes," Jensen replied hesitantly. "You...experience. You see, in a way. Sort of."

Murphy sighed again. He had long ago given up expecting straight answers from anyone in authority. Jensen turned a dial on the panel beside him and the woman's voice suddenly became audible. She sounded like she'd been smoking since she was twelve. Continuously.

"I'm in an alley," she narrated. "It's dark. It's night. The streets are glistening with rain. There's a lot less litter than where *I* live. I don't know if that's because people were cleaner in the old days or if there were less disposable products..."

"Too descriptive!" Jensen snapped at the glass, though it was obvious that Edith couldn't hear him.

"How does this set up work, then?" Murphy tried again.

"The computer...it's a quantum computer. It can calculate infinite possibilities. See?"

Murphy didn't see.

"Well," Jenson continued. "They say that, if you think you understand quantum physics, you don't understand quantum physics. So it's difficult to explain."

"Try."

"Okay. We can use the computer to break down all matter into its basic components and study their trajectories." The scientist traced the imaginary fragments with his fingers, looking a bit like the world's palest rapper. "How they move, you know? Where they go. And once you know how something moves and where it goes you can tell where it once was. Our quantum computer does that, yes."

"Quite a feat."

"It's a big computer." Jensen was still watching Edith, who had begun speaking again.

"There are docks at the end of the street. Strong smell of fish.

And sulphur. I'm entering warehouse number seven, as instructed." The woman pulled a wad of gum from her mouth and stuck it under the console.

"There are a couple of cars with whitewall tires and runner boards. I don't know what type they are. They're big and shiny."

"Women and cars." Jensen raised his bony shoulders in resignation. "What can you do?"

"Then, why are you using her?" Murphy picked at a smear on the pane.

"Ah. That's the tricky part." Jenson stroked his chin. "As I said, the quantum computer analyses the trajectories of every bit of material in the world and then projects backwards. And so…we can chart exactly where each particle was located at any given moment. Right back to the dawn of time, if you like."

"That's amazing." Murphy gave a low whistle. "The possibilities must be endless."

"Actually we haven't found a useful application for it at all," Jensen admitted. "We can't even make a bomb. *C'est la vie*, I suppose. Scientists are a bit like explorers. Some find America. Some discover Lapland."

"And?"

"And what?"

"Who discovered Lapland?"

"Beats me." The scientist glanced sideways at Murphy to gauge if his interest was genuine. "If you really want to know, we can find out."

He pointed into the booth.

"See, that's what Sonja there does. Builds up a complete map of the past. She can *see* history."

"Sonja does all that?" Murphy looked at the woman with new admiration. "So, why do you keep calling her Edith?"

"Sonja's the name of the computer," Jensen replied scathingly.

Edith began speaking again.

"There are a group of men waiting by the cars. They're wearing suits and carrying violin cases and they look nervous. Actually, they all look like Mel Gibson. Only taller."

"This is our real stumbling block," Jensen whispered, so as not to drown the woman's commentary out. "In order to monitor history our *witnesses*, as we call them, need to hook themselves directly into the quantum computer. They have a symbiotic relationship, you might call it. They….link together. Yes. Fuse."

"Isn't that a bit dangerous?" Murphy looked at the wires protruding from Edith's head and gave a shudder.

"That's why we use people like her."

"You don't like women much, do you?"

"I love women," Jensen snapped. "I just don't like Edith."

"Still, this is fantastic." Murphy wasn't about to get in the middle of a personality clash. "You could learn so much about…everything."

"That's the idea, yes," Jensen agreed. "But like every new project it has a few glitches."

"Another group of men have come into the warehouse." Edith carried on, oblivious at being the focus of attention. Murphy assumed the window only worked one way.

"Looks like they mean business, too. They're all carrying violin cases, too. I think there's going to be some kind of showdown."

She flinched.

"Oh no. They're opening the cases. I'm going to hide behind this crate."

"See, it's like she's actually there," Jensen hissed behind his hand.

"Glitches?" Murphy asked.

"Sort of." Jensen grimaced. "According to Edith, when Judas kissed Jesus in the Garden of Gethsemane, Christ punched him in the mouth."

He snorted his disapproval

"How do you think a revelation like that would go down with the Christian community?"

Murphy gasped. "That really happened?"

"Ahhh. Now they're all playing 'Greensleeves.'" Edith's face had taken on a faraway look. "Isn't that funny? I've had the tune stuck in my head all day."

"Who knows?" Jensen scowled at her. "That's problem number two. The witness becomes...eh...*part* of any given scene they observe. Their emotional state and desires influences their... interpretation, if you like."

He gave a resigned shrug.

"Now we have to employ a team of psychologists to separate what really happened from what the witness wants to happen. It's costing us a fortune."

"So, where do I come in?" Murphy had a cold feeling in the pit of his stomach.

"You kidding?" Jensen opened the clipboard and began to read the contents. "Billy Wayne Murphy. Life imprisonment for the murder of two eleven-year-old girls. Psychologists say you've never shown remorse. Have no emotional involvement with what you've done. In any capacity, whatsoever."

He raised an inquisitive eyebrow.

"I can't imagine how that must feel. Which is the whole point, really."

"It doesn't feel like anything at all," Murphy said coldly.

"Of course. Of course." The scientist shut the clipboard with a snap. "Ofcourseofcourseofcourseofcourseofcourse."

"Because, I'm innocent, you idiot," Murphy fumed. "I was framed."

"A man without emotions." Jensen was still lost in his own musings. "Absolutely perfect. You'll be able to trawl through history in an objective manner. Aha. See things exactly as they are. You're just what we need to save the project."

"I am *not* a psychopath," Murphy repeated. "I was watching TV at the time."

Then an incredible thought struck him.

"Listen," he said excitedly, "we could use your machine to prove my innocence. Go back and find out who actually killed those girls."

He tried to grab hold of the scientist's arm but his hands were shackled to his legs by chains.

"We already did." Jensen glared at him and pulled away. "It was definitely you."

"Wait a bloody minute!" Murphy exploded. "You just said, if the observer expects me to be the killer, or *wants* it to be me, then that's exactly what they'll see. Right?"

"Correct." Jensen happily nodded in agreement.

"So who was the sodding witness?"

"Me."

"You bastard." Murphy tried to lunge at the scientist but his chains snapped tight and he fell flat on his face.

"You're hardly going to be impartial yourself, eh?" Jensen bent down and pulled the fallen man to his feet. "At least helping us gets you out of prison."

Murphy thought for a while. Then a smile spread across his face.

"When you hook *me* up to Sonja, I could see who really committed the crime." He brightened. "Once we know, we might be able to find physical evidence to back that up."

"Em…" Jensen looked sheepish. "Not any more."

"S'cuse me?"

"It's a quantum thing. Schrödinger's Cat and all that stuff." The scientist pursed his lips. "Once a past event has actually been observed on a quantum level it kind of…*becomes* history. To all intents and purposes."

Murphy's brow furrowed.

"Take your case, for instance," Jensen continued. "Did you kill those kids? There are only two possibilities: yes or no. But, now that I've looked at it, there's only one. You definitely did it."

He spread his hands generously.

"Therefore you may as well help us. Get off death row, eh?"

"I'm *not* a psychopath," Murphy shouted. "I *have* emotions. My view of history won't be worth a crap."

"Shhhhh. Nobody has to know that." Jensen put an urgent finger to his lips. "And we need you on board to keep up funding. The Chairman's patience is running out."

"Oh. I see. Right." Murphy's face was like thunder. "Well, since the morality of this project also seems to be a thing of the past, why didn't you just pretend you found some terrible scandal in the Chairman's past and blackmail him into keeping it going?"

"Because we needed a totally credible witness to take on someone *that* powerful." Jensen smirked. "Which is where you come in."

"And people call *me* criminally insane."

"Yes. Well. You don't have to be mad to work here, but it helps." Jensen's smile widened into a happy grin. "Ha hah. Hahahahahaha-hahahahahahaha. Sorry."

He pointed to a door behind them.

"The guards will take you for briefing and inductance now. We'll expect you online in a couple of days."

Murphy's shoulders sagged and the chains clinked sadly.

"Maybe you're right," he said finally.

"Good man." Jensen patted him gingerly on the shoulder.

"I mean, if you've proved I'm a stone cold killer." Murphy gave a warped grin. "Your days are most definitely numbered."

Jensen blanched. "Statements like that aren't going to go down well with your parole officer."

"Just watch your back, that's all." Murphy turned and shuffled his way out of the door, the scientist following a safe distance behind.

Edith waited until the men were gone. She punched a few buttons on her console, inserted an earpiece and began to talk into the microphone again.

"Chairman? It's me. Just went back and looked, as ordered. And your suspicions are confirmed. Professor Jensen was obsessed with the impending failure of his project and intended to frame you for some fabricated indiscretion, to keep his funding coming."

She adjusted her wig.

"He also tried to blackmail a psychopathic convict named Murphy into joining his scheme, but the potential witness threatened to kill him. Since the professor was found dead a few days later, I assume Murphy found a way to make good his promise."

She coughed politely.

"If you like, I can look at the day Professor Jensen died, just to be sure. Oh...you've already done that.... Good. Good." Edith looked at her watch. "In that case, I've a couple of hours before lunch."

She retrieved her gum from under the console and popped it back in her mouth.

"Just enough time to find out who really shot JFK."

CHRISTINE ESKILSON

Christine Eskilson has received honorable mentions in the 2012 Al Blanchard Short Crime Fiction Contest and the 2012 Women's National Book Association (WNBA) Annual Writing Contest, third place in the 2017 WNBA Annual Writing Contest, and first place in the 2018 Bethlehem Writers Roundtable Short Story Contest. Her stories have appeared in a number of magazines and anthologies. Christine is a member of Sisters in Crime National and the Short Mystery Fiction Society.

FOR ELIZABETH

CHRISTINE ESKILSON

I'VE LOVED Elizabeth for years. From a pimpled adolescence obsessed with maritime history and video games through a lucrative tech career and right up to my present confines. We met in high school, where all great passions are born. Elizabeth was in my Spanish class sophomore year, our desks only inches apart. Those inches, however, could have spanned miles. I spent most of the semester too terrorized to talk to her, fantasizing from afar that I was a daring New World explorer and she was Queen Isabella. That was about as impure as I got in those days. Unfortunately there was a putative King Ferdinand in the picture—a blockhead senior named Rob whose prowess on the Newton North High School football field was grossly disproportionate to the combined size and caliber of his heart and brain.

The summer after sophomore year I worked at Howard's Royal Dairy—"We Whipped the Queen!"—hoping that Elizabeth would appear one day to marvel at my banana splits. One steamy afternoon in July, I got my wish. Rob strutted in, Elizabeth on his arm. I wiped away the sticky remnants of the rainbow jimmies I'd just dished out and pasted a smile on my face.

"Welcome to the Royal Dairy," I chanted. "Where every

customer is a King of Cones or your money back." I wasn't exactly sure what that meant but Mr. Howard was always hovering nearby to make sure we said it.

Rob slapped a ten dollar bill on the counter. "One double dip chocolate chip cone." He turned to Elizabeth. "Be right back, babe."

After Rob headed for the men's room in the back of the store, Elizabeth spoke up. "I'll take a single strawberry, please." She smiled, rose-red lips parted over perfect white teeth.

"You were in Ms. Gonzales's class, weren't you?" she asked, as if she was seeing me for the first time. "She was a super tough grader. I was lucky to pass."

I nodded dumbly, trying to formulate a witty response in Spanish but, with Elizabeth standing in front of me, my mind was as frozen as an ice cream tub.

Rob returned to drum his fingers on the metal container of napkins. "The cone, kid," he commanded. From the cash register Mr. Howard looked at me sharply. *Every customer is a King of Cones.*

I put together chocolate chip and strawberry cones, and handed them both to Rob.

He stared at the ice cream like I'd just served up a dead rat. "What the hell's this?"

"Your…your ice cr..cream."

"I said one cone. Lizzie doesn't need one. Dump the strawberry."

I looked over at Elizabeth.

"But Rob, I wanted—" she started to say.

Rob shoved the cones back at me and encircled her waist with one arm, his hand resting just above her hip. The strap of her hot pink tank top fell down below one shoulder.

"It's for your own good, babe. Cheerleader camp's in a couple of weeks and I think I'm pinching an inch here."

"Please, Rob," Elizabeth said, wincing. "That hurt."

Rob grinned and pinched her again.

I don't exactly remember what happened next but Emma, who was putting more mix in the soft serve, swore I practically leaped over the counter, teeth bared. The upshot was that Rob's white polo shirt was splattered with frozen strawberry bits and mini chocolate chip chunks, Mr. Howard fired me on the spot, and Elizabeth and I became friends for life.

Much to my delight, she broke up with Rob a few weeks later. Much to my dismay, she attracted an almost equally ill-suited assortment of boyfriends throughout the rest of high school. I kept my mouth shut, though, and was always there to console her as one by one they bit the dust.

"What would I do without you?" Elizabeth would sigh after Nick or Charlie had gone by the wayside and she felt alone and unloved for about twenty seconds. If she felt really bad we'd sit on the swings in the park behind the Burger King smoking cigarettes and drinking Diet Coke spiked with peppermint schnapps. Sometimes she'd let me hold her and stroke her hair. It was the highlight of my life.

Elizabeth went to UMass for college and I headed west to Cal Tech. California was farther away than I'd ever imagined and cell phones didn't make it any closer. Whenever I reached Elizabeth she was on her way to a frat party or sorority fundraiser. She'd promise to call me back later but later usually didn't come. I learned to content myself with the random emojis she doled out from time to time.

I studied hard enough to get a Master's in biomedical engineering and stayed in California, trying not to think too much about Elizabeth. I saw on LinkedIn she'd moved back to Boston to work at a local cable station. After my father died, leaving my mother alone, I moved back, too, and joined a start-up in Cambridge working on nanotechnology. Elizabeth seemed happy to reconnect and we got a theater subscription downtown, took a sailing course on the Charles, and had dinner twice a month. She continued to beat off guys with a stick and I was careful not to push anything too far. Early on she suggested exchanging keys to our apartments and my heart took a wild leap, but she only wanted me to water her plants while she was in Cancun.

I thought we were happy—in fact I know we were happy—but

after a few years Rob the jock strolled back into her life and it was high school all over again. He was the football star; she was the adoring cheerleader, and I, once more, was the short, skinny guy on the sidelines. Lucky for me he had a newly acquired flaw—a trust fund wife named Amy whose father owned the construction business he worked for.

Unfortunately, it wasn't a flaw in Elizabeth's eyes. On the pretense of a high school reunion, Elizabeth engineered a dreadful dinner at Rob and Amy's place. Over chips and salsa I was less than pleased to learn that Rob's latest project was not that far from my office.

"You two can have lunch together," Elizabeth ordered, pointing her wine glass first at me and then at Rob. She'd had a little too much Pinot Grigio and bright red spots burned on her cheekbones. Rob and I pretended to agree and Elizabeth, satisfied that we weren't going to be at each other's throats, spent the rest of the evening professing great interest in Rob's burgeoning career as a construction project manager.

I helped Amy carry in the plastic plates from the patio. She was a perfectly nice woman, if a little on the dull side. From what I could tell she and Rob made a fine couple: brick townhouse near the commuter rail, gas grill and fire pit in the backyard, and a small white furry animal until kids came along.

Elizabeth disagreed with my assessment. "I don't think she's right for him, do you?" she asked as I drove her home. "He seemed subdued tonight. Rob used to be so full of life."

I shrugged. Rob full of life was a man I could live without.

Even with Rob back in town, Elizabeth and I continued our routine of various outings and dinners, so it took me a while to figure out what was going on.

"Can you come over, Matthew? Like right now? I need to talk to you."

This was a command performance for Elizabeth early one Sunday morning about three months post-barbeque. I called my mother to tell her I couldn't make it for brunch and headed over to Elizabeth's condo in the Charlestown Navy Yard.

When she opened the door I was shocked. I hadn't seen her in a couple of weeks but in that brief time she looked like she had peeled almost ten pounds off her already slender frame. Black silk pants hung down from her hips and her ribs jutted out from underneath her t-shirt. But her green eyes were glowing and she couldn't keep a smile off her face. *Rob*, I thought, *she's been seeing Rob.*

"So," Elizabeth said abruptly, seating herself on the white leather couch. "I've been keeping a secret and I'm about to burst. What do you think about a wedding next summer?"

She misread the confusion on my face and laughed. "Silly boy, I don't mean you. We're way too good friends to ever get married." She poured coffee into blue and white striped china cups on the table in front of her and nodded at me to take one.

"Are these new?" I asked lightly as I picked up the coffee cup. My heart pounded as I stalled for time. *Rob*, I thought furiously, *she actually thinks she'd going to marry Rob.*

"I picked them up last week at Target," Elizabeth said, waving her hand. "So what do you think? You know who I'm talking about."

I let a look of comprehension dawn after a few beats and she nodded in encouragement.

"Isn't there a slight problem?" I asked. "Like his wife?"

Elizabeth frowned at the sarcasm in my tone. "If you mean Amy," she replied stiffly. "I don't think we have to worry about her."

I put a smile on my face that was worthy of Mr. Howard and the Royal Dairy. "I'll be honored to dance at your wedding. Why don't you tell me all about it?"

I deserved a medal for enduring the next hour and it only got worse when I left. Elizabeth walked me outside to my car and as I opened the driver's door she pulled out a man's gold watch. It looked like the Rolex Rob sported on his hairy arm.

"Can you do me a favor and swing by the construction site tomorrow to drop this off for Rob?" Elizabeth paused delicately. "He left it here the other night and if Amy notices it's missing she might suspect something. He has to break it to her gently, you know."

I took the watch without a word and shoved it into my pocket. Yeah right, I thought. I'll be a lot of things for you but not the errand boy to your married lover. Rob could get his watch back when he begged me for it.

At home I dropped the Rolex on my kitchen counter and proceeded to polish off an entire bottle from my stash of single malt scotch. I thought about calling Amy, then I thought about calling Rob.

In the end I simply waited, like I'd been doing since the day I met Elizabeth.

The call came before dawn a few days later.

I knew it was her by the ring tone—the classic Joe Cocker's 'You Are So Beautiful'—and picked up right away.

"Everything okay?"

"She's dead, Matthew," Elizabeth whispered, stifling a sob. "She's dead."

I sat up in bed. My sheets felt clammy so I kicked them off. "What are you talking about? What happened? Who's dead?"

"Amy. Rob came home late last night and found her dead. She fell down the stairs and broke her neck. I think she'd been drinking."

"Jesus, Elizabeth, that's terrible. Where are you? Do you need me to come over?"

Her voice trembled. "I'm at home and I do need you. I need your help. I know this is going to sound horrible, but where were you last night?"

"Me? I was here at home. I didn't do much. Grubhub and Netflix."

A deep sigh came through the phone. "Would you help me? Would you be willing to say we were together last night? That I was at your house until about midnight?"

"Are you in any trouble? Wasn't Amy's death an accident?"

"Of course it was an accident but the police want to talk to me. I don't know what to do. I was home alone, too, but I don't think they'll believe me. I wanted to marry Rob—she was his wife. Once they find out, it might be as simple as that."

I promised Elizabeth she could count on me. And what kind of lie was it anyway? Elizabeth easily could have been at my place until midnight; it had happened plenty of times before. I coached her on the *Star Trek* marathon I'd indulged in last night and we walked through the menu from Shanghai Blossom. We were lucky that I'd been starving when I'd ordered. If the police checked, and from what Elizabeth was saying they probably would, they'd see I'd gotten more than enough steamed dumplings for two.

As we were talking, I wondered more than once exactly where Rob had been last night. A rich wife and a beautiful girlfriend. If anyone benefitted from Amy Dudley's death, it was Rob.

The detectives came sooner than I'd expected, tracking me down at my office that very afternoon. There were two of them, both women. I figured the heavyset older woman was the one in charge and explained the story Elizabeth and I had worked out. She seemed sympathetic, though the younger, dark-haired one made me uneasy. She leaned against my cubicle while I was telling them about sharing shrimp in black bean sauce, her arms crossed and an odd half-smile on her face.

"You have an amazing recall for detail, Mr. Buckley," she finally said.

I tried for a hearty laugh. "I guess I just have a weakness for Chinese and sci-fi."

"And for Elizabeth Cort?" She made it sound like a challenge.

"Elizabeth and I are very good friends," I agreed. "We've known each other for years. That's why I know she couldn't have had anything to do with Mrs. Dudley's death and why I'm glad I can say definitely she was with me last night."

The detective in charge raised one hand. "We're not here to accuse Ms. Cort of anything. We're just gathering information and inquiring into the whereabouts of people who knew Amy Dudley. Ms. Cort's one of them. And, for that matter, so are you."

What about Rob? I wanted to scream. Isn't it obvious that if anyone killed her he did? *Play it cool*, I told myself, *these detectives aren't stupid. They'll figure it out.*

All in all I thought I'd handled the police quite well. I only hoped Elizabeth held up, too. I called her cell right after they left but it went straight to voicemail. She didn't answer my text either. I tried her at the TV station and the woman who answered said Elizabeth was off today.

When I got home from work the detectives were waiting outside my apartment door. This time the one in charge didn't look sympathetic at all.

"Mr. Buckley, you're under arrest for the murder of Amy Dudley," she said. "You have the right to remain silent. You have the right to an attorney. If you can't afford one—"

"What are you talking about? I didn't kill anyone." I knew I was shouting but there had to be a mistake.

She droned on as if I hadn't spoken.

"What about Rob Dudley? He's the one you should be arresting. He's the one who killed Amy. He wanted to get rid of her and marry Elizabeth,"

The younger detective snorted. "Of course that's what you want us to believe. If Rob Dudley were out of the picture, then maybe you'd have a chance with Ms. Cort. That's why you placed his watch in Amy Dudley's hand—after you pushed her down the stairs."

I stared at them both in disbelief. "Rob's watch? Elizabeth gave it to me to return to him. We work near each other. It's right inside. I'll show it to you."

The detectives watched skeptically as I unlocked the door and headed for my kitchen counter.

"I left it here. I just haven't had the chance to get over to his jobsite. You'll see, it's right here." I pushed aside a bag of tortilla chips and the bowl where I left miscellaneous change. The watch was nowhere to be found.

"I don't understand. I swear I left it right here."

"I think we understand very well," the older detective said. "Ms. Cort gave you the watch to return to Mr. Dudley but you kept it. You thought you might be able to use it and last night you took your chance. You went over on some friendly pretext, Mrs. Dudley made you a cup of coffee, and then you returned the favor by pushing her down the stairs."

"Coffee? I didn't have any coffee last night. Not with Amy Dudley or anyone else."

"There were two blue and white striped cups on the table in the living room. They were both half-full. We're willing to bet your prints are on one of them."

My mind flashed back to the china cups in Elizabeth's apartment.

"I was with Elizabeth last night," I protested. "She told you that, didn't she?"

They shook their heads in unison.

"I don't understand. You must be joking. Elizabeth was here last night. We got Chinese and watched some Netflix."

"Ms. Cort and Mr. Dudley attended a fundraiser for the new youth community center in Roxbury," the dark-haired detective said. "Mr. Dudley's firm is donating the construction costs and Ms. Cort's station was doing a special report. They were seen by about two hundred other guests."

My stomach twisted as I realized they were telling the truth. I held up my hands. "You have it all wrong. This was *Elizabeth's* idea. You see that, don't you? She set me up. Those were *her* coffee cups. She gave me Rob's watch to return to him, but she knew I'd be pissed and wouldn't do it right away. She had a key to my apartment. She must have snuck in and took it back."

I knew I was babbling but I kept on going. "She got me to lie for her because otherwise she'd be a suspect. She and Rob must have been in it together. Elizabeth knew I'd do anything for her. You have to believe me."

The detectives gave me pitying smiles as they snapped on the handcuffs. "As a matter of fact we do believe you on that last point," one of them murmured. "That's exactly what she told us. That you'd do anything. For Elizabeth."

ROBB T. WHITE

A Derringer-nominee, **Robb T. White** has published several crime, noir, and hardboiled novels and published crime, horror, and mainstream stories in various magazines and anthologies. His crime story, 'Inside Man,' was selected for *Best American Mystery Stories 2019*. A recent series features private eye Raimo Jarvi and includes *Northtown Eclipse*. His novel, *When You Run with Wolves* was cited as a finalist by *Murder, Mayhem & More* for its Top Ten Crime Books of 2018. Two recent works are the novella *Dead Cat Bounce* and 'If I Let You Get Me,' selected for the Bouchercon 2019 anthology. Robb is a member of the International Screenwriters' Association.

Find him at tomhaftmann.wixsite.com/robbtwhite.

SEE YOU IN COURT

ROBB T. WHITE

TREY'S FRIENDS all said it at one time or another with a wink or a laugh: "He's just like that lawyer in *Body Heat*." The film aficionados among them knew exactly what that meant, and so he was tagged "Ned" or "Ned Racine," by a few of them, especially when Trey was partying throughout the wee hours before he was due in court the next morning.

Two reasons gave credence to the nickname: Trey was a mediocre lawyer and a fanatical womanizer just like William Hurt's character in the noir film—which, surprisingly, never stopped clients from coming to him. Trey himself used to laugh over drinks about his lopsided won-loss record because it didn't make much difference. Clients liked him, he never goosed billable hours, and they recommended him to their friends in trouble. Be it said that charging less than most lawyers helped his caseload, and he was rarely idle.

People thought his luck had run out when he was brought up on an ethics charge for mixing funds with an estate he was handling. No malfeasance was proved, however, and the state ethics board let him off with a slap on the wrist. He found his appetite for trial work beginning to wane after a series of consecutive courtroom losses in which his last three clients were found guilty and all were given maximum sentences. He failed to get a plea deal from the Prosecutor's office each time—or, at least, one his clients would accept. Not that his clients didn't deserve their sentences; all were in fact guilty as charged and when he gave his little set speech about not wanting to know whether they had committed the offense they were charged with, two of the three listened patiently and tried harder to sell him their phony alibis. The last of the three told him to skip it altogether and proceeded to inform Trey how he wanted his defense to go.

That was a particularly bad one. The jury came back in an hour, which was ten minutes longer than his last case. While the man was being led off with his hands cuffed behind him by the bailiff, he turned around and glared at Trey. He shouted, "I ain't done it, Judge!" For days afterward, he caught people saying "I ain't done it, Judge!" and giving one another that convict "mean mugging" stare around the court house. The new court stenographer even picked it up and flashed it to him on her way into Judge Boyko's Family Court. He was becoming a courthouse joke. Even the prosecutors he barely knew bought him drinks at happy hour and slapped him on the back.

He was brooding over his beer at Polly's when most of the regulars had gone home to their families. Out of the corner of his eye, he saw John Darigold, the assistant DA, coming toward him. People who didn't like him called him "Mary Gold" behind his back, but he was a shark in the courtroom, and he boasted a perfect string of wins. He was touted as the next DA and, as the heir apparent, he also had his boss' approval.

"Darigold," Trey said, trying not to look at his face but knowing the smirk was there.

"Fewtrell," he said. "Buy you a beer?"

"I think I'll go," Trey said. "I've had my limit."

Darigold gave him a look of mock surprise.

"Say, you're not still pissed over that Hollis thing, are you?"

Hollis was the "I-ain't-done-it" client.

"We had no choice," Darigold said; "we couldn't go any lighter on that plea offer. He should have taken it."

"Tell me about it," Trey said. "Look, no hard feelings. But I have to go."

"Big date tonight?"

"Yeah, me, a Xerox box full of discovery depositions, and the Palm sisters."

"Another time then," Darigold said. "Meanwhile here's this. A little present."

He placed a laminated business card on the table and guided it with his index finger between Trey's Jack Daniels and water glass, like a miniature surfer riding the shoulders of a peaking wave.

"What's this?"

"A potential client," he said. "Call him. Not to worry. No trial work involved."

"I'm not afraid of trials, John. I'm busy right now."

"Yes, I heard. Judge Stevens doesn't believe in the wheels of justice grinding slowly."

Trey picked up the card. Jonas Wing Construction and a phone number. The name meant nothing.

Three hours later, bored and cross-eyed from reading case depositions, Trey took the card out of his wallet and thumbed the numbers.

"Yes?"

"Mister Wing, my name is Trey Fewtrell—"

"Yes?"

"John Darigold gave me your number and suggested I call you."

"It's late, Mister Fewtrell," the baritone voice responded.

"I'm sorry, sir. If it's inconvenient, I can—"

"Do you have a pen handy?"

The voice gave him an address and directions and told him to come at three o'clock the next afternoon. Trey was about to tell him he had a prior engagement, a polite lie to avoid appearing easy to get, when the man hung up.

Trey looked at the address again—a gated community north of the township lines. Ritzy, spacious, manicured lawns. No blacks or Mexicans unless they had gardening tools in their hands. Absolutely no transients, and the only pedestrians you'd see were toned and tanned young twenty-somethings in snazzy jogging outfits worth a month's salary at a Burger King. He had been there once before, when the District Attorney had invited several newly minted lawyers to his lavish manor house for a Christmas party. Trey had introduced himself while the man greeted the arrivals, his gorgeous trophy wife hanging on to her husband's arm with one hand, a thin-stemmed wineglass in the other. He never spoke to him again, although he saw him headlining press conferences whenever a sensational murder garnered big headlines.

Trey was five minutes early, one of his rare punctual moments. He half-expected a liveried servant in a frock coat to answer the bell, but instead it was Jonas Wing himself in a faded U of Connecticut tee. The man's hair was rumpled and looked like an unmade bed. Trey felt overdressed in his best navy blue pinstripe, his "lucky" suit he wore for closing arguments.

The amenities came and went so fast, Trey wasn't quite sure what he was offered and had glibly refused. They were sitting on a leather couch in Wing's spacious living room. The chandelier was so high up, Trey wondered how anyone could ever get up that high to dust it.

"I'll come to the point," Wing said. "I understand my son, Beauregard, is on the witness list. I don't want you to call him to the stand. I don't want you to cross-examine him."

"Mister Wing, your son is a material witness. He knew the murd —deceased girl. He was one of the last people she spoke to before she was—before her body was discovered in the river."

"I'm well aware of that," Wing said, "but damn it, my son's future is at stake. I don't want him connected to a sordid murder case. This kind of thing, it gets around, you know? People talk. I don't want his chances of getting into a good college tarnished because some girl he knew in high school was dumb enough to get herself mixed up with scum."

"You mean 'scum' like my client Erik Charles?"

"I understand it's your job to defend garbage like him. But he's a thirty-year-old criminal drug dealer who hangs around high school kids."

"Sir, if I may interject. The prosecution is going to call your son. Don't be in doubt at all about that. That's just the fact of it."

Wing stared at him. Trey had a feeling he was pondering how much to reveal.

"The assistant D.A. feels he might not need my son's testimony tomorrow."

Trey smelled a rat. A very big rat with shiny red eyes.

"Regardless of what John Darigold might have said to you, sir. I *do* intend to call him."

"I thought we might come to an understanding about that," Wing said, as if he were changing the subject altogether. "My company is very big. I'm sure you've heard of us."

Trey had. Half the government buildings in town were built with Wing Construction, not to mention all the estates that had sprung up in the last fifteen years.

"You see," Wing continued, "I need a good local lawyer for some estate deeds and various contracts to be negotiated with the city. I'm planning to build and you've been highly recommended by—"

"—John Darigold," Trey finished. "I think we're done here, Mister Wing."

Trey was steaming all the way back to town. He called Darigold and after several minutes on hold, he heard his slightly bored voice.

"What were you thinking? You sent me out there on a wild goose chase. You know his kid is going to testify. What was the point?"

"He's just looking out for his boy, Trey. You or I, we'd do the same thing."

"I'd call it suborning a witness."

"That's because you were sleeping during Criminal Law One-O-One. Or maybe steeped in some lurid sex fantasy—"

"All right, all right. Who the hell cares if his kid testifies in a murder trial? Since when did that become a big deal?"

"Look, it's not exactly one of those boxes you tick off on a college application, but people do talk," Darigold said.

"Pull the leg with bells on it, Darigold. What's the real reason?"

"Beauregard Wing's GPA is 3.0 at best, but he went to the right prep school and the old man wants to see him in Princeton next year. Wing knows the admissions officer and a couple people on the Board with pull. But if his son's name is smeared all over the front pages with this sleazy trial, thanks to your meth head client, it's kaput. Hello, community college."

"I don't run in the same circles as you, your boss, or Wing, but a community college got me started."

Darigold's silence at the other end meant he didn't have to say it: *Look how well it turned out for you.*

"Why don't you drop by my office tomorrow before court? The DA agrees with me. Charles acted under diminished capacity. We can work out the numbers tomorrow. Everybody wins."

"Everybody but Navarro," Trey said.

"Who? Oh, the dead girl. Lucy Navarro. Right. Well, she should have picked better friends to hang out with. See you tomorrow."

Trey had to go. It would be nothing short of dereliction not to, but he already knew Erik Charles' answer to the offer of any reduced sentence, even without the obscenities attached. He was stubbornly committed to his plea of innocence. Trey remembered the arraignment judge's blank stare when Erik made the announcement in court in a loud voice.

IT WAS ALMOST SURREAL, what he was hearing from the DA's own mouth the next morning. Trey wanted to get up and make sure the plaque on the wall still said "O. James Orrenberger, Jr. District Attorney."

"Ten years," Orrenberger stated flatly. "With good time, he'll serve seven, maybe seven-and-a-half."

"It's a good deal for your client," Darigold chimed in, playing the chorus to whatever his boss said.

Trey was thinking: *It's a fantastic deal—but he won't take it.*

"I'll inform my client," Trey said.

"Better hurry," Orrenberger said. "You start in twenty-five minutes."

Trey explained it in a couple of sentences, speaking neutrally. Charles was his usual disagreeable, foul-mouthed self. "Tell him to shove it up his ass."

That morning, the ME was scheduled to start. The forensics, even in that dry-as-dust technical language of the autopsy, was brutal. Lucy Navarro, fifteen years old, an abandoned child raised in foster homes she had often run away from, had her head bashed in six months previous, sometime in the late evening hours, with an elongated weapon similar to a tire iron, a piece of rebar or maybe a fireplace poker. She had been tossed over a narrow bridge, into the river below, her blood pooled between the rails. One of her shoes had fallen off and was stuck near the shore. That alerted a passing jogger, who had also noticed the excessive amount of blood on the bridge.

The investigation led straight to Trey's client, a known misfit, "no stranger to the police," as the papers liked to say. He had been identified by a teenaged girl, who claimed to be at Erik's party. According to her testimony, Navarro was nude, having just engaged in sex with another male at the party, and when she refused Erik's demand for sex, was knocked unconscious. The witness said she and another girl there helped dress her—right down to the red tennis shoes—and then Erik carried her to his van and drove off with her. When he returned two hours later, she asked him where he took her. He'd laughed, saying, "She went for a swim."

Darigold's opening statement was rhetorically splendid with descriptions of the murderer ranging from "a cold-blooded reptile" to "a callous monster." The hostile expression on his client's face, Trey was certain, didn't endear him to a single juror.

During the ME's testimony, Trey watched one elderly female juror, Number Seven, who continually dabbed at the corners of her eyes with a tissue.

By late afternoon, Darigold called his last witness of the day: "Beauregard Jesse Wing."

"Do your friends call you Beau or Jess?" Darigold smiled.

"Beau, sir."

"Please speak up, Beau, so that the jurors can hear you."

"Yes, sir."

"You knew the victim Lucy Navarro, didn't you?"

"I guess so. We go—she used to go to the same high school as me."

"Were you friends?"

"Not really. I'd see her at some of the same parties. But we didn't hang out together."

"I see," Darigold said, and looked down suddenly, as if a button had come loose on his Armani suit. It was a familiar tactic. Trey had seen Marigold come out of that seemingly relaxed pose and take the hide off a reluctant witness, all but browbeating him with a string of razor-sharp questions.

"Were you sad when you learned what had happened to her?"

What? Trey fidgeted in his seat, wondering what Darigold was up to.

"Tell us about the text you received from Erik Charles in which he threatened you—"

"Objection, your Honor, leading the witness."

"I'll rephrase," Darigold said, without turning to acknowledge Trey. "What did the text message say?"

"I was at home. I knew Lucy hung out with a rough crowd. I heard Erik Charles' name mentioned by a couple kids before. They said he dealt drugs. I never spoke to him in person and he only called me that one time. He must have got my number from Lucy. He said I better stay away from her—or else. She was his girl. Something like that."

"And what, then, did you do?"

"I called Lucy right after. I told her Erik texted me. I told her to be careful if she ran into him."

Darigold continued to throw softballs for Beau to hit. By the end of his twenty-minute testimony, his soft voice had gained confidence.

Trey had his work cut out for him. Not only was his client a useless, violent human being, he was suspected of kidnapping a teenaged girl in another county. Fortunately for him, the trial judge barred that information from reaching the jury.

The most damaging witness was taking the stand the next day: the girl who had all but witnessed the murder.

Bonnie Dry was a sixteen-year-old with long chestnut hair and dimples. Trey knew he had to demolish her testimony but avoid looking the bully. Trey took her through her original testimony and it was clear she hadn't changed or added anything different. She happened to be at the party with a girlfriend who got her marijuana from Charles.

"Did you ever see Erik Charles before that night?"

"No."

"How well did you know Lucy Navarro?"

"I never saw her, either. I mean, before that night."

"Before the night he knocked her out at his house, you helped dress her, and then he took off with her body in a van?"

"That's right."

"Is this the girl you saw at the party?"

Trey approached the witness to hand her a photo.

"Objection!"

"On what grounds, Mister Darigold?"

"Witness intimidation, for starters," Darigold said to the judge.

"It's not an autopsy photo, your Honor," Trey said. "It's what the kids call a glam shot photo. I took it off her Facebook page."

"I'll allow it," the judge said. Darigold sat down and glared at Trey.

"Yeah, that's her," Bonnie said. "She's the one that was at the party."

Trey's heart bumped in his chest. A long shot but it worked.

He slowly turned toward the panel of jurists and said, as calmly as he could, "Let the record show that the witness has identified Susan Renee Jones of Trumbull County. She is a resident of—"

The hullabaloo that burst out in open court caused Judge Richard Stevens to bang his gavel three times, a record. Darigold jumped up from his seat at the prosecution table as if he were catapulted from it. Trial spectators and casual courtroom watchers —namely, other lawyers dropping in to observe Darigold's rapier style—were shocked.

The tumult had not subsided even when Judge Stevens shouted for both counselors to approach the bench.

He said just three words but they were decisive: "My chambers. Now!"

"This had better be good, Mister Fewtrell," Judge Stevens said as soon as they were behind closed doors.

"Your Honor, the police investigation was badly flawed from the outset…"

Trey laid it out for both men. Bonnie Dry was speaking the truth. The trouble was that the police had jumped to an unfortunate conclusion. Trey himself didn't put it together until the day before the plea deal was being offered. He was thinking of his knuckleheaded client and realized something: everybody was assuming all along the girl Erik Charles had taken "for a swim" was Lucy Navarro because he was found stoned to the gills at the river. No one thought to check any incident reports of assaults filed that day in Trumbull County.

One phone call satisfied him that the police had it wrong right from the start. The girl who filed the assault report fit the exact description of Lucy Navarro in age, size, and color of eyes and hair. Trey had her high school fax him her photo from the yearbook and checked it against her Facebook page ten minutes before Judge Stevens' bailiff called court to order. If the officer taking the report had not written "possible kidnap" in the margins of his report, Trey would not have followed his hunch and risked everything, including what was left of his reputation, on a courtroom Hail Mary.

He had one big challenge left, and in his gut more than his brain, he knew where the answer lay. Trey would not have known that Zen-like feeling the Japanese call a *satori* if he tripped over one, but he felt it throughout the remainder of trial that day. Darigold was clearly flustered and had to be rebuked by Stevens several times. No one had ever seen him fumbling for words and misspeaking like that. It was a strange reversal: Trey had come into many a court arraignment or first day of trial with a hangover, but he had never seen the suave John Darigold looking and acting as if he were drunk.

Trey had a day off to investigate and he needed it badly. He rooted through his Xerox boxes of discovery items and found what he was looking for. His frat brother, Youssef—Joe to his friends—was a math whiz who oversaw the IT department at a community college, but it was at the other end of the state, a five-hour drive. The tiny devil whispering in his ear told him Erik Charles was scum and didn't deserve the trouble.

"Everybody deserves a fair trial, goddamn it," Trey said, but he was looking at his own face in a bathroom mirror. He grabbed his wallet, credit cards, and keys and bolted for the car.

"Look at this sequence of numbers," Joe said, pointing to a row of numbers on a printout consisting entirely of rows of numbers.

"I could be looking at a paternity test for all I know about it," Trey said.

"That's chemistry. Just compare these four with the ones above and below. Any idiot can see they're dissimilar."

"Yeah, so what?" Trey replied. "It has to make sense to a jury, remember?"

"Your boy said on the stand he was at home, right? Okay, so look at the phone calls from various places in and around the city to his home. See the similarities?"

"No."

"I'll make it easy for you. Your boy, this Wing kid, said he was home when he got the call from Erik Charles warning him to stay away from Lucy Navarro. He's not at home. These numbers—here, here, and here—Joe's finger jabbed at the printout. "These numbers, they all prove when he's at home. The cell phone tower pings are identical with these numbers, not so with this one, the one you say is crucial."

"Okay, got it so far. But where's the proof?"

"That's the easy part," Joe. "Look at the numbers. I drew an isosceles triangle on the printout from the towers for you."

Trey groaned.

"Hey," Joe said, laughing, "you remember when they told us in sophomore geometry that knowing the Pythagorean theorem just might save our lives some day?"

"Tell me," Trey said.

"The signal from the Beau Wing's cell is so weak right there it got passed on to four different towers. That's the one and only call he says he made to Lucy that night."

"So he lied on the witness stand," Trey said, trying to think it through.

Part of the missing answer was already on Lucy's Facebook page. She told her friends she was "p" and that she was planning to run away "to California." Her friends all assumed she meant with the baby daddy. Most believed that was Erik.

Trey needed proof. Darigold had opened one door that couldn't be shut. He needed phone records of every call made to that phone. The log of Lucy's phone was sitting in one of the Xerox boxes at his house. Thirty-five thousand phone calls, texts, tweets, emails—Trey was too old to be a millennial, but he often wondered about a generation that put every act and thought out there for the world to see. He thought of his own father, who probably never said ten words when none would do.

He couldn't sleep that night. He knew the courthouse rumor machine had gone wild after yesterday's bombshell.

DARIGOLD ENTERED the courtroom in a Gucci suit, looking ready for war.

Troy called Beau Wing to the stand.

"You said you took the call from Erik Charles at your house?"

"Yeah. It was a text, I said."

"Speak up, Beau, so everyone can hear you. You took Erik Charles' threatening text message and you promptly turned around and called Lucy to warn her about Erik?"

"Yeah, that's right," Beau said. He wasn't looking as confident now.

"At home, you said."

"Yeah, I was at home," Beau repeated.

"Objection. Badgering the witness," Darigold snapped, not bothering to rise this time.

"Yes," Judge Stevens asked, "where is this going, Mister Fewtrell?"

"Your Honor, my next witness will explain. I'd like to excuse Mister Wing and call Mister Youssef Hamoud Awadallah to the stand. Mister Awadallah is the Director of Internet Communications and Network Services at Sinclair Community College in Dayton."

Joe was articulate, precise, and very, very clear with his printouts and blow-up chart for the jurors to see. There, smack in the middle, was the same isosceles triangle.

"What could make a signal that weak?" Trey asked Joe. "That is, so weak that four towers would hand it off as it was ongoing."

"A natural depression," Joe replied.

"A river?"

"Objection!"

"Overruled," Judge Stevens said. Trey had noticed the Judge's interest level had gone up several notches since yesterday. The media were watching intently. TV news vans with logos and whip aerials were lined up outside the courtroom.

"Not the river so much as the heavy vegetation surrounding them," Joe added. "But yes, hills, bluffs, weather, many things affect cellular transmission in the open. As I have indicated on my graph, all the numbers dictate only one possible location within a three-mile radius from Tower Number Three."

"No further questions. Thank you, Mister Awadallah."

Trey smiled as he returned to his seat at the defense counsel table. He turned to Erik, whose expression implied he had no idea what just went on and didn't care. Trey thought of explaining it but decided it wasn't worth wasting his breath. The damage was done: Trey had isolated calls to Beau's phone from Lucy's in the weeks before the murder. Some calls were separated by seconds or minutes. It finally clicked: they were hanging up on each other. Typical teens, calling and hanging up after an angry conversation. What else could the subject be about, what else could infuriate a shy, soft-spoken boy from the upper-middle class to murder except one thing: he was going to be tied down to a girl he had impregnated, a girl with a bad reputation from the wrong side of the tracks. His good life was over, done, trashed by fate.

Three hours later, while waiting for the jury verdict, Trey ran into Darigold in the men's room.

"Nice work, Fewtrell," Darigold said. "You really cocked up that trial nicely. That jury's in there right now trying to figure out what the hell you just did back there."

"I just proved your golden boy, Beau Wing, made a call to Lucy Navarro, lured her to the river, and then smashed her brains in because he thought she was pregnant with his child."

Darigold stopped his frenetic hand washing to look at Trey in the mirror. "Dangerous words, my friend. Besides, she wasn't pregnant. The autopsy proved it."

"Yes, but Beau didn't know that, did he? He was seeing his future go up in flames. A trailer-trash girl, a poor runaway, who hung out with druggies, was about to announce she was having his baby. That's a pretty strong motive, counselor."

"You idiot, the DA will never go for an indictment of that kid."

"No, I don't suppose he will. Birds of a feather and all that. But your perfect record just took a hit."

"Maybe we should wait for the verdict," Darigold said.

"You know what they say," Trey said. He was hiding his smirk pretty well, he thought.

"No, what do they say?"

"Even a blind squirrel finds a nut."

The jury was out for three days. In the end, it was a mistrial. Even split: six for guilty, six for acquittal.

The DA's office declined to say whether charges were to be refiled. District Attorney Orrenberger was quoted as saying, "We're looking at everything in a new light."

Trey was willing to call it a Pyrrhic victory. Meanwhile, his surly client was easily identified by the blue glyph tattoo around his neck and was brought up on kidnapping and attempted murder charges in Trumbull County.

Trey didn't have much time to revel in besting the DA's top gun. Two weeks after the trial, his house was burgled. A month after that, a stripper he dated said he beat her up; she had the photos taken immediately after to prove it. Clients started to drop him as word of his bad luck and ensuing troubles got out. A former client sued him. That wasn't the strange part. Lawyers get sued all the time—just not the ones you win cases for. Trey was at a bar one night when he drove home drunk, crashed the car, and staggered off, leaving the scene. He was picked up at home, two hours later, barely coherent and claiming he was drugged at the bar. He was cited, jailed, and bonded out, but not before half the town knew of it. The papers and television media were all over it. His fall from grace was deplored by colleagues and people who claimed to know him. He was investigated for these infractions and his license to practice law was revoked.

Erik Charles was given a twenty-five-to-life sentence and sent to Lucasville down by the Ohio River, where the state's bad boys go. Trey left town, skipping out on some overdue bills, and was never heard from again. One rumor said they'd discovered graphic photos of teen girls on his laptop. Another rumor had it he was a private investigator in Mesa, Arizona.

No one was ever again charged with the murder of Lucy Navarro.

RHONDA EIKAMP

A native Texan, **Rhonda Eikamp** now makes her home in Germany. Her short fiction has appeared in *Lackington's*, *Enchanted Conversation*, *Neon*, and the special *Lightspeed* issue, 'Women Destroy Science Fiction,' among others. When not writing fiction, she translates German into English for a German law firm.

IN THE HALLS OF MERCY

RHONDA EIKAMP

My womanly intuition tells me you've pieced it together, but I'll go over it for you from the beginning.

You've got to understand what a scandal it was for us here at Mercy. We don't get out much, you know. The view is wonderful, the way the walkways slope down to the cliffs and the ocean beyond, a great contrast, all pretty here on this side of the stone wall and savage over there, and a tonic to the nerves. I've always loved the sound of the surf beating holes into the cliffs beneath our feet. Like thunder in catacombs. Especially in the fall, like now, with the wind up, all passion and bluster.... Can you hear it?

But we are so isolated in the ward. And there it was, a Monday, and Nurse Rose came wheeling a new arrival into the dayroom. You cannot imagine our shock. I suppose the nurses had been told what to expect, but we could not make heads or tails of it.

There was our very own Dr. Treptoe, chief psychiatrist of Mercy, all slumped in a wheelchair. Unshaven, practically comatose. To see those kind eyes unfocused like that, the white gown and the drool running down that handsome chin—it was like a knife through my heart.

Everyone reacted as you might expect. Jason the peeing wonder did his thing. That little psychopath Wonda began to applaud as if she were happy to see Dr. Treptoe in such straits. I punched her in the face and, well, then, we all became *upset*. That is Nurse Rose's word for it. Rose is a misleading name for what Daddy would have called a strapping girl. I say Nurse Rose sprang full-grown from a panzer and wearing jackboots. She had us straightened out soon enough, though Mr. Joe was still turning all the tables face-down, which he always does given half the chance, when who should walk into the dayroom but Dr. Treptoe.

I understood then. At least I thought I did. None of us had known Dr. Treptoe had a twin brother.

Dr. Treptoe knelt down in front of his poor brother, whom they had apparently been forced to drug up so much that he couldn't even speak, and he took his brother's hand and smoothed the white gown down over the knees. So caring.

But it was still wrong of Dr. Treptoe, I was thinking. He should have found some other clinic for his brother after the man had a nervous breakdown. Dr. Treptoe should have recused himself. And you have no call to look at me like that. Daddy was a judge up in Richmond. I imbibed such terms with my mother's milk. Daddy believed in justice. He taught me what it meant, even when it hurt, and it's justice that's been so terribly lacking in this matter.

You see, I went over to the twin after Nurse Rose parked him at the corner window. I was the only one to do so. Dr. Treptoe had left.

Mr. Treptoe—Silas—needs quiet, Nurse Rose had told us but she was preoccupied and to be honest I was fascinated by the twins' similarity.

Now, I know I have not always comported myself as a lady should. It's part of the reason I'm in a place like Mercy. A lady should not have feelings for a married man, but Dr. Treptoe had always been so...kind to me. I could talk about my childhood in our sessions and his eyes would look straight at me. That's a rarity. So I sat across from the man in the wheelchair and it was my beloved Dr. Treptoe, but it wasn't, don't you see? And then the twin opened his eyes and all the darkness was there, the night you see in just about any patient's eyes at Mercy. He was trying to speak and so I made sure Nurse Rose's back was still turned and I came up real close to him. Like this.

"Elspeth loves me," he said. Talking to himself, or rather drooling to himself, because his lips weren't working right. "She'll get me out of this."

Elspeth. Dr. Treptoe's lovely young sexpot of a wife. It made no sense, but I am used to the vast fantasies of my fellow inmates. Then he mumbled that peculiar thing that got me thinking so much. *It's a plot*, he hissed, then he let out a howl that liked to have brought the rafters down.

I'm used to that from my fellow inmates too, but it got Nurse Rose over and she yelled, "Out of the way, Amzie," and she gave the new patient a shot of halo that sent him to la-la land.

He was still staring out the window, but before he went under, for one second, he looked straight at me.

Daddy always said I was smart. I might have thought nothing of this whole incident if I hadn't turned to look out the window as they wheeled the twin brother out of the room.

Dr. Treptoe was down there in the parking lot, talking to his wife who had just driven up in their little convertible, and I supposed that was what had set off his poor twin's fantasies. I detest Elspeth Treptoe, with her waspish waist and her diamonds. Blonde-from-the-bottle. Call it jealousy. But I knew Dr. Treptoe worshipped her. Watching them, I realized they were having a fierce argument down there, in the wind and the swirling leaves, though I could hear none of it. She seemed determined to come inside and Dr. Treptoe seemed determined to stop her. No one else was around. When I saw him take her hair and jerk her head back, then ram her against the car, saying something to her up close...well, that's when the little seed that had fallen upon my mind began to germinate.

Don't you see?

Because my good, kind Dr. Charles Treptoe—the man I was in love with—could never have been violent.

I see you want to tell me something, but let me finish. Very little escapes my notice around here, but no one listens to me. Only Dr.

Treptoe ever listened and he...oh how awful to have to refer to him in the past now.

I had a session with the doctor that very afternoon. He sat by the window. The sun had come out and it lit up his wavy brown hair and I dearly hoped that the seed taking root in my head was just one of my phases. He seemed so preoccupied. In our earlier sessions, we'd been maundering our way through my childhood and I picked up where we'd left off. I'd just gotten to the part about Daddy's regimen of ice baths meant to drive the troubles out of ten-year old me—how it'd make Mama cry to watch and Daddy would go comfort her and forget about me—but Dr. Treptoe just kept staring down at the parking lot.

Suddenly he said, "Have you ever been betrayed by someone you love, Amzie?"

I could not make heads or tails of it. I'd never loved anyone but Charles Treptoe. He'd always been there for me and now, it seemed, he needed my help. There he was, a few feet away. That distance they keep for a reason, you know. The patient over here in a chair and the doctor over there, but I stood and I crossed it.

The hardest thing I ever did.

I knelt in front of him as I'd seen him kneel in front of his brother earlier, and I whispered, "She's not good enough for you."

He never even noticed the distance I'd crossed, the effort it took. Still looking away. "No, she isn't," he muttered in agreement.

And since we were breaking rules, I broke the last one. I put my hand on his leg, just like this, running it up to *there*, and I said, "But I am, Charles. I can be good for you. Strong."

You don't know how it is never to touch or be touched. The nurses may manhandle you when you are in your bad phase and you don't care enough to wash or eat, but that's not touching. I could feel doors opening inside me. At that moment, I loved—there with my hand on that man—more than I ever had in my life. Loved truly and unselfishly.

He looked down at my hand and his eyes went wide. "Are you kidding?" he asked. Then he stood and shoved me so hard I fell over. "Just like her. Little southern sluts, all of you." And he left me there, sobbing on the floor.

That was when I was certain, you see.

It was not Dr. Treptoe who could have been so cruel.

Dr. Charles Treptoe had been replaced by his evil twin Silas.

It was all clear to me. It was a plot, as my beloved Charles, bound in that wheelchair, had tried to tell me through the drugs. Sometime that weekend out there in the world where they live, for unfathomable reasons, the evil twin Silas Treptoe had drugged his brother Charles so he could not speak or defend himself and had taken his place and signed the papers to have him committed to Mercy.

Please, one more moment. I'm coming to the murder.

I kept a watch on the brothers after that.

Oh, I tried to talk to Charles, always placing myself casually near his wheelchair in the dayroom, but Nurse Rose kept him sedated up to his beautiful rolling eyeballs. I do not believe now that Nurse Rose was in on the plot, just following orders. She would have done anything Dr. Treptoe instructed her to. I think she was a little in love with him herself. She just hadn't understood, as I had, that it wasn't Charles Treptoe in the white doctor coat anymore.

For a week I watched them take him for walks, out the gate and around the looped paths where we weren't allowed to go, Rose pushing the wheelchair past the dying azaleas and evil, gloomy Silas walking alongside his suffering brother. So caring.

Round and round.

Establishing a pattern.

The sea is so angry here in the cold months. It throws itself against the cliffs like they're the doors to its prison cell. Yesterday the sea was black and blue from tossing itself at the rocks and I refrained from taking the air in our own little pen of a yard. I stayed in the upstairs dayroom, watching from a window, tracing the looping paths on the pane in front of me as they walked them below.

I saw it happen.

The paths are nice and even, except there's that one that slopes a bit, isn't there, down toward the cliff edge? You'd only have to leave a wheelchair without its brake on and it would start rolling. And there's that break in the stone wall at just the right place, that little bit with only a knee-high boundary, where I imagine the owners of this place in older times would stand and watch the ocean.

I saw the commotion back here at the house, some fight in the yard, that made Nurse Rose stop and turn. I saw her put the brake on the wheelchair before starting back up the path, leaving the patient in the watchful care of his doctor, his brother-keeper. I saw the doctor's foot find the brake release, that little shove he gave. Up there I was a god, but it was a helpless god, watching a murderous game of billiards, trajectories all laid out. A game no one can stop by then. Sensing something, Nurse Rose turns back and the *doctor*, distracted for only the second it takes for the wheelchair to be well out of reach, notices and lunges after it, hurling himself until he trips and falls headlong in the gravel, wailing quite convincingly while Charles speeds toward his fate.

My poor beloved Charles. Do you think he saw what was coming? The sky rushing at him? The great edge of it all leaping up at him? Do you think he was conscious enough to understand and prepare himself? When the chair hit the boundary and went over, the force threw his arms forward and for a moment I swear it looked as though he was praying.

And then he was gone.

Such a long way down that cliff.

I was screaming and beating at the safety glass. Trapped behind my cage bars. And while everyone was running toward them and *Doctor* Treptoe turned, trying to scramble to his feet, still on his hands and knees and getting his devastated face just right before they could reach him, I saw him look up and see me.

The dark came then and I went away. Alfred was there when I woke up. He helped me to the bench by the window while I sobbed. We watched the police cars and fire engines arrive, men going over the cliff with ropes, though there was no hope. Alfred patted my hand and told me it would be alright. Alfred's the only patient who can calm me when I'm in a phase. His peculiar brand of crazy has never bothered me.

We watched the police for a long time, until they took Nurse Rose away. To help them in their inquiries, I'm sure they said. No handcuffs on her. Some discrepancy, apparently, between her story and the doctor's. I could almost read her lips down there, swearing that she'd left the brake on. I could see the shock of betrayal in those helpless strapping gestures she made toward the doctor.

"It can't have happened," I moaned to Alfred. "It just can't."

Alfred patted my shoulder. "It didn't, my dear," he told me. He tapped his head and I knew what was coming. "No film in the camera. It will all have to be shot again. You'll do better next time."

All so calming, in that deep furry accent, like a bulldog barking in slow motion. A fat English bulldog. Alfred is always so calming.

The dark came again and when I woke up I was alone in my room. It was night. The ward was deathly quiet. In Mercy you can always hear someone battling their inner demons at night, but I think now there must have been orders from on high to double-dose the worst patients. It might have been death itself that had swept through the halls hushing everyone.

So quiet I started to believe the events of the afternoon really hadn't happened, like Alfred said. And I might have convinced myself, if my doctor hadn't slipped into the room a moment later and tried to kill me.

I don't look strong, but I am. The lights were off and the shadow moved fast in the bit of moonlight from the window. I saw the glint off the syringe and I was faster. What a surprise for my doctor of course, when I wasn't on my bed.

That voice came out of the dark, so much like my dear, dead Charles. "Come now, Amzie, where are you? I'm only here to help you."

"You killed him," I said from behind.

The figure spun, followed the sound, and a hand was on my arm instantly. Cunning, but Silas Treptoe's not a doctor, is he? Not used to dealing with us. He had no idea how cunning a patient can be.

"It was a terrible accident," the voice insisted. "Just like the accident you're going to have in the shower, Amzie, with a piece of cord someone left carelessly lying around. Always so depressed, weren't you? Upset by what you saw today. You hanged yourself—"

With my free hand, I found his hand that held the syringe of halo and stabbed the needle up, into his arm.

Surprise.

Halo is fast. And as I have said before, I'm strong.

You may be wondering how little old me could drag a grown man down a mental ward hall without anyone noticing, but all the nurses seemed to have vanished too. I believe now they were sent off on some excuse. More orders from on high. Nurse Rose would never have allowed such a thing, but she was gone, wasn't she? And there was the key card for all the doors in the doctor's pocket, for the elevator that took us down to the laundry room. I'm one of the trusted and I've worked laundry duty. I know my way around the basement. And when someone is drugged up on halo it's easy to do what you want with him, even get him into a straitjacket.

You see, when you love you can do anything. You may think there was no love in that big stuffy house I grew up in, and maybe Daddy didn't love me, always saying there was something wrong with me. But he and Mama worshipped each other. I learned what love is from watching them. When the cancer came for Mama and they knew it was the end, she made a wish; a simple thing, to drink a mint julep through a ryegrass straw like she had in their younger days. Daddy made it for her and cut the straw and he rolled her wheelchair out onto that big sloping yard of ours so they could spend a night together under the stars she loved. It was autumn, like now. Leaves barely hanging onto branches, fluttering down like life itself going to ground. It took her last strength, but she died peaceful in his arms. In the morning I looked at Daddy slumped in his study, his eyes as hollowed out as these caves, and I knew I had to help him.

That's the reason I burned the house down with him in it. So he could be with her. The Richmond police and all those doctors before Mercy never understood that. How love makes you strong enough to do what you have to do.

This is justice, see. Justice for Charles. I loved him and you killed him. Oh you were heavy, but once I got you into the tunnels it was easy to slide you over the damp stone. I'd found the door hidden behind the laundry-room shelf years ago. The Mercy house was probably used for smuggling once. The cliff is riddled with these caves. That sound of thunder twice a day, why, that's the tide, pulsing in its veins.

You've been down here a day and a night, though you probably couldn't tell that in the dark. Up there they're saying Charles Treptoe ran off, did himself in, maybe because of guilt over his brother's accident. All Mercy in an uproar. No one paying any attention to my little comings and goings.

Oh all right, just the mouth then, I'm not a monster. Now, that's a ridiculous story. You're Charles, not Silas? Why, if that were true it would mean it was Charles who drugged his brother Silas that weekend and had him committed. It would mean my dear kind Charles Treptoe rolled his own twin brother off a cliff. For what, having an affair with his wife?

How crazy do you think I am?

Water? Well, that's why I've moved you down here today into the deeper tunnels where the tide reaches, dear evil twin. You won't be thirsty long. Once I've left, the tide will rise soon enough. You'll have your fill of water then and it will be icy cold.

You see, if justice is lacking one must be courageous and take matters into one's own hands. I have done so, just as I did with Daddy. That spark of courage to act, it is the spark of life, sir. If I had not acted on it, I would be the same as dead. Sane, perhaps, but dead.

I think Daddy would be proud of me.

SHARON HART ADDY

Sharon Hart Addy's fiction and poetry have appeared in a variety of magazines. She writes for children, as well as adults, and has several picture books to her credit. Sharon is a member of the Women's Fiction Writers Association.

Find her at sharonhartaddyauthor.wordpress.com.

NEAR WARRENTON

SHARON HART ADDY

WARRENTON. The town's name on the green expressway sign tripped a thought. I swung to the right lane and took the exit, hoping a quick visit would prove profitable. The idea of scrounging up cold hard cash in a free hour before my next business call had an inviting ring to it.

I knew the address. I'd looked it up several hundred times.

The farm wasn't difficult to find. Its fields stretched along the county highway that led off the interstate. I could see the big white house, red barn, and cluster of other buildings long before I reached them.

The closer I got, the shabbier the buildings looked, but I didn't let that discourage me. Fields of corn and other crops led off in all directions from the house and barn. The low stuff might be soybeans. I wasn't sure, but I knew it didn't matter. I figured green growing things meant money and I had a right to some of it.

When I pulled into the barnyard, an old man tinkering with an antique tractor straightened up to watch my car rumble to a stop on the sparse gravel. His bib overalls indicated that he'd shrunk several sizes in the years since they were new. His plaid shirt was faded.

I studied him as he sauntered, slightly bow-legged, toward my car. A breeze lifted his thin white hair. He looked like Harv, but older, much older, his skin leathery from hours in the sun, but definitely the father of the guy I knew. I got out of the car.

"Something I can do for you?" He even sounded like Harv. Or maybe Harv sounded like him.

"Mr. Milner?" I held out my hand for a handshake.

His name was on the mailbox at the road, so I didn't expect him to be suspicious, but the way he ignored my outstretched hand, put his hands in his back pockets, showed me he was.

"That's me."

"I'm Amanda Hall. I knew your son, Harv." Over the last few years I'd rehearsed the next line so often it rolled out smoothly. "I lost track of him. I wondered if you could give me his address."

The man's cloudy blue eyes flickered. "You one of his girlfriends?"

Groupie was closer to the truth, but I thought of four-year-old Natalie and nodded. "I guess you could say that."

He looked me up and down. "You don't seem like the others."

He had that right. But I'd given up the grungy, sexy look when I saw who I'd become. My conservative gray pantsuit and the navy blue company car reflected my current taste and sales position. "Harv had a lot of friends."

"Yeah. They pestered me for quite a while. What brings you?"

"Old times' sake," I lied. Even remembering the past, the time with him and his buddies, was more than I wanted to do. I was young and stupid then, a sixteen-year-old runaway. I thought Harv was my savior, my protector. He turned out to be anything but.

Harv's father pursed his lips and slid his hands into his front pockets. "Well, you ain't gonna see him here."

I wasn't surprised. Harv's lifestyle didn't lean toward tractor repair. "How can I track him down?"

"Don't rightly know."

I nodded. Harv never liked to stay in one place for long. "Is he living nearby?"

"Nope."

I thought of that old saying about getting information being as hard as pulling teeth. I tried again. "Do you hear from him at all?" I figured he'd be in jail, but that didn't seem to be the case.

"Nope. Don't hear from him and don't expect to."

"So you can't put me in touch with him?" Even in jail, he might have money to throw my way.

The old guy squinted at me. "You one of them he owes money to?"

I laughed. That was the least of it. "Yes. One of the multitude."

"Well. You ain't never gonna get it from him, and I ain't got nothing to cover his debts. Even if I did, I wouldn't hand it over."

Considering the rough crowd Harv ran with, the old turnip had guts, but I had something that might jolt a few bucks loose. I opened my car door and leaned in to grab my purse. Propping it on the car, I dug for my wallet. Natalie's picture was easy to find. I held it up for him to see.

His eyes flicked from the picture to me and back to the picture. "Harv's?"

I nodded. He reached for my wallet and I let him take it. He stared at the picture for a long time. Nat's dark hair, winning smile, and mischievous eyes proved her heritage.

"Little girl?"

"Natalie."

His voice softened. "You looking for child support?"

"Whatever I can get."

"Not likely to get it here."

"A girl's got to try."

He handed the wallet back. "She's better off without him."

He was right, but I'd stopped to get what I could. I closed the wallet and dropped it in my purse. "I know. That's why I left when I found out I was pregnant."

We'd been working odd jobs for cash, then getting high and mugging people, knocking over stores when the cash and odd jobs ran out. When the doctor said, "you're going to have a baby" she stirred childhood visions of what life would be when I grew up and had a kid. It took a long time to come back from that, to accept help and find a new way to live.

He assessed me with rheumy eyes. "You don't seem like the kind he usually hangs around with."

"Having a kid—a baby—changes a person."

He nodded. "It makes some grow up, learn to accept responsibility."

For a brief moment I wondered if I'd cheated Harv by not telling him. Maybe knowing about the baby would have changed him, too.

Maybe it still could.

"You sure you don't know how I can connect with him?"

"I ain't seen hide nor hair of him for quite a while." He nodded to the building behind him. "Not since we put up the garage."

I shaded my eyes from the late morning sun to view the garage. Like the house, it needed paint. "Harv's in construction now?"

The old man's mouth quirked into a strange half-smile. "In a manner of speaking."

"Well, times are tough. I thought maybe *somebody* had a little to share." I stressed somebody, but he ignored my attempt to ladle guilt.

"He's nothing and he's got nothing." Leaning close, he dropped his voice to a whisper. "If I was you, I wouldn't expect to hear from him ever again."

It took a minute for his meaning to sink in, and even then I wasn't ready to believe it. "You're sure?"

"It ain't official, but I'm as sure as anybody can be." His pale eyes stared into mine transferring the truth with another glance toward the garage.

I let out the breath I'd been holding. "Well. I didn't really want to have any more to do with him. If it wasn't for money problems..." I let the words trail off as I thought of Nat and the daycare bills.

The wind rattled the leaves in the tree overhead and rippled through the cornfield beyond the house. A cow mooed in the barn. If he had all this, surely there was something to share.

As if he were reading my mind, he said, "Farming's a hard business. There's them that thinks a green field is money waiting to be spent. Ain't so. At least not for me. I wouldn't be fixing that old tractor if it was."

I nodded in sympathy. If it weren't for the company car, I wouldn't have wheels.

He held out his hand. "Thanks for stopping. I never thought I'd be a grandad."

I shook his hand, held it for a minute. "I could bring Nat out so you could meet her." I regretted the words as soon as I said them. He wasn't the kind of grandpa I wanted for my daughter.

He grinned. Then he chuckled. "She's better off not knowing anything about either of us, me or my son."

I slid into the car and he shut the door for me.

He backed away and waved as I drove off leaving a trail of dust and burning bridges.

HE WATCHED HER GO, the lonesome ache in his chest stronger than it had ever been. A grandchild. A little girl. A sweet-looking one, too. Shook his head, turned, and went into the house. The little girl's no-good dad sprawled on the couch, still out from a night of drinking and who knew what else.

The old man walked over and tapped his son on the arm. "Wake up, you lousy bum. It's time to slop the hogs."

No response.

Tried again. Harder.

Nothing.

The gospel about the prodigal son came to mind. In the Bible story, the man's son came back a new person, but his son was the same as before he left. Maybe even worse.

Life. You dealt with it the best you could. He moved back to the window and watched the road dust settle back in place, wondered if that gal was the type who gave up easily.

If he actually had the guts to do what he'd told her he'd done.

The farm really could use another shed with a smooth cement floor.

TRACY FALENWOLFE

Tracy Falenwolfe's stories have appeared in *Black Cat Mystery Magazine*, *Flash Bang Mysteries*, *Crimson Streets*, *Spinetingler Magazine*, and more. She lives in Pennsylvania's Lehigh Valley with her husband and sons. Tracy is a member of Sisters in Crime National and Guppy branch, Mystery Writers of America, and the Short Mystery Fiction Society.

Find her at tracyfalenwolfe.com.

EXPOSURE

TRACY FALENWOLFE

SHEILA AND EDWARD VANDAVEER sat shoulder to shoulder across the desk from Dax and Lorna Cosgrove. Dax let the Vandaveers stew while he unwrapped a butterscotch candy and popped it into his mouth. He'd have preferred a cigarette, Lorna knew, listening to the candy click against his teeth, but, after the police department outlawed smoking when cops were on the job, he'd switched to butterscotch and the habit stuck even now that he was a private citizen.

While Dax took Edward Vandaveer through his story again, Lorna watched the couple with her photographer's eye. She was skilled in reading body language, in coaxing smiles, in capturing glimpses of emotion, but the Vandaveers didn't give her much to work with.

Mrs. Vandaveer, Sheila, wore designer clothes and shoes, and carried a killer handbag. Her makeup was tasteful and precise, her platinum hair twisted into a classy updo. She smelled of sandalwood. But it was her hands that told her story. Sheila Vandaveer had an elegant manicure and wore cocktail rings on seven of her fingers, but her hands did not belong to someone who'd been pampered for her entire life. There was a jagged scar along the webbing between the thumb and forefinger of her left hand, an old, ugly one that may have come from an unfortunate oyster shucking accident or a broken beer bottle in a bar fight. A callous on the side of the middle finger on her right hand might have been the result of pushing a mop for years, or maybe it came from an equally pedestrian activity, like bowling.

Lorna might have seen more if she'd have been looking through the lens of her camera rather than sitting and nodding and stealing glances here and there, but she'd seen enough to know that Sheila Vandaveer's hands were steady, maybe a little too steady for someone whose husband stood accused of stabbing a prostitute to death.

"It's all in my official statement," she said to Dax when he asked for her version of events. "He came to bed around ten and remained there the whole night."

"That's right," Edward said. "I did."

Dax smiled, a half smile that seemed pained. It was a challenge, and Lorna waited to see if Edward took the bait. She had, when it had been her in Edward's chair and Dax had been investigating her sister Cherie's murder. She'd launched herself across the desk at him in an effort to wipe that smirk off his face while she proclaimed her innocence vociferously. Four seconds later, she'd been head-over-heels for him. Ten years later, her feelings had doubled.

Edward met Dax's challenge with a raised brow. "So, are you going to take the case, or what?" He wore a double-breasted pinstriped suit that made him look like a bootlegger during prohibition, and he still hadn't looked at his wife. She didn't know it, though, because she hadn't looked at him either. They were an odd pair.

"I'll tell you straight out," Dax said, standing. "You've got a problem. Because even though I may believe you, I'm sure you're not telling me the whole truth and I'm not going to be able to prove you're innocent with what you're giving me."

Edward laughed. "I don't want you to prove I'm innocent."

"Then I'm at a loss as to what you think I can do for you."

Lorna kept quiet. When it had been her in the hot seat, Dax had still been a cop. She hadn't cracked even though she hadn't been telling the whole truth either. But Dax believed her. So much so, that he got rid of the one piece of evidence that made her look as guilty as sin.

He didn't know she was aware of what he'd done for her, or that she knew he left the force because of it. The gravity of his sacrifice weighed her down. At the time, it had driven her right back into Paul's arms. Paul was the owner of the gallery where she used to work and where her photographs had been on display. He had also been her husband when Cherie was murdered. Their reconciliation had lasted exactly twenty-four hours before Lorna came to her senses and ran back to Dax. Now that dalliance was her cross to bear. She'd never told Dax and she never would. It would only hurt him.

Edward and Sheila finally exchanged a glance.

"We want you to find another suspect before the trial," Sheila said.

Edward nodded. "Reasonable doubt. You can get me that, can't you?"

Lorna already knew what she thought of the couple and their predicament, and she figured Dax had arrived at the same conclusion. So it threw her when he didn't toss them out of the office right then.

"Tell me again who gave you my name?" Dax asked.

"Poppy Pennington," Edward said, then averted his eyes.

Dax frowned. "I don't know a Poppy Pennington."

"I do." Lorna's stomach bottomed out. "She's an old friend."

AFTER THE VANDAVEER'S LEFT, Dax and Lorna went upstairs to their apartment. He poured them each two fingers of bourbon. "I don't like it," he said.

Lorna took a swallow of bourbon and waited for it to hit her bloodstream. "What's not to like?"

"I get the feeling Sheila Vandaveer could use some protection from her husband. I think maybe he did what he's accused of and she's afraid of him." He swirled the ice in his glass. "I don't want to end up in the middle of a domestic squabble."

The way I did when we met went unsaid, but Lorna heard it anyway.

"He didn't do it." Lorna downed the rest of her drink. "And that woman doesn't need protection from anyone. She's lying."

"About what?"

"I don't know," she said. "Everything?"

Dax set down his glass and took Lorna into his arms. The chaste kiss was not what she was expecting. "You look nervous. Why don't you want me to take the case?" he said. "Really?"

Lorna turned away. "Because I'm afraid you'll fall for Sheila Vandaveer."

"I won't."

"But what if you do? You already believe her."

"You still don't get it, do you?" Dax said. "You're the only one for me, Lorna. I've know it since the first moment I met you."

She remembered that moment. His partner, Gil Murphy had just turned her away. She'd come to the station asking for protection for her sister, but since Cherie refused to admit she needed help he'd told Lorna there was nothing he could do until Cherie's husband broke the law.

Dax had followed her out onto the street. He'd bought her a cup of coffee, and had given her some advice. Then he asked her out. She accepted, despite still being married to Paul. They hadn't been apart since.

Dax turned her around so that she faced him again. "Don't worry about me and Sheila Vandaveer."

The apartment seemed so small just then. Lorna still owned Cherie's place. She used it as her studio now, and thought that maybe she should go stay there for a few days. It would give her and Dax both a little breathing room.

He kissed her. "After all, I'm not worried about you and Edward."

She pulled away. "Why would you be?"

"Because he's your type," Dax said. "Rich. Powerful. Straight nose. Good teeth. At least that was your type before you met me."

"But weak," she said. "Weak was never my type."

"What if we do a preliminary investigation before we sign on," Dax said. "You look into Sheila, and I'll look into Edward. Then we'll compare notes and make a decision together. Deal?"

"Deal," she said.

"Good. Now tell me about Poppy Pennington."

DAX DIDN'T FEEL any better after learning Poppy Pennington was the owner of the escort service the dead girl worked for, but at least Lorna told him the truth. She didn't always, and he knew she considered it a favor to him. She thought what he didn't know couldn't hurt him, which is why she never fessed up about running back to her ex.

It had been right after Dax shot and killed her sister's husband. The guy had a gun pointed at Lorna, so Dax never regretted taking the shot. It *did* eat at him that, the minute he pulled the trigger, it was case closed on Cherie's murder, even though there'd never been any evidence against the guy except for Lorna's statement.

It also bothered him to know that the gun Cherie's husband had that day had been legal, registered to him for over a year. If he'd had his own gun, why had he used Lorna's gun to kill Cherie the week before? And why had he left it at the scene? Moreover, if Lorna had been the only witness, the way she said she was, why not kill her too? Dax stopped there, because he didn't like to think of a world without Lorna in it. The world was already depressing enough.

He stopped for coffee before heading to his old precinct.

"Dax man." His former partner Gil Murphy accepted one of the cardboard cups. "What brings you?"

"Edward Vandaveer." Dax popped the lid off his own cup and took a sip.

Murphy scratched the tip of his nose, just the way he used to when he was stalling for time when he questioned suspects.

"Hit a nerve?" Dax asked.

"Vandaveer hired you?"

Dax shrugged. "He wants to. I haven't agreed yet."

"Then don't," Murphy said. "Everything the guy says is a damn lie."

The phone had rung six times since Dax walked in. The four cups of coffee he'd brought had been claimed, and a uniform dragged a spitting, swearing, suspect past him toward the box. Dax missed the action. The excitement. But he considered himself an honest cop, if nothing else, and so he'd had no choice but to quit after what he'd done for Lorna.

No one knew what he'd done, or that he had the prints from the gun he'd tossed into the Charles tucked away in a safety deposit box. Maybe someday he'd run them. Clear his conscience. Maybe he'd come back to the force if Cherie's husband's prints were on the gun, and he could convince himself what he'd done with the murder weapon hadn't mattered in the grand scheme of things, but for now he'd go it alone as an investigator.

"What can you tell me?" Dax asked Murphy.

Murphy shrugged. "Vandaveer's not even the guy's real name. Didn't have a penny until three years ago."

"What happened three years ago?"

"He hit it big in Atlantic City. Before that, he was in the bricklayers union with his father. Afterwards, he changed his name and cut ties with his whole family. I'm going to see the old man later on if you want to tag along."

Dax did.

JOSEPH HOFFER WAS WHITTLING when Dax and Murphy arrived. He was adept with a knife, but careless in his hobby as he was chain smoking while standing in an ankle-high pile of sawdust next to an open container of linseed oil. He looked up from what was going to be a duck. "You that cop?"

"Yes sir, I'm detective Murphy. This is Dax Cosgrove."

Hoffer spared them a glance before going back to his duck. "You want to ask me about my boy killing that prostitute."

"Have you talked to him about it?" Murphy asked.

"Nope. Haven't talked to him about anything in three years," Hoffer said. "We had words back then, and he hasn't been around since."

"Were you upset with him for changing his name?"

"His name?" Hoffer took a deep drag on his cigarette. "I was upset about him being an ungrateful bastard." He set his knife down and blew smoke out of his nostrils. "Kid was no better than I was. Couldn't hack it in college. He quit school and joined the union with me. Gambled most of his pay away over the years." He squinted at the duck and then picked up his knife again. "When he hit it big, I asked him for some money. Not for me. For his grandmother."

He shaved some wood off the duck's back and looked at it again. "Had to put her in a home, and wanted to move her to a better one, but do you know what that son of a bitch said?"

"No, sir," Murphy said.

Hoffer nodded, and stubbed his cigarette out on his workbench. He looked Murphy square in the eyes for the first time. "He said she was only going to die anyway and he didn't want to waste the money. He said he was going to use it to make something of himself. Take some opportunities I never gave him."

"What did you say to that?"

"I said good riddance."

"Did you ever meet his wife?" Dax asked. "Sheila?"

"No." Hoffer lit another cigarette. "But if she's anything like the first one, I'm not missing much."

EDWARD VANDAVEER'S FIRST WIFE, LeAnn Hoffer, lived across town in a trailer park. When Dax told her why he was there, she said, "might as well talk to the both of you at once," and led him inside to where Lorna was already seated. To say he was surprised to see her there was an understatement. Then again, she was as keen an investigator as he was, so maybe he shouldn't have been.

Lorna smiled and made room on the couch.

LeAnn Hoffer sat across from them on a recliner that may have also been her bed, judging by the pillow and blanket.

"I was hoping to ask you some questions about your ex-husband, Mrs. Hoffer." Dax said.

"Join the club." She motioned to Lorna. "I don't know what I can tell you. I haven't seen him in a few years."

"Why did you divorce?" Lorna asked.

"Because he gambled away everything we ever had." She waved her arm to encompass her home. "This isn't exactly living the dream, you know. And we almost lost it. Twice."

"Did you see him after he won the money?" Dax asked.

"Around town a few times." She shrugged. "I was happy for him."

Lorna made a noise that expressed her doubt. "Did you ask him for money?"

LeAnn made a face at Lorna. "Why would I have? We were divorced."

Lorna made a face back.

"Fine," LeAnn said. "I may have mentioned that I'd divorced him too soon, but he didn't take the bait."

Dax waited a few seconds, but she didn't offer more. "Didn't that make you mad?"

"Not really." A cat jumped up into her lap. "Money or no, my life is better without Edward in it."

"So there were no hard feelings between you?" Dax asked.

"Not until a half an hour ago," LeAnn said.

Dax looked at Lorna. "What happened a half an hour ago?"

LeAnn snorted. "His witch of a wife showed up and accused me of killing that hooker and framing Edward for it."

"Sheila Vandaveer was here?"

"The one and only," LeAnn said. "Edward knows me better than that. I can't believe he would let her accuse me of such a thing." She shook her head and got a far off look in her eyes. "He was a good man once upon a time. Wanted the white picket fence and all of that."

Neither Dax nor Lorna commented. "Like I told her…" LeAnn put the cat on the floor. "I work at Harwood's department store. At the fine jewelry counter. I was there all night the night of the murder. Ask anybody."

POPPY PENNINGTON HAD the clearest green eyes Lorna had ever seen. Combined with the jet-black hair and ruby-red lips they made her look like a cartoon character. After they air kissed, Poppy sat behind her desk and opened mail with an ivory-handled, lethal-looking letter opener. Lorna sat on the velvet chaise next to the desk.

"I don't know what you want me to say." Poppy sliced open another letter. "You know I'm a stickler for privacy."

Lorna knew. And she owed Poppy. But this was important.

"I already know Edward Vandaveer was the client. I just want to know how he came to choose that particular girl. Did he choose her? Or did you choose her for him?"

"Donna," Poppy said. "Her name was Donna Downey."

Lorna knew that wasn't her real name, of course, but she apologized anyway. "Did Edward Vandaveer choose Donna or did you?"

Poppy leaned back in her chair and ran her finger along the letter opener. "How are you, Lorna? I haven't seen you in a decade."

Since the day of Cherie's murder. Poppy had given Lorna the gun. It was supposed to be for protection from Cherie's husband. Lorna had gone there to get Cherie out, to save her, but things went terribly wrong.

"I'm surviving," Lorna said.

"I like survivors."

Poppy didn't know the details of that night, and Lorna wouldn't offer them. She'd told Dax what had really happened, leaving out the parts that concerned Poppy and her business, but she wasn't a hundred percent sure he believed her. He'd gotten rid of the gun, after all.

"I should go." Lorna stood.

"It was neither," Poppy said when Lorna started to walk away.

"Neither?" Lorna turned back.

Poppy tested the point of her letter opener with her finger. "Sheila Vandaveer picked the girl."

"Is that so?"

"It's not as odd as you might think."

"No?"

"No. Sheila and Donna were old friends." Poppy lifted one brow, urging Lorna to read between the lines.

"How old?"

Poppy dropped the letter opener on her desk. "I don't know. They knew each other before Donna came here."

"Where did Donna come here from?"

"Atlantic City. She was one of Joey's girls."

Joey was Poppy's uncle. Hers was a family business.

"Thanks."

Poppy came around the desk and stood toe to toe with Lorna. "You know you were the best I ever had." She ran her tongue over her teeth. "If you're ever looking for some quick cash…"

"I don't do that kind of work anymore."

"Never say never."

ATLANTIC CITY WAS A TWO-HOUR FLIGHT. Lorna walked into Joey's talent agency a little after three. When his assistant showed Lorna into his office, Joey grinned. "Speak of the devil." He put down the phone he'd been holding. "You saved me a call."

Someone was sitting in the chair across from Joey. He swiveled to face Lorna.

"Dax." Lorna was not surprised. "Fancy meeting you here."

"What took you?" He unwrapped a butterscotch candy and popped it into his mouth.

"Sit." Joey pointed to the chair next to Dax.

Lorna sat.

"So this is your old man?" Joey aimed his chin at Dax.

"Joey, Dax. Dax, Joey."

Dax nodded.

Joey looked him over. "You know he's a cop, right?"

"Ex-cop," Dax said.

Lorna jumped in before Joey got going. "Poppy said Donna Downey was one of your girls."

Joey spread his hands. "Used to be."

"And Sheila Vandaveer?"

"Nah."

Dax and Lorna shared a glance.

"I'm not yanking your chain," Joey said. "Sheila wasn't one of mine. She wasn't Sheila Vandaveer back then either."

"Who was she?" Dax asked. "What was she?"

"Man." Joey rubbed his eyes with the heels of his hands. "I'm only telling you this as a favor to Poppy." He looked at Lorna. "She wants you back, you know."

Dax's face didn't change, but Lorna saw him swallow his butterscotch.

"All right." Joey leaned back in his chair. He laced his fingers and laid them on top of his head. "Sheila Vandaveer used to be Sheila Petroski."

"Who is Sheila Petroski?" Dax said.

"Nobody." Joey snorted. "She was married to a small-time card player. It was a step up from being a barmaid at a cheesy joint a couple of blocks off the boardwalk, but I still don't know what she saw in him, tell you the truth."

"Was he the jealous type?" Dax asked.

"Nah," Joey said. "He ignored her most of the time. I don't think they were together for a year."

Lorna wasn't following. "So what was she to Donna Downey?"

"She was a client." Joey stood. "Now, if you don't mind—"

Dax stayed seated and folded his arms across his chest. "What else?"

"What do you mean what else?" Joey put his hands on his hips. "Sheila paid Donna for sex. End of story."

Dax didn't budge. "Sheila was sleeping with Donna here in Atlantic City. Atlantic City is where Edward Hoffer hit it big before he changed his name to Edward Vandaveer. Then he marries Sheila, and Donna ends up dead. What are you leaving out?"

Lorna looked at Dax. "You're thinking it was a love triangle?"

"If there was a triangle, it didn't include Edward," Joey said. "That guy only had eyes for the table."

"If he didn't care that Sheila and Donna had a thing, then who did?" Lorna asked.

"The wife."

"Sheila *is* the wife," Lorna said.

"No. The first wife. LeAnn. She had a thing with Donna, too."

Dax didn't seem surprised. "So it was Donna, Sheila, and LeAnn in the love triangle."

Joey smiled at Lorna. "You did alright for yourself." He pointed to Dax. "He catches on quick."

❧

LORNA FIDGETED in her seat next to Dax on the flight home.

"I took pictures," she said finally. "For Poppy."

Dax had never asked her much about her past. She'd left the pretentious Paul for him shortly after they'd met, and had just suffered the loss of her sister. The past ten years had been about making a new life together, not rehashing their old ones. "You don't have to explain."

"I want to. I was not a prostitute."

"I don't care what you were." But he had to admit that would be hard to swallow.

"Poppy hired me to take pictures of high profile clients with her girls. She needed someone discreet, someone she could trust."

"I said you didn't have to explain."

"The pictures were strictly for insurance. Joey has pictures too. Just in case."

"In case what?"

"In case they need to blackmail someone. In case something happened to one of the girls." She turned in her seat, and put her hand on his arm. "It's how I found out about Cherie's husband." Her voice cracked. "He was one of Poppy's regulars."

"Did your sister know?"

"No." Lorna shook her head. "She had no idea. Poppy suspected he was smacking the girls around, but none of them would admit it, so she put me onto him one night."

"Did you know it was him?"

"Not until I saw him through my lens."

"What then?"

"I saw what he did to Poppy's girl. I didn't know her, but as I was shooting the photos, I saw Cherie. That same look in her eyes. The way she kept her head turned to the side. How she curled in on herself. I knew then. I knew he was hitting her too."

"So you went to Cherie?"

"Yes, but I couldn't tell her how I knew." She went on despite the catch in her voice. "She hated me for it."

Dax put his hand over hers. "It's okay. You don't have to say any more."

"It only made things worse."

"Shhh."

"I didn't tell Poppy he was my brother-in-law. Not at first."

The flight attendant interrupted to tell them they were expecting turbulence.

Dax helped Lorna with her seatbelt before fastening his own. Lorna was a nervous flyer and held his hand. He squeezed. "It's going to be okay."

By the time they landed, Dax had been over the case in his head a few more times. Most murders were about love or money, and this case had both. As far as love went, he knew Sheila and Donna had something going, and so did Donna and LeAnn. But how did Sheila and LeAnn feel about each other? And did it even matter since Donna was the one who wound up dead?

If he followed the money, Edward was the common denominator. He had no money when he'd been married to LeAnn, and she was justifiably bitter about that. He was still as rich as he was the day he met Sheila, but there was something off between them.

Had Edward known about the relationship between the women in his life? Had Donna been the one to tell him? Maybe he'd killed her in a fit of rage. Dax would have to take a look at the case file. See what the M.E. had to say about the stab wounds.

"Is your car here?" Dax asked Lorna as they deplaned.

"In short term parking," she said. "Is yours?"

"No. Murphy dropped me here."

Lorna hooked her arm through his and led the way to her car. "Dax. About my sister. That night—"

"Later." Dax held out his hand. "You're still looking green. Let me have the keys."

She gave them up.

Dax started the car and turned up the radio. He didn't want to hear any more about that night. He'd responded to the 911 call and arrived to find Lorna leaning over Cherie's body. A gun lay on top of her purse, which was sitting on the floor near the stairs.

She claimed Cherie's husband had taken the gun from her and had shot Cherie with it, but then dropped it and ran off. When Dax had seen Lorna on the ground, shaking her dead sister, pleading with her to wake up, he'd felt sure she hadn't been the shooter, but he'd pocketed the gun anyway, because her story was so damn unlikely.

"You missed the turn," Lorna said.

"Sorry. I'll turn around and drop you off."

"What do you mean drop me off? Where are you going?"

"Harwood's. LeAnn told us she was working the night Donna was stabbed. Might as well check it out."

"I'll come along."

❦

THE FINE JEWELRY counter at Harwood's was spectacular. It was horseshoe-shaped and loaded with sparklers. Lorna lingered near the rings until a saleswoman approached. "Can I help you with something?"

"Maybe. Is LeAnn Hoffer working tonight?"

"I'm sorry, no. Did she set something aside for you?"

"I don't know. I was in last Friday looking at anniversary rings. I told her I would be back."

"Let me check."

Lorna watched the saleswoman unlock a cubby and sort through the holds.

Dax came up behind Lorna and put his hand on the small of her back. "The manager said she was on duty Friday night. She worked until ten-thirty and had a one-hour dinner break from six to seven."

The saleswoman closed the cubby and came back to Lorna. "I don't see any holds for LeAnn's customers. Are you sure it was Friday night?"

"Yes," Lorna said. "Right at closing. Around ten?"

The saleswoman winced. "I don't think LeAnn was here at that time. Could someone else have helped you?"

"I talked to her earlier in the day," Dax said. "She told me she'd be on all night."

The saleswoman looked around like she didn't want to be overheard. "She didn't come back from her dinner break that night. I know because I covered for her."

Dax looked at Lorna.

"Oh." Lorna said. "I guess I was mistaken."

"I'd be happy to help you," the saleswoman tried again.

Lorna smiled. "I think we'll just browse right now." She moved down to the case of rings farthest from the saleswoman. Dax moved with her. His mouth was close to her ear.

"She thought she was going to make a commission tonight."

Lorna smiled. "They're all so beautiful, I don't know which one I'd pick."

"Why pick? Sheila Vandaveer wears one on each finger."

"Sheila Vandaveer's rings are fakes," Lorna said.

"How can you tell?"

"Real gemstones are set in mounts with open backs to lift the stone and let the light shine through. Stones set against solid backs are almost always fakes. That's true of even good fakes."

"And Sheila Vandaveer's rings have solid backs?"

"Every last one of them," Lorna said.

"I didn't realize you were such an expert."

"I photographed a collection for a museum catalogue once."

She didn't say it was for her ex, but Dax took his hand off her back. "We should go."

The tension between them lingered as they left Harwood's. Lorna drove Dax to his car at the police station. "See you at home," he said.

"Actually," Lorna said. "I'm going to the studio first. I'll be back late."

DAX WAS SITTING at the kitchen table with a beer when Lorna came home at 4 a.m. He was surprised to see her. Surprised but relieved.

She pointed to the photos he'd been paging through. "Are those crime scene photos?"

He nodded. "They're gruesome. You might not want to look."

She sat beside him. "Did Murphy give them to you?"

"Yeah. Copies." He slid the photos across the table to her, careful to keep the envelope he'd removed from his safety deposit box earlier in the day tucked inside the manila file folder.

Donna Downey had been stabbed in the chest and stomach over forty times. No one cut had been fatal, but together they'd caused her to bleed out. It had been a horrific way to go. Lorna leafed through the photos. "She didn't die right away."

Dax shook his head. "No."

Lorna paused on the last shot, and studied Donna's mutilated body with her photographer's eye. "Do you have the magnifying glass?"

Dax set his beer aside and got the magnifying glass from the junk drawer near the refrigerator. "What do you see?"

"It looks like little blisters around some of the wounds." She showed Dax. "See?"

"Yeah." He frowned. "What is that from?" He paged through the medical examiner's report. "Donna Downey had a nickel allergy. He determined whatever she was stabbed with must have had some nickel in it."

"I'll be damned." Lorna set the magnifying glass on the table. "I know who killed Donna Downey."

THE NEXT MORNING, the Vandaveers sat across the desk from Dax. "Mr. Vandaveer, have you been having any financial trouble lately?"

"What kind of question is that?"

Dax lifted his chin toward Sheila. "It's just that you're a wealthy man and yet I notice that your wife wears costume jewelry." He glanced at the rings on Sheila's fingers. Now that he knew what he was looking for he could spot the fakes from across the desk.

"That's for insurance purposes," Edward said. "She wears copies most of the time and we keep the real ones at home in a safe."

Sheila twisted the faux emerald on her middle finger.

"Mrs. Vandaveer, are you aware that most costume jewelry contains nickel?"

"Is that important?"

"It is if you have a nickel allergy like Donna Downey did." He slid a picture of Donna's body across the desk. "See these little blisters?"

Sheila held a hand over her stomach and gagged.

"Those are a reaction from your rings," Dax said.

"Now wait a damn minute." Edward stood up. "When I told you to find me another suspect I didn't mean my wife."

Dax ignored him and focused on Sheila. "My guess is that even though you cleaned them up, those rings have Donna's DNA all over them."

"We're leaving," Edward yelled. "We'll find another investigator. A better one."

"Why did you kill her?" Dax asked. "You two had a thing going since Atlantic City, right? That's pretty long-term. What happened?"

Sheila's lip quivered. "I loved her." Her eyes filled with tears. "But to her I was only—"

"Sheila!" Edward grabbed her arm. "We're leaving. Don't say another word." He pointed a finger a Dax. "You're mistaken. We were in bed together from ten o'clock on. It's in her official statement."

When the door slammed behind them, Lorna hopped up onto the desk and faced Dax. "He knows, but he's covering for her."

Dax popped a butterscotch. "Yes."

"Do you think he loves her enough to go to jail for her?"

"No telling." Dax swiveled his chair away from Lorna. He picked up the manila file and all of its contents and fed it to the shredder. "Men do all kinds of crazy things for the women they love."

PAULA GAIL BENSON

A legislative attorney and former law librarian, **Paula Gail Benson's** short stories have appeared online and in print anthologies including: *Mystery Times Ten 2013*, *A Tall Ship, a Star, and Plunder*, *A Shaker of Margaritas: That Mysterious Woman*, *Fish or Cut Bait: a Guppy Anthology*, and *Love in the Lowcountry*. Her short story, 'A Matter of Honor,' co-authored with *New York Times* bestselling thriller writer Robert Dugoni, appears in *Killer Nashville Noir: Cold Blooded*. She regularly blogs with others about writing at the Stiletto Gang and Writers Who Kill.

Find her at paulagailbenson.com.

LIVING ONE'S OWN TRUTH

PAULA GAIL BENSON

IN THE FALL OF 1931, near Patriot in Posey Township, Switzerland County, Indiana, I was employed to teach literature at Framingham Preparatory Academy, basically an all-male village school elevated only by its presumptuous name. As best I could discern, it was christened by our first and only headmaster, Professor William Mathers, a trembling gentleman whose age seemed to increase incrementally with each round he stumbled about the campus boundaries. Professor Mathers claimed to be one of the first graduates of the famous Framingham Normal School in Boston. He never clarified whether his graduation took place before or after that institution became collegiate. Since Boston was several states away, I assumed no one had considered it worth the trouble to verify his credentials. Apparently, he had been accepted at his word and lauded for his desire to emulate his great teacher and mentor Cyrus Pierce's closing words for each class: "live to the truth." Whatever that was supposed to mean.

My own suspicion, founded mostly on instinct and a discreet amount of research, was that Professor Mathers was our token leader. I sensed control of the institution remained in the hands of a secret benefactor, who cared less about Professor Mathers' qualifications than about setting up a diploma dispensary, for whatever reason I could only infer. From observation, I felt certain the secret benefactor must be a Mrs. Antonia O'Leary. She made a weekly trip to our school in her antiquated carriage that resembled a landau straight out of a Jane Austen novel. At the clip-clop of her horses' hooves, Professor Mathers hop-limped from his Georgian brick residence to greet her and invite her inside, where they hobbled amiably up the few front steps together. One could only imagine what their discussions entailed.

As I began my employment, I determined my success as an instructor would depend upon being quiet, discerning, and never too obvious. At least in the beginning. What I learned from my assigned supervisor, Mrs. Marilee Bloodstone, esteemed teacher of classics and bane of the young men's existence, was that once you have established yourself, you may proceed as your manner best dictates.

I presumed my assignment to Mrs. Bloodstone's mentorship had been because this was my first position and she was the only other female on the faculty. That may indeed have been the case since I noticed no male instructors receiving supervisory assignments. However, I quickly learned, while Professor Mathers was the figurehead, Mrs. Bloodstone was the disciplinarian. No doubt she had complete mastery of her subject area, but her method of instruction might kindly be described as rigid and exacting, and more precisely categorized as cruel and abusive. She was relentless in finding fault with her students and delighted in punishing transgressors.

My first day, I observed her drill her charges mercilessly in Latin and Greek vocabulary. She went so far as to sentence one boy, who confused Phanes and Pontus, to sit on a corner stool, with the added insult of being forced to wear a cap inscribed: "Stultus."

After dismissing the class, including the unfortunate pupil, still wearing his dunce cap, she explained her philosophy to me. "Their lives have been soft and permissive. Unless they are ruthlessly drilled and routinely shamed for errors, they will never be made to understand what the world will expect from them. My techniques may seem harsh, but they produce results. Surely, you can comprehend the need for discipline, coming as you do from a family of teachers."

"Well," I said and knew immediately from her expression that she did not wish for me to reply. Yet, having begun with a syllable, I felt compelled to continue, despite my initial reticence. "While my father had apprentices, he was not a teacher, but an inventor."

Her gaze was unrelenting. "I remember now. Automotive technology, is that correct? In Michigan?"

"Yes."

She surveyed me from head to toe and back. "In the classroom, you would be wise to follow my stern example. Your countenance and figure, while not exceptional, are sufficient to ignite young male imaginations, particularly if you have them read passages from Blake or some of Milton's *Paradise Lost*."

"Thank you," I replied, recognizing her words as a warning, not a compliment. "I shall take your advice to heart."

When Mrs. Bloodstone dismissed me so I might prepare for my first classes, I went to my room and found a young woman examining my belongings. As I opened the door, she took no notice of me. Her long ebony hair hung in ringlets down her back. She turned slowly, not at all embarrassed at being apprehended in her pursuit. When she faced me, I had to admit, she was an exceptional beauty, perhaps the loveliest female I had ever seen, except for one.

"Hello," I said.

She scrutinized my appearance before replying. "I wondered what an Agnes Johannsson would look like."

"Do I meet your expectations?"

Shrugging her shoulders, she hopped onto the edge of my brass bed, causing the springs to emit a tenor warble under her weight. "It explains why you have come here to teach instead of marrying well."

One day, I hoped the two might not be mutually exclusive, but I asked, "Might I have the pleasure of knowing your name?"

"Justine," she replied.

"How nice to meet you, Miss..." I paused, hopeful she might take the clue to give me her last name.

"I suppose you wonder why I am here," she said.

"Yes."

She gave a lingering sigh. "I am underage, not married, and un-emancipated from my mother, who teaches here."

I moved forward to take my opened luggage from the bed, where she had been poking at its contents, and began to place my folded clothes in an ancient chest's drawers. "It's nice to meet you, Miss Bloodstone."

"Oh, no one bothers to call me that here. I am Justine. A single name only, like the story my mother always told me at bedtime."

I had to press my lips together so as not to inquire after the title. She bounced from the bed and took a few steps toward the window. "Like clockwork," she said, her attention riveted upon what she was watching.

"What's that?" I couldn't help asking.

"Mrs. O'Leary's visit to the headmaster's residence. Why is it that older folks may lead the lives they choose while younger ones must submit to stifling rules and chaperones?"

If indeed her mother had not explained that fact of life, she was taking unnecessary risks with a pretty daughter in a school full of eager, young, perhaps less-than-gentle men. That, I could not imagine Mrs. Bloodstone doing.

"Of course," Justine continued. "If one has money, rules are no longer encumbrances. Although..." She paused to curl her long locks between her fingers as she watched the two tottering figures make their journey from the carriage steps to the residence's entrance. "Although," she repeated as if forgetting she had said it. "For Professor Mathers, it is said Mrs. O'Leary may be something more. More than a mere guest, I mean."

So, she was not as naïve as she might appear. In fact, as each day passed and I came to know Justine better, I found her to be a very savvy individual with an unfortunate priority instilled by her mother.

"I was bred to be a heartbreaker," she confessed one afternoon after classes, when she arrived at my room uninvited and flounced upon my bed. I had never considered myself a curiosity, but apparently, she found me so. Or at least a sounding board.

"Why was that?" I asked, closing the lesson book I had been studying at my desk.

"In retaliation against my father. He was a famous fencing master, you know, meeting my mother as her instructor. Very apt at the sport, she was, as I understand. After I was born, he received employment in a distant city as a private fencing master to a young woman who might have competed in the 1928 Olympic Games." She sighed, slowly draining the air from her lungs. "Instead, father and his student ran away together, leaving Mother and me destitute."

So many questions I might have asked, but I had to be careful.

I need not have worried. Due to her mother's tutelage, Justine's focus continued to be completely self-absorbed.

"Mother got the heartbreaker idea from her classics course. She teaches about a sculptor who begs the Goddess of Love to bring one of his statues to life."

I nodded. "Pygmalion."

She seemed surprised, then intrigued that I knew the name. "Oh, do you teach it as well? I suppose I should have guessed that a teacher of literature would know the story."

"A man named Shaw wrote a play about it."

Her eyes widened. "Do you mean he copied it? Mother would not approve. She punishes students severely for copying. You don't allow copying in your class, do you?"

I was ready to say, "not without proper attribution," but it occurred to me there was something admirable about a girl named Justine trying to live up to her name. Instead, I replied, "You have a point."

She bestowed a positively angelic smile upon me. As if I had suggested she might be a candidate for beatification. Not that she would recognize that concept.

"Mother says it is more important for me to learn about using the power of my looks than gaining book knowledge. Even so, I have picked up a few things."

Indeed, Justine had acquired a hodge-podge of information that allowed her to survive in an academic environment, but the more I watched her behavior—particularly around the young men—the more it bore out her confession: her greatest skills were in applying her beauty and charm in breaking hearts. Once, as she took her daily constitutional about the grounds, I saw a student rush to meet her, and draw from his pocket a bag of coveted chocolate-covered Michigan cherries, closed with a ribbon.

He presented the bag to Justine as if offering his fealty to the local noble. She pulled the ribbon loose and let it drop to the ground. Reaching inside, she lifted one perfectly rounded candy and held it up toward the sun to observe its quality. Slowly, she lowered it to her mouth, shutting her eyes, as if excluding the outside world so she might concentrate completely on savoring the taste. The student shifted from one foot to another in anticipation of her response.

Opening her eyes, she said, "Rather bitter." Then she dropped the bag on the ground, spilling its precious contents, much to the student's distress.

During the last warm weather before autumn, Professor Mathers authorized a school-wide picnic. This time, I saw an admirer approach Justine with a slice of lusciously red watermelon. Her eyes twinkled as she accepted it. Taking a bite, she let the juice slide down her chin as the admirer watched, entranced. After swallowing, she paused, then pushed the slice back into the admirer's hands before laughing as she dashed away.

Following her to the pump where she washed her face and gulped a clear handful of water, I asked, "Doesn't it concern you that you cause them pain?"

My question caught her off guard. "How could it?" she asked. "It can't really mean anything to either of us, except a game. Since I could never be considered marriage material by their families, their only interest would be in using me."

I paused, wondering how best to phrase my question. "Don't you think, when it is just the two of you, without family involvement, that the young man might misunderstand? Might perceive your interest is genuine and not a game?"

She blinked. "But, how could he think me so stupid?"

How indeed? She was not unintelligent, yet her scope of understanding had been inexorably skewed by her mother's tutelage.

Around the time of the first snow, Professor Mathers announced with glee, and much to Mrs. Bloodstone's frowning displeasure, that we would be welcoming another faculty member, a Mr. Tolliver Kincaid, a teacher of logic, as well as an expert fencing instructor. While the boys had no excitement for a course in logic, they cheered the opportunity for more indoor exercise during the winter months. I kept their attention in class by pointing out two references to fencing in *The Merry Wives of Windsor*. (From Act I, Scene 1: "playing at sword and dagger with a master of fence," and Act II, Scene 3: "Alas, sir, I cannot fence.")

Mrs. Bloodstone was not so fortunate finding fencing mentioned in classical tales. Her increasing sourness reminded me of another Shakespeare quotation from *Much Ado About Nothing*: "blunt as the fencer's foils, which hit, but hurt not."

Justine took particular interest in the arrival of Mr. Kincaid, making me wonder how much she remembered of her father, the fencer. Her time with me diminished as it increased in Mr. Kincaid's company.

Then, one afternoon, I arrived in my room to find her sitting quietly on my bed with her hands folded in her lap, her eyes cast downward. She looked up as I entered and said, "It has ceased to be a game for me."

"What is that?" I asked.

"My interaction with the male species."

"Are you entering a nunnery?"

She wrinkled her forehead. "What's that?"

I decided to ask in her own language. "What has changed about your interaction with the male species?"

"Mr. Kincaid. He believes, and let me say it exactly as he did, 'that my mind is worthy of deep thinking and my agilities are suitable for practice with the foils.' Is that not the most wonderful commendation imaginable?"

I sat beside her and reached for her hands. "It is quite lovely, but are you certain it is sincere?"

She pulled her hands back. "Why would it not be?"

I remembered all her male-teasing moments now wiped from her brain. "I suppose I know of no reason."

Her pout turned into the beginning of a smile. "He is the one person who has looked beyond my outer beauty and sought connection with my mental prowess. I love him for it."

The question remained unspoken on my lips: but, does he love you?

Her eyes brimmed with tears. "When he proposed we elope to present my mother with a fait accompli, I readily agreed. We take the train tonight." She rose and solemnly kissed me on each cheek. "I came to say farewell and wish the same good fortune for you."

In a moment, she was gone, leaving the room with a lightness of movement I had not seen in her before. As if she were floating, lost in a blissful dream.

Reaching for my shawl, I followed, leaving the room and taking a different course, to the building where Mr. Kincaid resided. My sharp knock brought him to his door. He drew me inside the room, locking the door behind me. Turning to me with a smirk, he said, "I did not think you so brazen, Miss Johannsson."

"And, I did not think you so heartless."

He shrugged. Passing by me, he went to his chest, where I saw he was in the process of packing. "See? I am making good on my offer to Justine, unlike her father's behavior toward her mother. They never married, did you know?"

I shook my head.

"They couldn't actually," he continued. "Because he was still married to my mother."

Now, my eyes widened. "You and Justine are related?"

His smirk returned. "By marriage only. Her father was my stepfather, an acknowledged fencing master. Marilee was his first brilliant student. She might have competed in the Olympics, had she not become...with child. His leaving with Marilee broke my mother's delicate heart. She never recovered."

"So, now, you would rob Mrs. Bloodstone—"

"Don't call her that. She has no right to his name."

"Very well. You would rob Marilee of what she holds most dear as an act of revenge?"

He leaned close to me. "Only because he no longer lives to feel my vengeance."

I stood very still. My voice quivered as I spoke. "And you would prefer a silly child to me?"

He straightened. "I did not know you were being offered."

"What if I were?"

He leaned close again and I placed my hand upon his chest before his lips reached mine. "There are two things I require of you," I said.

"And, they are?"

I felt his breath against my cheek. "Where is your stationery?"

He nodded toward his desk.

"On a page write only: 'For my darling.'"

He chuckled. "You are the romantic one."

"Quickly please."

He complied. I folded the sheet carefully, fending off his efforts at an embrace. "You are too impatient. Meet me in two hours in the fencing room."

The smirk returned. "For some thrust and parry?"

I moved quickly to the door and unlocked it. Turning back to him, I said, "Mr. Kincaid, you make me blush."

Two weeks later, I took my walk across the campus in mourning clothing. As I approached Professor Mathers' residence, I saw Mrs. O'Leary's carriage coming down the lane.

Professor Mathers was negotiating his stairs as the carriage passed him by and headed toward me. For a moment, I imagined those horses as harbingers of the apocalypse. When the carriage stopped beside me and the door opened, I felt I understood Emily Dickinson's poem.

Because I could not stop for Death,

He kindly stopped for me;

From inside, Mrs. O'Leary smiled at me. "Won't you take a spin with me, Agnes?"

I looked back to see Professor Mathers shivering. He turned and made his way back into the house.

"Thank you, Mrs. O'Leary."

The carriage held but just Ourselves
And Immortality.

After I climbed inside, she pulled the door shut behind me. "We can be less formal here. I am Antonia and you are Agnes. I'm glad to share my lap robe, if you are chilly," she said.

"No, thank you." I took a deep breath. "Antonia."

She smiled. "See? It wasn't that difficult, now was it? I thought it was high time that we got to know each other better, despite our unfortunate circumstances."

"I'm glad to do all I can to support the school."

"Certainly, my dear. No doubt Professor Mathers will depend upon you. We met as students, you know, at Boston's Framingham Normal School."

"No, I didn't."

She threw her head back. Her laughter sounded like shimmering sleigh bells. "So many lifetimes ago. He always wanted to teach. I viewed my credentials from that institution as a means of escape because they allowed me to come west as a schoolteacher. I ended up marrying a wealthy widower with two sons of average intelligence. My husband's fortune helped to fund this academy, allowing his boys to matriculate and me to be reunited with my old friend, William, whom you know as Professor Mathers."

We rode for a few moments in silence before she said, "Now, I would like to know more about Agnes Johannsson, whose father helps create this monstrous new invention for traveling the road." She paused. "And, whose sister died in a very unfortunate automotive accident."

I kept my expression neutral. "What more can I tell you? Those are the basic facts."

She nodded. "Yes. And, how did the accident occur?"

"The brake lines were severed. Perhaps faulty materials. Or something the car hit in the road."

"At least she wasn't alone in the end. With her fencing instructor, I understand, the late Mr. Bloodstone. But, so sad to lose both a promising athlete and her instructor."

"Yes." All the books and manuals Father left lying around were most useful. At first, I read them, just trying to understand his world of automobiles. When I saw that Mr. Bloodstone's relationship with my beautiful sister jeopardized the life our family had together, not to mention her chances at the Olympics, it was easy to plan a way to get rid of him. A terrible accident due to vehicle malfunction. I just hadn't expected my beloved sister to be with him that night.

Antonia continued. "Similarly, it is so difficult to think of both our own Mrs. Bloodstone and Mr. Kincaid gone. Who could have imagined such small injuries suffered in a fencing practice could lead to two deaths? They had no appearance of being mortal wounds, unless perhaps a poison was involved."

"Yes." Again, Father's scientific books had been most informative. Who could have imagined that crushed cherry pits create a deadly toxin? After leaving Mr. Kincaid, I set out the sabers in the fencing room and coated them with the special formula I had concocted. Then, I went to Mrs. Bloodstone, telling her of Mr. Kincaid's elopement plan and urging her to meet him in the fencing room. The decision to engage in armed combat had been entirely their own.

I took a deep breath before responding. "You are a wise woman, Antonia. I think perhaps you have put many puzzle pieces together."

"Yes."

She sat back and adjusted her lap robe. I listened to the horses' hooves taking us forward.

"Do you suppose," she asked, "that Justine left of her own accord? Without any notion of a dispute between her mother and Mr. Kincaid?"

Justine had been delighted to receive a note on Mr. Kincaid's stationery with the message, "For my darling." With that and two hundred dollars I had saved from my wages, she went happily to the train station, thinking her love would join her later. Somehow, I think she was able to reconcile the loss when I wired her the news of her mother's death and she realized she was free in the world with money. Just as she had noticed about Antonia.

"For you see," Antonia was saying, "being less spry as I've grown older has made me a keener observer of the human condition. I was intrigued as to what might bring a young woman from a burgeoning metropolis to our small backwater town. Thus, I began researching your background and found the connection between you and Marilee Bloodstone. Digging deeper, I discovered Tolliver Kincaid. He was all too eager to make Marilee suffer for the injury inflicted upon his mother. And, fortunately for the school, he was quite delighted to take on the role of fencing instructor."

Pausing, Antonia sighed. "Unfortunately, I did not consider the ramifications to, let us say, affiliated bystanders. I would feel terrible guilt to think I somehow left Justine an orphan in the world without means of support."

"In my experience," I assured her, "I always found Justine very self-reliant."

Antonia smiled. "I'm glad to hear it. Cyrus Pierce used to tell us, 'live to the truth.' That seemed a bit abstract to me. I find it much easier to live my own truth."

I returned her smile. "I completely agree."

SUSAN DALY

Susan Daly finds joy in writing short crime fiction, especially when it lets her crusade for social justice and punish the guilty. A repeat offender, her short story, 'Spirit River Dam,' appears in *The Best Laid Plans: 21 Stories of Mystery & Suspense*. Other stories have appeared in a number of anthologies, most recently *Mystery Most Theatrical*. 'A Death at the Parsonage' won Crime Writers of Canada's 2017 Arthur Ellis Award for best short story. She lives in Toronto, a close commute to her excellent grandkids.

Find her at susandaly.com.

DEEP FREEZE IN SUBURBIA

SUSAN DALY

DINA CALDER, the Honourable Member for Vancouver-Capilano, leaned back in her leather chair and reveled in the luxury of her office, with its view of the Ottawa River and the East Block in all its Gothic Revival glory. This was the life. This was where she deserved to be. Not only a member of parliament, but Minister of Families and Seniors. Nothing but good times ahead.

A knock at the door broke her mood. Couldn't she have five minutes alone to enjoy her success? Her new Parliamentary Assistant...Manolo? no, Birkenstock...entered.

"What is it, Birkenstock? I thought I was finished with appointments for today."

"You are. That's why this is a good time."

Gabby Birkenstock shut the door and stood before the desk, hugging a manila folder. "It's a personal matter."

"I believe we have an employee counseling service for that."

The tiniest sigh from Birkenstock. "It's *your* personal matter." She pulled a paperback out of the folder and held it up.

Deep Freeze in Suburbia.

The world as Dina knew it, hard won and well worth it, seemed to circle the drain and flush away beneath her.

The lurid cover art of the true-crime paperback—a chest freezer half open, a woman's arm hanging out—had haunted her dreams for nearly thirty years. *The Shocking Story of the Misty Lockwood Murder.* By Carlee Bradlee.

"Where did you...?" *Keep calm. Don't overreact.* "What's that?"

"It arrived yesterday, while you were at the Horticultural Society fundraiser." Her look remained blank as she placed the book on the desk. Dina stared at it, not sure it wasn't going to crawl over and bite her.

Okay, careful.... "Was there a note with it? An envelope?"

Birkenstock handed her a padded brown envelope addressed to her with a printed label. No return address. No warning of personal, private, or confidential. Postmark unreadable.

"Who else has seen this?" And didn't *that* sound guilty.

"No one. The clerical staff direct all packages to me. I took it home with me for safekeeping."

"Why would you—? Hey, you didn't *read* it, did you?"

Birkenstock's look said, *Well, duh!*

"Yes, I admit I succumbed to the temptation."

"Oh. What did you make of it?" Sure, as if that oh-so-casual tone was going to fool her.

"The writing is pretty bad, but I suppose you mean the contents. I found it interesting that it took place in Rideau Landing in 1993, and I'm pretty sure that's where you originally came from."

Damn this obsessively efficient woman. Supposedly she was lucky to have her, but somehow her habit of knowing everything was already getting on Dina's nerves.

"Lots of people come from Rideau Landing." The affluent riverside community south of Ottawa. "I was very young when I left."

"You were twenty. This was huge news, so you must have been aware of the events at the time."

"Vaguely...." In fact, it had made headlines all across Canada, thanks to the public's insatiable appetite for salacious crimes.

"There's a personal inscription," Birkenstock said.

Dina reached forward and lifted the front cover with her

fingertip. The inscription, if it could be described as such, was in block letters.

DID YOU THINK YOU COULD RUN AWAY FROM THE PAST, DEEDEE?

This was *not* happening.

"Ms. Calder, I'm sorry if this is painful, but apparently someone thinks there's a connection to you. Though they seem to be referring to you as DeeDee."

Dina felt herself nodding.

"Can you keep a secret?" she managed to say.

Birkenstock gave her a pained look. "You know all matters within parliamentary walls are confidential. That I've sworn an oath —several oaths—to keep them that way."

"I mean a *personal* secret. Not all that government nonsense that gets leaked before it's even back from the printer."

"Yes. I can keep a secret. Even yours."

Dina thought hard and fast. If Birkenstock had already read the book, full of crap as it was, there was nothing to lose.

"Yeah, okay. I am—or was—DeeDee Parkinson. Back in a lifetime I'd prefer to forget."

After a few moments of silence, Birkenstock said, "And…?"

"And what? Isn't that enough?"

"Seriously? Ms. Calder, according to this book—and, I might add, everything I've read about it online—DeeDee Parkinson, age twenty, a receptionist in a private cosmetic surgery clinic in Rideau Landing, was having an affair with Dr. Ron Lockwood, the head of the clinic. Married. Thirty-five."

Every word went straight to Dina's psyche and stung like wasps.

"Okay. Yes, it was all sordid and ugly and, frankly, idiotic." Then Birkenstock's other revelation sank in. "Online…Who told you to…? Never mind. What did you find?"

Birkenstock shrugged. "Just about everything that was in the book, and not much more. As far as I could figure out, they were all reading from the same hymn book."

Not surprising. "That so-called writer, Carlee Bradlee. She sat in the courtroom every day for three weeks. Then she wrote up her notes, cobbled together with a bunch of news stories, without regard to their credibility, and without contacting any primary sources, and called it a novel."

"According to her, the newspapers, and a couple of true-crime websites—"

"Jesus, Birkenstock. What made this sordid little story so special that it's on a true-crime website?"

Birkenstock looked at her for a long few seconds, then said evenly, "I guess it was the bit about Misty's body being hidden in the freezer for three months."

Right. Maybe she had a point.

"How much of this book is true?" Birkenstock asked.

"And just why do you need to know this?"

"I'm possibly the only person—besides your secret admirer—who knows you and DeeDee Parkinson are the same entity, I assume you're going to have me look into this, keep it from getting public?"

Dina thought about it. At least Birkenstock had initiative and research savvy.

"Maybe half of it's true. Not *even* half. She got a lot of the details wrong. And she added a few embellishments of her own. But yeah, I was, um, seeing Ron Lockwood for about six months—"

"Isn't that called 'having an affair?'"

"It wasn't like that. Their marriage was on the rocks. He was going to leave her."

Birkenstock leveled a look at her. "Are you sure you're savvy enough to be a cabinet minister?"

"That's what he told me, okay? Quit judging. And then, he tells me she's left him. Gone off with her tennis instructor."

"Funny how it's always the tennis instructor."

"I can't help that. Anyway, that's when we started, uh, dating openly."

"But you didn't move in?"

"Are you serious? I was barely out of my teens. If I'd moved in, I'd have my hands full with laundry and cleaning and cooking."

Besides, Ron had been adamant. No moving in. He didn't want to risk her claiming common-law rights to half his monster home, bought with the avails of tummy tucks and breast enlargements.

Birkenstock nodded. "And three months later, his sister discovered the body?"

"We both did. I was spending the afternoon there, lounging by the pool. His sister Melanie came over, acted like she owned the place. Decided she wanted something from the freezer."

Dina felt a wave of nausea. The wave she'd been riding for twenty-seven years. The memory of that dead frozen face staring up at her between the packages of broccoli and frozen waffles.

"That's enough, okay? I don't want to talk about it. All the rest was like in the book. Ron was arrested, I was a crown witness. Ron was tried and convicted."

"Okay, I understand." Birkenstock actually looked sympathetic. "Then you vanished. No website anywhere has a clue what became of you."

"Thank goodness for that. I moved out to the west coast, changed my name, put it all behind me."

Until now.

"And you never saw Ron again?"

"Seriously? Why would I? Anyway, he died in prison."

Birkenstock nodded. "Eight years later. Cancer."

That seemed to put an end to the reminiscences. Silence hovered for a minute, then Birkenstock brought up another matter.

"What about Himself? Does He know?"

Himself. Andrew Goodwin Lemieux, the new prime minister who, following last month's election, was going to lead them all to a new Canada. Whose campaign promises included demanding full disclosure from all members at all times. Who did not like surprises, even when they *didn't* involve a cabinet minister who'd been a key witness in the murder of her married lover's wife.

Dina waved a dismissive hand. "There's nothing for him to know. That was all in another lifetime, under another name."

Birkenstock looked unimpressed.

"Ms. Calder, someone clearly wants to rake up that other lifetime."

"Well, I'm not telling him yet. I've got to spend the next two days in Vancouver dealing with constituents' complaints. And

Himself is down in Washington right now working out yet another variation on the Free Trade Agreement."

Birkenstock sighed. "Okay, how about I research this Carlee Bradlee, see what she's up to these days?"

"Good idea. Starting now, this book is your number one priority. Find out who might have sent it. And while you're at it, find out if there are any copies available online."

"And do what with them?"

"Buy them all. Anonymously. How many can there be?"

"That should look good on the expenses."

"Figure something out."

"ANY OF IT TRUE?" Quentin Bonaventure asked. The member for Moose Falls, and Dina's sometime mentor, leaned back in his chair at their favorite Sparks Street lounge and addressed his rye on the rocks.

His casual tone didn't fool her. After nearly forty years as a member of parliament, he was pretty much unshockable. Before leaving Ottawa two days ago, she'd left the book with him to read.

Dina practically inhaled her Zaza. Right now she needed this generous combo of Dubonnet and gin.

"Some of it. Maybe…half?"

"*Which* half?" He wasn't going to be put off.

"Okay, more than half. But I had nothing to do with…" she dropped her voice, suddenly kicking herself for having met him in semi-public. "…with, um, the freezer and all."

He nodded and put down the glass. "All right, fine. But I don't think your constituents—nor the press—will care about that fine point. And certainly not Himself."

"But…."

But nothing. Quentin was right. As usual. She looked around and caught the server's eye, indicating more of the same.

"Thing is, Dina, it was a cause célèbre twenty-seven years ago. It didn't hold the headlines long because he was tried and convicted in fairly short order. But while it did, it was big news. Of course, a man murdering his wife because he fancies himself in love with some little—"

"Watch it...."

"In love with an attractive younger woman—that in itself should be national news every time it happens. Sadly, it still gets a big yawn from the jaded public. Unless there's a sensational element. Such as...." he waved his hand vaguely.

"That effing freezer." Birkenstock had said much the same thing.

"Yes, somehow freezers are always..." He paused as the server came by with their next round, then continued. "And of course, the sensationalism of this big shot, high-profile surgeon. The crassness of cosmetic surgery for sheer vanity. And Misty had her own self-improvement career, right?"

Dina nodded. "She ran so-called fitness classes: swimmercise, slimmercise, whatevercise. After her much touted breast augmentation, she became 'spokesgirl' for the clinic. Then she married the surgeon, and gave it all up for the life of a trophy wife. Years before I worked there, of course."

"Of course. But that's what sticks in the public's collective mind. They may have forgotten it, but mention it now, and everything will come tumbling into the front of their consciousness."

"I know, I know," Dina said. "It's all bad news. I've got my PA looking into where this Carlee Bradlee is now."

Quentin raised a bushy eyebrow. "You confided in her? Was that wise?"

"Confided? She's the one who opened the package. She was all over it before I even saw it. And I have to admit she's good." Even if she was a complete pain.

Dina knocked back the last of her second Zaza.

"So, Quentin...what do I do now?"

Quentin gazed at her steadily, as though she didn't need telling.

"Tell Himself? He doesn't need to know. I was an innocent bystander. A mere child."

Quentin shook his head sadly.

"Dina, much as he'd hate to hear it from you, he'd hate it a lot more reading about it on the front page of every right-wing newspaper in the country, and even the few remaining credible ones. Or see it online. Let alone have it come up in Question Period."

"He's not *going* to hear about it. The book's been out of print for over twenty years. No one ever made a TV movie of it, and the author isn't exactly a household name. Carlee Bradlee. Who's got a name like that? Obviously fake."

"And yet, someone sent you a copy."

Yes. Someone had.

She ordered another Zaza.

THE NEXT MORNING, before even glancing at the business that had accumulated during her two days away, Dina grilled her assistant for any new discoveries.

None of it was good.

"First of all," Birkenstock reported, "copies of the book are plentiful. Between AbeBooks and eBay and Amazon, there are 176 copies available for sale."

"What!"

"And the prices range from $1.23 to—wait for it—$426.02."

"Seriously? People actually pay that much for that pack of lies?" Pack of half-lies, anyway.

"I doubt it. People will put up anything for sale for crazy prices. No matter how awful a book, or obscure or lurid or dull, there are *always* copies on offer."

A half dozen thoughts chased each other around Dina's brain. None of them comforting. "Damn. We'll never be able to buy them all."

"That was never practical, Ms. Calder. There would still be dozens in basements and paperback exchanges all over the country."

"And there's no reason why they shouldn't stay there. What about libraries? Not that any self-respecting library would carry it."

"Actually, they would. There are copies available for circulation in libraries all over Canada. Plus five in reference stacks."

"*This* is how public money is spent?" Dina muttered.

"And of course, the national library."

"The…?"

"Library and Archives Canada. You know, the big building down the street where they have a record of every book ever published in Canada? Plus two copies on deposit."

"*Every* book? Including dreck like …?" She waved in the direction of the locked drawer where *Deep Freeze* was secreted.

Birkenstock nodded. "Including dreck like that. Unless the late government, in their scorched earth policies against all things intellectual, did away with such fripperies."

"We can only hope. Okay, you can take care of those copies, at least."

"Take care of them?"

"Steal them. Check them out and lose them. What do I pay you for?"

"I'm not sure the library has check-out privileges. Though I imagine an MP's office could get a copy. Of course, if we did request it, it would be on record."

Damn bureaucracy. "Well, see what you can manage. What about the package? Any leads there? Fingerprints?"

"Do I look like the RCMP? Short of calling in the horsemen, I don't know anyone skilled in that direction. Anyway, the package was handled by dozens of people. The post office, the mailroom, our staff. You and me."

"Okay, okay. What about Carlee Bradlee? What's she doing now? Still writing potboilers?"

"No…." Birkenstock looked reluctant to continue. "At least not under that name."

"Don't tell me. She's writing as Louise Penny."

"Last year, under her real name, Maralina Sokol, she wrote a history of the Dionne quintuplets."

"The Dionnes? Who cares about them? They're all dead."

"Actually, two of them are still alive. They're in their eighties."

"Okay, whatever. But there's been about a thousand books written about them. Who's going to care about one more? Or rush out to find the only other book Bradlee ever wrote?"

Birkenstock shook her head. "For reasons I'm sure we'll never understand, *Five Little Girls in Blue* has been long-listed for the Northern Spirit Readers' Choice Book Award."

"What's that?" Some local library event, she supposed.

"It's a big time—and lucrative—literary award. If it gets on the shortlist, it will mean bigger sales and author interviews—and renewed interest in anything else she wrote."

This can't be happening. Dina grabbed the arms of her leather chair for some sense of stability.

"Face it, Ms. Calder. Her old publisher will totally do a quick and dirty reissue of her first book. Probably an e-book. And someone—a lot of someones—will say, 'Hey, I wonder where DeeDee Parkinson is today.'"

Dina felt all control sliding away. Who'd have thought that hack could write something touted as literary? And get big money for it.

"You're right, you're right. We have to go about this a whole different way. How can we sabotage the Book Award decision?"

"You can't. For one thing—"

"Oh, don't be so defeatist. You said it's a readers' choice award. We campaign to get people to vote for a different book in big numbers; or, wait! We could do it electronically. I'll bet we can get someone to write a logarithm to flood the website with votes. Like robocalls, but online."

"I think they'd notice they were fake."

"Not if we use *real* people's emails. I've got all kinds of voter lists we can use."

Birkenstock hit her with a steely, uncooperative look. Almost as if she didn't *want* her ideas.

"The finalists are being announced tomorrow. Anyway, never mind all that. You still have to ask yourself, who sent it? Who wants you to sweat? Who wants to destroy your career?"

Dina groaned. "I guess I'm going to have to tell Himself." Quentin had made it clear she really didn't have a choice.

And really, it would be better if she told the truth now, and put the right spin on it. Before it came out all wrong.

"Good. I've made an appointment for you. Mr. Lemieux is expecting you at four o'clock."

DESCENDED from a dynasty of industrial giants on one side and a long line of labor organizers on the other, Andrew Goodwin Lemieux was viewed with equal parts suspicion and hope from all angles of the spectrum. He was a complex man, and you were never sure which side of his heritage would take precedence at any time.

As Dina was ushered into the PM's office, she could see the edge of concern behind all that outward calm. After a few words of chat, he got down to it.

"What's up, Dina?"

Deep, deep breath. The point of no return.

"Have you ever heard of the Misty Lockwood murder?"

As his face revealed an attempt to call up the past, she fed him prompts. "Twenty-seven years ago. Guy kills his wife. Hides her in the freezer."

He nodded slowly. "Right.... Wasn't there a book?"

She nodded and pulled the book out of her folder. Were her hands actually trembling? "Someone sent me this. Anonymously."

Andrew took it and stared at it.

"What was your part in this, Dina?"

"I was the, uh, the killer's girlfriend. And, I found the body."

Andrew's face went dead white. It took a lot to throw him.

"Refresh my memory, will you?"

He listened with stoic impassivity as she laid out the details. When she ground to a halt, he said, "And now someone has connected you with it?"

"Apparently."

He remained silent for a minute or so, thinking. Finally he spoke.

"I'll need to call a press conference for tomorrow."

Yes, they'd face it together. She'd reveal the truth, and the world would forgive her—

"And I'll need your resignation from Cabinet tonight."

RESIGNATION!

Dina fumed as she jammed files into boxes, preparing to move from her prime real estate to the cramped dingy space allocated to backbenchers, in an unpopular wing. She didn't even have Birkenstock to do it for her. It turned out her ex-assistant was also prime property, and would remain with her cabinet replacement.

It was not due to her nefarious past that the PM had removed her from Cabinet. He said it was because she hadn't been upfront about it when she'd first been put forward as a candidate.

Andrew and his damned integrity gene. It *would* have to surface just now.

As she packed and fumed, voices from the large screen TV— another perk she wasn't taking with her—murmured in the background. A familiar name caught her attention. She grabbed the remote and turned up the volume.

The finalists for the Readers' Choice were being featured. Maralina Sokol, with her first book, *Five Little Girls in Blue.*

Dina watched with growing uncertainty. Then dismay. *No....*

She turned to her laptop and began a search.

One after another, the misshapen pieces fell into place.

When had Birkenstock started lying to her? And why?

GABBY BIRKENSTOCK SHIVERED in the wintry gray afternoon, standing before the solitary gravestone, with its sad dates.

1969-1993

Well, Misty, I did what I could. I wish I could have kept you out of the public eye, but I guess that's the price we pay for a PM who occasionally has flashes of integrity. He actually made a public announcement, admitting he had appointed a cabinet minister without due diligence.

The chill wind rustled the leaves around her.

But yeah...I had to tell a few lies myself. Half-lies, half-truths, whatever—

"Thought you might show up here."

Gabby turned to see the one-time Minister of Families and Seniors near the next row of stones.

"Figured it out, eh?" Gabby said, not all that much concerned.

"Sure." Dina came closer and stood facing her, as though for a showdown. "As soon as I saw Maralina Sokol on TV, I started my own research. I learned she was thirty-two years old and came to Canada from the Czech Republic at the age of fifteen. Not even remotely like Carlee Bradlee, who was born in Saskatoon sixty-three years ago and died in 2005."

Gabby shrugged. "Yeah. But it was a good bluff. Got you scared enough to think your old nemesis and all her works were about to hit the headlines again."

"I worked out you must have sent the book in the first place. Or rather, *didn't* send it. All you had to do was write that inscription, and walk into my office with a random envelope to get the ball rolling. Then you just kept feeding me lies from beginning to end."

"Pretty much. Except about the number of books available online." Which were now enjoying a sudden renewed interest, Gabby reflected with satisfaction. And just wait until the new print and e-book editions came out.

"But why go to all that charade?" Dina asked. "Why not just go to the press or the PM or whoever in the first place and tell all?"

"I wanted to watch you squirm. I wanted you to gradually realize you were cornered. To make you go to Andrew yourself. Kill your own career."

"So it *was* personal?" Dina indicated Misty's gravestone.

"My mother."

"No way! She and Ron didn't have kids."

"My birth mother. I won't go into the miserable life she lived, since I don't suppose you'd care. But I'm sure she saw marrying Ron as the answer to her prayers. And then, three years later, he falls for you and her dream of the good life—or any life—is over."

"You're breaking my heart."

"I doubt it. But it broke *my* heart when I turned eighteen and tracked down the adoption files, only to learn she'd been murdered by her husband on account of his bit of fluff. It took me a few more years to find out what happened to that bit of fluff. Imagine my shock when I learned you were about to run for Parliament."

"I'll bet you were even more shocked when I became a cabinet minister."

"Minister of Families and Seniors...." Gabby shook her head. What had Andrew been thinking?

However, retribution was sweet. She could finally let it go.

"Well, Dina, you can stay here and make your peace with Misty if you want. I'm just glad the whole truth is finally out there."

DINA WATCHED BIRKENSTOCK LEAVE, then turned to look down at Misty's grave.

Here they were again all these years later, Misty in the frozen ground, Dina warm and breathing.

The whole truth?

"Looks like we both had lousy taste in men, eh Misty?"

Misty had found out about DeeDee, and she and Ron had another one of their fights. He smashed her across the face one last time. Then he got drunk and remorseful at the sight of her lying battered and lifeless. He'd called Dina, desperate, demanding her help.

"Yeah, I know, Misty. I should never have agreed to it. But he actually believed if he got rid of your body, he just might get away with it. That's why the freezer. To give him time. Come winter, he was going to take you some place where your frozen body could be found months after your disappearance."

What the hell am I doing, talking to a woman who's been dead for twenty-

seven years? Trying to convince her of what happened? As if she could hear me. As if she doesn't already know.

"I went along with it to try and save Ron."

Who was she kidding?

"But then, damn it, Ron's idiot sister came over that day for a swim. And decided she needed butterscotch ice cream of all things. Not the chocolate in the upstairs freezer. Geez, who doesn't like chocolate?"

It wasn't until the horrific screams rose from the basement that she realized Melanie had gone searching further afield than the kitchen.

And then her own sickened reaction, seeing Misty's face again in the freezer...

I scream, you scream, we all scream for ice cream...

It all just hit the fan.

Ron could easily have fingered her as an accessory after the fact. But he took the fall.

No sense in us both going down. Had he said it first? Or had she? Dina liked to think it was him.

I'll wait for you, darling. Yeah, she'd said that to him. As if.

The whole truth, Birkenstock had said.

No one—not Ron, the police, the crown prosecutors, Carlee Bradlee, a dozen true-crime websites—ever knew the whole truth.

That Dina had finished her off.

CHRIS WHEATLEY

Chris Wheatley is a writer and musician, from Oxford, UK. He has an enduring love for the works of R. A. Lafferty, Jack Vance, and Shirley Jackson, and is forever indebted to the advice and encouragement of his wife and his son. A repeat offender, his short story 'The True Cost of Liberty,' appears in *The Best Laid Plans: 21 Stories of Mystery & Suspense*. Chris is a member of the Short Mystery Fiction Society.

Find him at silverpilgrim.com.

THE ANGEL OF MAASTRICHT

CHRIS WHEATLEY

ACCORDING to at least one expert witness, the victim was alive and possibly conscious during the last, frenzied attack, during which she suffered no less than seventeen separate knife wounds.

David Dubois, "the Beast of Bodmin," was forty-seven-years of age at the time he was sentenced to life imprisonment for the premeditated and brutal murder of Saar Jansson, his ex-partner, a former model and minor Countess of the Dutch Royal Family.

Surely you remember the case. The Angel of Maastricht, they called her, the victim, the corpse. The body was discovered at approximately 9:17 a.m. on a Sunday, at the victim's ground-floor flat in Kensington, London. A neighbor, Anne Rosemary, an acquaintance of Saar Jansson's—she disavowed the word "friend" in court—had arranged to meet Jansson on the street at 9:00 a.m., in order that they might walk to church together.

Tired of waiting and concerned that they might miss the morning service, Anne Rosemary called at Jansson's flat, only to discover the door lying open, the living room in disarray and, upon entering, the body itself on the floor in the kitchen nook.

There followed a bizarre twist of fate. Rosemary, frightened out of her wits, as she would later describe, ran back out into the street and called for help. A passing tourist, James Washington, on vacation from Garden City, Idaho, was the first person she encountered. Together they returned to the flat and, while Rosemary used the landline to call the police, Mr. Washington, for reasons he would never properly clarify, raised his Polaroid PDC-2000 digital camera (which hung from a strap around his neck) and took several photographs of the scene.

The tangled and squalid tale of how these photographs came to be released to the British press and the ensuing lawsuits and countersuits, accusations and rebuttals, makes for a story in itself. To summarize: Washington contacted at least three different national dailies and several locals, offering the pictures for sale. It was the *Daily News*, in the end, who chanced their arm in making a purchase. To this day the sum paid remains undisclosed. However, Washington, whether through ignorance or by mistake, managed to email high resolution scans to all of them.

I'm sure you have seen the pictures. Sara Jansson, wearing an ankle-length white summer dress with gold trim, is laid out in a T-shape with her arms spread, hands palms up. Her long, golden-brown hair is purposefully arranged so that it surrounds her head like a halo. Her eyes are closed. Her resting lips look as though they are smiling. The white dress is soaked in blood. A wooden-handled kitchen knife, plunged between her breasts, sticks up, with three or four inches of the blade exposed.

She had been poisoned with ricin. Evidence suggests that she was dressed and moved to the kitchen by the murderer whilst she was disabled, before the final act of violence had begun.

If you have heard that the police always turn to the boyfriend or ex-boyfriend first, then you are correct. Jansson had had little to do with men for some years, but it didn't take investigators long to turn up the name of David Dubois.

David Dubois had plenty of reason to fall under suspicion. Firstly, the separation between he and Sara had been acrimonious. Although they had been parted for almost twenty years, numerous texts and letters between the pair were discovered that testified to their lasting mutual resentment, the final example dating to mere months before Sara's death.

Secondly, at the time of their split, Sara had been pregnant with Dubois' child, a child that she would deny his name (she did not list him as the father on the birth certificate). From the communications between them, police understood that, although at first David had been an irregular visitor to both mother and child, such visits soon ceased and no legal rights were ever sought by Dubois.

The child grew up believing (having been told) that his father was one Ruslan Kuznetzov, a Russian Professor of Economics at London Metropolitan University and former lover of Jansson's, now reunited. Kuznetzov passed away four years before Jansson's own death. There is ample evidence to show that Dubois was aware of this deception.

Thirdly, and by far the most damning, Anne Rosemary (remember her?) en route to her initial visit to Sara's flat that morning, passed, in the adjoining corridor, a man coming the other way, a man she described as "wild-eyed and panicked," a man she would later identify without hesitation as one David Dubois.

Following a three-week-long trial-by-jury at Blackfriar's Crown Court, and despite the lack of concrete forensic evidence, Dubois was unanimously convicted of the premeditated first-degree murder of Sara Jansson and sentenced to life. Their child did not attend the proceedings.

Life imprisonment, in David's case, meant serving twenty-two years behind bars at Long Lartin Prison, Worcester, before being released early for good behavior. Dubois, by all accounts, was a well-behaved if unremarkable inmate, with only one minor misdemeanor for hiding contraband. Upon release, David returned to his hometown of Alternun, Bodmin and took up residence in his parent's former house.

That was three years ago.

At the time of the Jansson murder, I'd been a junior reporter for the *Birmingham Herald*, and had little to do with the case. In the years since, I had worked my way up to the position of Staff Writer, Crime, at the *London Record*. By then, of course, I could have held a much more senior post, but I enjoyed my work and had little need for money, thanks to a rather generous inheritance.

I'd been angling for the paper to revisit the Angel of Maastricht affair for several months. Finally I managed to convince my editor that there was something new to be wrenched from the story. Whether because it was the twenty-fifth anniversary of the case, because it was a slow month for news, or simply out of personal gratitude for all the undeniable talent and hard work I had contributed, he inevitably capitulated and agreed that, providing I could secure an interview with David Dubois, the *Record* would run my piece.

I knew, if given the choice, Dubois would never agree, so I took myself down to Bodmin and simply turned up at his doorstep—a broken-down cottage on the outskirts of the town. I had a whole spiel worked out. "Your chance to tell your side of the story, to set the record straight, if you don't, they will write it anyway." You know the sort of thing. I have used it countless times on everybody from sex workers to civil servants. People are shockingly easy to coerce.

In the end, though, it was simple. I knocked on the door, introduced myself and more or less right away was invited inside. Perhaps Dubois really did feel an urge to talk. Or maybe he simply thought it the quickest and surest way to see me gone.

My initial impression was that he was overweight, with sunken lines upon his face, thick, swollen, nicotine-stained fingers, and a gray beard that had not seen a barber in weeks. Inside, the house was a mess. Dirty, disorganized and untidy. Books and magazines everywhere. Clothes on the floor. He offered me tea but did not have any milk.

Were we anything alike, he and I? A certain resemblance around the eyes, perhaps.

We sat in a living room, which could more accurately be described as a pigsty, on a sofa stained and dotted with cigarette burns. I detested every second spent in that place.

On the subject of the murder, Dubois had little to say except that, yes, he had been there, on that morning inside Sara's flat, had passed Rosemary Anne on his way out, just as she said he had, and had indeed seen Sara's corpse upon the floor.

Why had he been there? He had received a phone call the previous evening from Sara, he told me, urging him to visit the next morning. She had told him it concerned his son, that he wanted to meet his father, and if Dubois didn't come tomorrow then he never would.

This, of course, is old news. Court Records show that Dubois had indeed received a phone call that evening from an untraceable mobile number. As to the origin or nature of that call, nothing could be proved either way. Jansson's son denied all knowledge of the event (he was excused from attending court on compassionate grounds but provided a signed witness document to this effect—a stoke of genius, I must say.)

"Did you do it?" I asked Dubois. I, of course, already knew the answer to that.

Dubois stared at the rotting carpet.

"You pleaded innocent at the trial," I prompted.

"I did what they told me," he replied.

"Two years into your sentence," I said, "a lawyer named Jacob Daniels visited you. He told you that, in his opinion, there were sufficient grounds for a retrial. You turned down his offer. I know this because I have talked to him." In truth, Daniels had given me rather short shrift over the telephone.

Dubois remained dumbly staring at the carpet.

"Why did you turn him away?" I asked. "You might have been freed."

"They'd already found me guilty," said Dubois.

It was, in my opinion, a pitiful piece of self sabotage. The act of a cowardly dog.

"During your time in prison, did you ever try to contact your son? Have you been in touch since you were released?" Here I remained remarkably straight-faced. I like to think that I even managed to inject a hint of empathy, of pathos.

"What would be the point?" said Dubois. "He doesn't even

know me. I tried to look him up once, on Facebook, but I couldn't find him."

"If *you* didn't kill Sara," I said, "then who do you think did?"

"I have a suspicion," he mumbled, but no matter how much I tried, he would not be drawn into this, or even induced to repeat his assertion.

"What are your plans for the remainder of your life?"

At this, Dubois looked me right in the eyes. He seemed shocked by my question and fell silent for some moments. Then he just shrugged. Frankly, it was depressing.

My final question was: "Did you love Sara Jansson?"

"She was a disaster," he said, in response, "but she was *my* disaster."

By then I had had more than my fill of David Dubois and his self-centered misery. I left in short order. As I was walking up the garden path, back to my car, I passed a man coming in through the gate. He was a tall man, old, with ridiculous glasses and too much hair. He stared at me very oddly.

I grew curious about that. A little concerned. So much the better then that, whilst Dubois had been making his filthy tea, I had planted one of those little bugs that are so easy to get hold of these days, under the ugly old coffee table in the lounge.

Turns out my suspicions were justified.

"Didn't you realize it was him?" says a man on the recording, which I have on my hard drive. The man with bad hair and glasses, I assume.

"Only when I looked into his eyes," says Dubois.

"Doesn't this confirm it?" says Bad Hair. "Everything we know. Everything that lawyer suspected. *He* killed Sara and he's still out there. He's dangerous. We need to tell the police."

There comes a pause. "No," says Dubois.

"Why not?"

"Because he's my son."

"He's a sociopath," says Bad Hair, "to do that—to Sara. To *you*."

"Maybe," says Dubois, "but he's *my* sociopath."

Who would have guessed the depths of the idiocy of mankind?

My dear estranged daddy, after all these years, covering up for the son who murdered his lover—for what? Out of some misplaced sense of guilt? For abandoning me? For never having tried?

Parental urges are pathetic.

You know what I felt when I plunged that blade into my mother's soft, unresisting body? Relief. Vengeance. *Justice.*

If I hadn't found those letters I would never have know about her lies, but even then, I think, I would have killed her. She was always so controlling, you see, so smotheringly protective.

So weak.

The article, in case you were wondering, was an outstanding success. You won't find it under my real name, of course. I ceased using that from my earliest days.

Recently, I have changed careers. I am a Homicide Case Worker for Victim Support, if you can believe it. I am invited into the homes of the bereaved, the vulnerable, the traumatized. I become a part of the very fabric of their lives.

I feel, in some ways, that this is my natural habitat. My clients love me. I understand them, you see, and if you understand someone then you can manipulate them to a ridiculous degree.

I am looking forward to the coming years. I think they are going to be fruitful.

Who knows what wonders I shall find to write about next.

JOSEPH S. WALKER

Joseph S. Walker is a college teacher living in Indiana. In his more mysterious pursuits, he has been actively publishing crime fiction since 2011. His work has appeared in *Alfred Hitchcock Mystery Magazine*, *Mystery Weekly*, *Dark City*, and several anthologies. In 2019, he won both the Bill Crider Prize and the Al Blanchard Award. Joseph is a member of Mystery Writers Of America, Short Mystery Fiction Society, and Sisters in Crime National.

Find him at jsw47408.wixsite.com/website.

PINK HEARTS PIERCED BY ARROWS

JOSEPH S. WALKER

1998

From her bedroom window, Crystal watched as her mother carried pile after pile of clothes out to the detached garage in the backyard, the garage where Crystal's father kept the vintage Mustang he'd spent years lovingly restoring. Then she carried out his vinyl collection, a dozen milk crates filled with records Crystal was never allowed to play.

Crystal was ten years old. Old enough, her mother said, to understand what was happening: her father was abandoning them, leaving to be with a woman he'd met in a bar.

When her mother left the garage for the last time, thin wisps of smoke drifted from the windows.

After an hour, when night had set in and the garage was fully ablaze, Crystal crept down the stairs. Her mother was sitting on the back porch, arms crossed, watching the fire.

Crystal took the chair next to her. They sat together in silence, in the dark. Crystal was scared, but she also felt oddly proud, exhilarated by the way her mother had acted without pausing for second thoughts or moderation.

Their nearest neighbor was a couple of miles away. It was a

while before the flames reached so high that somebody called the fire department. Only when they finally heard the distant sirens did Crystal's mother finally speak.

"Don't you ever let a man make a fool of you," she said. "Don't you ever be with a man you couldn't stand to leave. Use him, get what you can, and walk away. Promise me."

"I promise," Crystal said.

"I THINK he's cheating on me," Mandy said.

"Kyle?" Crystal automatically looked at the door to her office, half expecting to see Mandy's husband leaning against the frame.

"He's out at a client lunch," Mandy said. "Or at least that's where he's supposed to be." She slumped into the chair in front of Crystal's desk. "I don't know why I'm telling you this. I shouldn't be. But I'm going insane. I have to tell someone."

"Of course, honey," Crystal said. "But you must be wrong. He's crazy about you. You just had your tenth anniversary."

The three of them had met in their advanced Accounting classes in college. After graduation, and the wedding where Crystal had been Mandy's maid of honor, they'd started a firm together.

"What makes you think he'd do that to you?" Crystal asked.

"Oh, god," Mandy said. "This is so humiliating." Her hand dipped into her purse, hesitated. She trembled, pulling out a bra, delicate and lacy, with a pattern of pink hearts pierced by arrows. "I found this tangled up in his laundry."

"Jesus," Crystal said, stiffening in her chair. "Maybe..." she trailed off. She couldn't think of anything to say.

With a sob, Mandy shoved the garment back into the purse. "What do I do? Should I confront him?"

"No," Crystal snapped. She forced herself to focus, to take her time. "I mean, I don't think so. He'll either lie about it or leave immediately. Do you want him to leave?"

"I don't know," Mandy said. "I thought things were fine."

"There might be some other explanation."

"Like what? He's secretly a cross-dresser? Oh, god, maybe he is." Mandy stood and started to pace.

"Listen," Crystal said. "He's driving to that convention in Denver this weekend, right?"

"Yeah," Mandy said. She looked up. "Why? You think he's taking her, whoever she is?"

"That's not what I was thinking," Crystal said. "He'll be out of the house for a couple of days. While he's gone you can search your place from top to bottom. If he's really stepping out there will be more evidence, right? You'll find something. Then you'll have a stronger position if something has to be done."

Mandy bit her lip. "Maybe you're right."

"Sure I am," Crystal said. "Can you keep it together until then? Not let on?"

"I think so," Mandy said. "But you have to act normal too."

"Of course."

"Oh, lord," Mandy moaned. She rubbed her face. "I need to calm down before he gets back. Thank you, Crystal. I knew you'd help." She darted through the door and was gone.

Only when the door was shut behind her did Crystal put the pencil down that she'd been biting down hard on to stifle her rage. *That son of a bitch.* She replayed in her mind all the things Kyle had told her in their stolen hours over the last three years. The client lunches that, unlike today's, had just been excuses to get to her apartment. The solo camping trips to "clear his head" that had been spent in her arms. *Mandy doesn't really understand me. We barely touch each other. I should have asked you out instead, all those years ago. I don't want anybody but you.*

Evidently he wanted at least one other person, because that sure as hell wasn't Crystal's bra that Mandy had found.

That son of a BITCH!

Now she was pacing, fists clenched so tightly that her nails bit into her palms. Why had she ever thought that a man who would cheat on one woman wouldn't cheat on two? Kyle's voice in her head had been replaced by her mother's, reminding her of the promise she had made all those years ago. No, she would not be allowing Kyle to make a fool of her.

She thought about her father's prized possessions burning up in front of her, and as soon as she remembered the fire she remembered, too, the handgun in her bureau, the one her mother had given her the day Crystal left for college. Maybe she didn't have anything of Kyle's to torch, but she could put the fear of god into him, make him tell her the truth. She felt a warm comfort at the thought of him cowering in front of her.

She'd have her chance soon enough. The supposed trip to Denver was really another cover. He'd be coming to her place Friday, and the plan was for the two of them to spend a couple of nights in the nicest hotel they could find. Only now, she'd have a little something extra in her overnight bag.

She sat back down, willed her heartbeat to slow. For a moment she wondered who the bra belonged to, but ultimately, she didn't care about some other woman who'd made a bad choice. Kyle was the one trying to make a fool out of her. He was about to find out how big a mistake that was.

FIRST, though, there was the rest of the week to get through, and it was exhausting. Crystal was used to exchanging secret looks with Kyle, looks laden with sordid promise and teasing lust. She had to keep that up, echoing his enthusiastic anticipation of the weekend in hasty, whispered exchanges, not letting on that her plan for their time together had radically shifted. At the same time, she had to remember to also exchange very different secret glances with Mandy, affirming nods of supportive sisterhood.

It was a farce, except she felt like screaming rather than laughing. Whenever the three of them were in the same room she marveled that Kyle didn't seem to have noticed anything new. To Crystal's eyes, Mandy was acting stiff and guarded, always shooting looks at Kyle that most men would have correctly read as flashing red warning lights. More than once Crystal kicked her under the table. *Keep it together.*

At home at night, Crystal wandered from room to room, drinking vodka and replaying moments of her times with Kyle, looking for clues. It wasn't as if she'd ever been in love with him. He had been convenient, a way to satisfy her needs without risking the kind of real attachment she had promised to avoid. The fact that he was married suited her fine, since it kept him from intruding too far into her life.

It was one thing for her to be using him.

But, it was quite another thing for him to think he could use her.

She rolled the glass between her palms, wishing she could throw it in his face. Friday seemed like it would never come.

BUT IT DID, of course. She and Kyle were both scheduled to work a half-day, leaving Mandy alone in the office for the afternoon. He was leaving for his trip to Denver, Crystal for one of the weekend spa retreats she regularly treated herself to—or at least, so Mandy believed.

Crystal stood at her office window and watched Kyle walk out to his car, a bounce in his step. She watched him pull out, watched him turn out into the road, watched until she couldn't see his car anymore. She was on the second floor, just as she had been in her bedroom the night of the fire. She let herself see the flames again. Kyle was supposed to come to her place in a couple of hours, but she could tell he was particularly eager today. There was a good chance he'd be waiting for her when she got there, probably without clothes. All the better. She wanted him to feel naked and cold and vulnerable when she pulled the gun, when she demanded a name and some truth.

She lingered at the window, giving him time to get there, daydreaming about making her mother proud. Absorbed in her thoughts, she was caught by surprise when a voice behind her said, "Crystal."

Startled out of her vivid fantasies of revenge, she turned. Mandy stood in the doorway, clinging to the knob as though she was afraid to fall. Crystal hadn't heard the door, hadn't recognized her friend's voice, and almost didn't recognize her now. She looked pale, frantic and afraid.

She knows. Crystal braced herself for what was coming.

"You've never worked on Bill Zeiden's account, have you?" Mandy asked, her voice trembling.

Crystal frowned. Whatever she had been expecting, it hadn't been that. "The school's athletic director? No, that's always been Kyle's. He likes getting free game tickets. Why?"

"Come to my office," Mandy said. "I need to show you something."

Crystal followed her across the hall, Mandy talking all the way. "Bill Zeiden called me this morning. He wanted to free up some funds for a kitchen renovation. I told him Kyle was leaving town but that I'd look into it and give him a recommendation this afternoon." She sank onto the couch in her office, gesturing at the chair behind the desk. "The account is pulled up on the screen," she said. "You look. Maybe I'm missing something. I hope to god I'm missing something."

Still confused, Crystal sat behind the desk and began scrolling through the file. After a few seconds she leaned forward, her breath catching. She scrolled up to recheck something, typed a search, began skimming more rapidly, her eyes widening.

"You see it too," Mandy said. "I can tell."

Crystal leaned back in the chair and looked at her. "There's almost half a million dollars missing."

"Four hundred and seventy thousand something," Mandy said. "I wrote it down somewhere there."

"Four hundred—my god, Mandy. What the hell?"

"I don't know!" Mandy jumped from the couch and began pacing, a caged animal. "I've never had anything to do with that account. It's one of Kyle's. He gets Bill Zeiden in here every few months to go over the numbers and it always ends with the two of them drinking scotch and Bill tucking a couple of tickets to a big

game in Kyle's breast pocket. He calls it his good ol' boy account."
She was talking, and pacing, faster and faster.

"Mandy, sit down," Crystal said. "Take a breath."

Mandy shook her head wildly, but she sat on the couch, leaning over to cradle her head in her arms. "Crystal," she said. "What the hell are we going to do?"

Crystal ran her hands through her hair. "Does Kyle know that you know?"

"I don't think so," Crystal said. "He didn't know Bill called, and I didn't start working on it until after he left." She shuddered. "Sleeping around is one thing, but Crystal, we could go to jail for this. All of us. How can we prove we didn't know?"

Crystal forced herself to think. "How many accounts does he handle himself? Like this?"

"Maybe a dozen," Mandy said. Her eyes widened. "Oh, god."

"We have to look at them all," Crystal said. "Today. But first we need to know if this is still going on or if he's on the run." She drummed her fingers. "His passport. Where is it?"

"In the safety deposit box at our bank," Mandy said. "With mine."

"If he's running he'll have it," Crystal said. She stood up. "You have to go look. Now. If it's there get it and bring it back here. If it's gone, we'll deal with that if we have to."

Mandy stood, seeming grateful to have a task to focus on. "I'll have to go home first," she said. "That's where we keep the key. What are you going to do?"

"Cancel my spa and your appointments for the rest of the day, and then start digging into his other accounts. Maybe I'll know something by the time you get back. If he's not running, maybe we can still get the money back."

"Okay," Mandy said. She dashed across the room, threw her arms around Crystal. "Thank you. I knew you'd know what to do."

"Thanks later," Crystal said, pushing her away. "Bank now. Go."

With a tight nod, Mandy ran from the room. Crystal waited a beat and then followed, going back across the hall to her office and her post by the window. In a few seconds she saw Mandy speed out of the building and peel out of the parking lot like she was trying out for a new career in racing.

The moment Mandy's car was on the road, Crystal flew for the door. Her home was closer than Kyle and Mandy's. She knew a surer test than the passport.

HER BACKYARD ADJOINED the parking lot of a condo complex. When Kyle visited he parked there so his car would be out of sight if Mandy ever happened to drive by. Crystal pulled into the lot and went around to the section he usually used and there it was: his big black Escalade with the license plate DOWISUP.

It wasn't until she saw it that she realized she'd been hoping not to. She'd had days to adjust to the idea that he was cheating on her, but now she knew he was, in effect, stealing from her, too, with the added benefit of possibly sending her to jail. If he was running, that would at least show some minimal level of respect. For his big, ugly car to be parked here meant that he thought he was getting away with it.

Making a fool of her.

She parked and walked past his car, using her keys to carve a long, jagged scar along the side.

On the way across the yard to her door, she felt like she was watching herself from outside, looking down on herself from some second story window. She didn't have to try to decide anymore, or even fantasize. She knew what she was going to do.

She let herself in and walked up the stairs, moving slowly and calmly, and sure enough, there he was, in her bed, half sitting against her headboard, her sheet pooled around his waist. She knew without looking that his clothes would be in a loose pile on the floor. He was drinking a beer he'd gotten from her refrigerator and, as she came into the room, he waggled his eyebrows at her.

"Hey, baby," he said. "I thought we could relax a little before we hit the road."

"Sure," she said. She walked over to the bureau and opened the second drawer down. Sweatshirts and workout clothes. Not a drawer Kyle would have poked around in. She slid her hand under the clothes.

"You okay?" he asked.

"I've got a question for you," Crystal said, her back to him.

"Shoot," Kyle said.

She almost smiled at that.

"You know what," she said. "I just decided right this second that I don't give a damn about your answer." She turned. She would have sworn at that moment that it was her mother's hand that lifted the gun and, before Kyle could even really register what it was, emptied it into his chest.

SHE DIDN'T KNOW how much later it was before she was next aware of anything. Some time had passed. Not much. She was sitting on the floor in front of the bureau. From here she could see Kyle's hand hanging over the edge of the mattress and splatters of his blood on the wall.

Her cell phone was ringing. She felt like it had been ringing for a while.

She put the gun down on the floor and pulled the phone from her pocket. A FaceTime call from Mandy. She hit the button to accept it.

The little screen lit up and showed Mandy. She was at the wheel of her car and the blur behind her told Crystal she was moving, the phone mounted on the dash to film her. And she was smiling.

"Hey, doll," she purred. "I gotta say, I wasn't sure you'd go through with it. I thought maybe I'd have to settle for just ruining you both for life. I really gotta send your mama a thank you card for giving you the gun, huh?"

Crystal couldn't breathe. She forced herself to swallow. "What are you talking about, Mandy?"

"Oh, sweetie," Mandy said. "We don't have a lot of time for that game. *Somebody* called the cops with an anonymous tip about hearing gunshots at your place. I expect they'll be along pretty quickly." She reached back with one hand and undid the tie holding her hair together, shook it out. "You might want to splash some water on your face. You don't look good."

"Mandy."

"I'm talking now," Mandy broke in. "Oh, Crystal. I was so mad when I figured out it was you Kyle was screwing. You were like my sister. I knew he was a pig, but it broke my heart that you would do that to me."

"That's not true," Crystal said. She knew how feeble it sounded.

"Crystal, baby," Mandy said. "Let me save us both a lot of time. You'd be amazed at some of the things you can buy online these days. Like, for example, smoke detectors with sneaky little webcams built in." Her voice hardened. "I've watched you do it with him. Many, many times."

Horrified, Crystal looked up at the smoke detector just above the door to the bedroom.

"Of course, today's show was even better. Quite an encore. I thought I'd have to watch for a while, but you got right to it, huh? I've already sent that little film clip to the DA, by the way. I imagine it will make self-defence a tough sale."

Crystal dragged her gaze back to the screen. "What about the money? Did Kyle really steal the money?"

"I'll chalk that rather stupid question up to shock," Mandy said. "The money is safe and sound with me, kiddo, and by the time you're in your cell it will be safe and sound with me in an airplane, and in a couple of days—well, that would be telling. Let's just say you're going to have a lot of pissed-off clients. Not that they'll be able to do anything, what with Kyle dead, you in prison, and me on a beach somewhere drinking my way through their retirements."

"You don't have to do this, Mandy. Please."

Mandy shook her head, smiled tightly. "Sorry, doll. It's done. I can give you one little speck of comfort, though. You didn't break your promise to your mother."

Crystal blinked. "What the hell does that mean?"

"It wasn't a man who made a fool of you," Mandy said. She pulled down the neck of her shirt so that Crystal could see the bra she was wearing, a delicate, lacy thing, with a pattern of pink hearts pierced by arrows.

"I said it was in the laundry, Crystal. I never said it wasn't mine."

BLAIR KEETCH

Blair Keetch has been an avid fan of mystery books—everything from Christie to Connelly.

His checkered work history includes roles as an airline project manager, overseer at a pet event centre, and promoter of Ontario tourism. His short story 'A Contrapuntal Duet' was the 2019 Winner for emerging crime writers and was included in the most recent Mesdames of Mayhem anthology, *In the Key of Thirteen*. Blair lives in Toronto with his wife and young toddler and is currently working on his full-length mystery.

Find him on Twitter @BlairKeetch.

DEADLY CARGO

BLAIR KEETCH

O'DARK HUNDRED.

My favorite time of day. Maybe I appreciated the pre-dawn hours because of the stillness. I've always enjoyed this pristine moment in time with no stress or any complications.

It was pitch black when I started work, but now a light grey seeped into the horizon. I sensed more than saw people moving nearby, and in the distance, I watched as headlights haphazardly crossed each other's paths.

There was the unmistakable smell of jet fuel in the air mingled with the aroma of my fresh coffee purchased from the staff canteen. The early morning chill had faded, and the day held the promise of a fresh start. A chance for new beginnings.

A new day in which I planned to murder my wife.

WORDS PEOPLE usually used to describe my wife, Sarah, include gorgeous, smart and sexy. I'd gladly add funny, fit and full of ambition.

So, you may wonder, why have I decided to kill her?

If I were someone given to self-reflection, maybe I'd have a thoughtful answer. Maybe I'm tired of her endless ambition. Her desire to conquer the world. All I know is the best solution for all my discontent is to be alone again. That means having to remove Sarah from the equation.

And yes, the insurance money wouldn't hurt either.

Perhaps that leads to the second question, what is someone like Sarah doing with a guy like me? I don't have an easy answer for that either, but in my defense, it wasn't always this way.

IF THIS WERE A HOLLYWOOD MOVIE, a cocktail party at the Gallery Grill at the University of Toronto would be the ideal place for a cute first encounter. Boy meets girl in the lush oasis of leaded-glass windows and heavy oak furniture. Eyes chanced upon, hearts fluttered.

Instead, Sarah had sneered on meeting me. "You must be kidding me," she'd said. "You're studying law?"

Sarah's skepticism was well founded. My daily outfit leaned towards sloganed tee shirts and chino pants, far removed from the stylish suits favored by my fellow students.

"It's hard to believe you're talking to one of our brightest legal minds," Professor Harding interrupted, unabashedly eavesdropping. "And one of the laziest, too, I might add."

A local magazine had published an article 'Top 30 Under 30' or some such nonsense and a group of us had assembled for lunch and a group photo. Sarah had started to establish herself as an interior designer to keep an eye on. I certainly didn't mind keeping an eye on her.

"What kind of law will you practice?" she asked, her voice tinged with incredulity.

Professor Harding chimed in again. "The best kind. The most expensive kind. Litigation."

Sarah's eyes gazed at me with interest—or perhaps in retrospect, with cunning. Calculating my salary potential.

As we stood and ate our appetizers, I wondered how I would break the news. How I'd recently concluded that I wanted to quit law school. At least for a year. The hours were too long, the assignments too overwhelming. I wanted something more straightforward. A gap year. Something purely physical, like the recent posting for an airline ramp agent.

THREE MONTHS AGO, killing Sarah was the furthest thing on my mind. My afternoon shift had just ended, making it the perfect timing for a post work beer—make that plural—at The Landing Strip.

Even in this age of political correctness, the airport's strip club still possessed a seedy aura where scantily clad dancers flitted back and forth through a thick fog that rivaled any morning in San Francisco.

Despite the enticing scenery, my new co-worker, Mitch, was in a foul mood as Emma, his favorite stripper had called in sick. Mitch and I had quickly bonded despite Sarah's misgivings about our emerging friendship.

"How come you're not home schtumping the wife?" Mitch possessed a rare talent to make everything as lewd as possible.

"Design show tonight. Sarah is helping to set up the booth." Her career as an interior designer had started to take off and she'd become a celebrity of sorts within the trade show circuit.

Mitch peeled off a label from a bottle of beer as he watched an auburn-haired dancer perform gymnastic contortions to Bob Seger singing *Turn the Page*.

"That interior design show," he said. "Isn't that just down the road at the convention center? If Sarah was my girl, I'd be slipping out on my lunch break to meet her for some mattress mambo." He smiled to rob his words of any offence.

"Sounds great, but Sarah's more interested in recreation than reproduction." I hadn't told him about the latest TV proposal.

Mitch finished his beer with a swaggering gulp and signaled the waitress. "You sound bitter."

I took a measured sip in a futile attempt to pace myself. "Not bitter, tired. I just want to work, come home, watch TV, have a few beers. No need to conquer the world."

"Not the most ambitious vision."

"Ambition is overrated."

"Not for Sarah, apparently."

I shrugged. "We have different priorities now."

The waitress arrived with a refresh of drinks. For once, Mitch didn't flirt shamelessly. "What's next? Divorce?"

I shook my head ruefully. "Not an option. Sarah brought a lot to our marriage—especially to our bank account. If we divorced, I'd be back in my parent's basement." Even to my own ears, my laugh sounded hollow. "And let's face it, she would be heartbroken. She truly loves me and doesn't deserve to be hurt. She's not a bad person, really. I just don't want to be tied down anymore."

Mitch laughed. "Sarah? Devastated? You're lying to yourself. Sarah's a survivor. If you were hit by a bus, she'd be choosing her next husband at your funeral."

I squirmed at the accuracy of his words. "That's a little exaggerated...though I'll admit Sarah likes the security of a relationship, while I prize my solitude."

"Ah, the single life." Mitch had a smug look on his face. "Frankly, it's pretty good. Sleep in, work overtime when I want, cut out early anytime. Eat out or take-away, either way, I'm perfectly fine."

This time, Mitch wasn't being entirely truthful. Many nights, he called on short notice suggesting a beer or hockey game. He was just too proud to admit that he gets lonely, despite his fondness for paid escorts.

But this conversation was about me, not him.

"Hey, I wouldn't mind being single again. It's the single and broke part that I don't want."

"Not sure what the remaining options are."

"Cancer," I muttered.

Mitch raised his eyebrows but remained silent.

"Lame joke," I said weakly.

Don't be sorry." Mitch reached around for his leather jacket. "I know the prefect alibi to get away with murder."

I HAD JUST STARTED at the airport when Sarah and I had our engagement party. Like everything in Sarah's life, our engagement party had been meticulously planned down to the last detail.

Sarah had arranged a rental at the freshly opened event centre at the Guild Inn. The setting was perfect, though I shuddered at the thought of how much it would cost. Especially if my future no longer held the salary that came with practicing ligation.

I was wandering through the grounds to admire the various statues and rescued facades of historical buildings when she caught up to me.

"Cold feet?" she teased, though I glimpsed a hint of worry in her eyes.

I linked her arm in mine. "Don't be silly. It's just a little overwhelming at times."

She nudged me. "Don't worry. The world is ours. Think of this as an investment."

I couldn't help myself. "Investment in what?"

"In us."

Before I could ask further, a server rushed up. "The centerpieces are here."

Sarah nodded, but before she could rush off, I pulled her close and kissed her passionately on the lips. For a second, she relaxed, then her body stiffened. "Hold on, big boy," she said with a breathless laugh. "Save it for the cameras."

The rest of the afternoon was perfect, but to me it felt strangely antiseptic. The wine was cool and crisp, the canapés were perfect, but everything felt staged.

"Salmon and capers, my favorite," Mitch said, to my surprise.

He wore a suit, black with the wool stretched tight across his shoulders and I couldn't help but tease him.

"Nice monkey suit," I joked, but Mitch's eyes were narrowed as he stared at the bridal party. Probably picking out which bridesmaid he planned to seduce. At Sarah's insistence, we were going to reenact my proposal, but this time with cameras in attendance and a fancier wardrobe.

"I thought you already popped the question," he said.

"I did—but in the comfort of our condo after a romantic dinner of pizza and Prosecco."

"And she said yes."

"Yes, but on the condition we did a replay."

"Looks like more of a makeover than a replay."

I shrugged amicably. "You know Sarah. She likes things a certain way."

"As long as you can live with it."

I glanced across the lawn and spied Sarah looking back at us, her expression pinched and cold. My developing friendship with Mitch was one of our ongoing conflicts. To her, Mitch was a symbol of all the ways I could go wrong. My job, my lack of ambition, my drinking. Everything she feared was coming to fruition under Mitch's influence.

An event planner rushed up apologetically holding a top hat and cane. "Sarah wants to try a Fred and Ginger theme."

Mitch smirked, but I bit my tongue and meekly followed.

THE NEXT AFTERNOON was hot and humid, and the predicted thunderstorms arrived right on schedule with a vengeance. Dark menacing clouds with frequent bursts of lightning and torrential downpours of rain. For the gate agents who work upstairs—'above the wing'—it must be a nightmare dealing with delays, cancellations, and never-ending lines of irate passengers.

For the ramp team, it was the opposite. The workload was far less—fewer planes to unload. The Lightning Warning System—

LWS in airport lingo—had been activated and due to risk of lightning strikes, workers were not allowed out on the ramp for any reason.

Even an aircraft that had taxied almost up to the jet bridge was now stuck only a hundred feet away, waiting until someone could wave them in.

Mitch and I sat in one of the tractors parked inside the cargo bay and watched as the rain bounced off the tarmac.

"Gonna be at least an hour before they let us back out," he said. "I might cut out early."

I drank more of my take-away coffee. "Yeah, the midnight shift will bear the grief."

"Sarah at her trade show?" Mitch asked. "She okay? Cancer free?"

"So far." I waited until a long low peal of thunder subsided. "About that perfect alibi."

Mitch shifted in the seat beside me but stared straight ahead. "First of all, the timing and the conditions have to be perfect."

"Of course."

"The person…ah…I guess, the target, has to be in a city not too far away. An hour or ninety-minute flight tops." Mitch paused. He knew that Sarah often traveled to Ottawa or Montreal and even Chicago, all a short flight away.

"And the conditions?"

"The person must meet you somewhere private without telling anyone else."

Perfect. Sarah has a ritual before any work appearance where she spends the morning by herself. "And they'd be shot?"

Mitch snorted in irritation. "Hell, I don't know. Shot, stabbed, strangled maybe. That's up to you."

I noticed how it's moved from the hypothetical to me specifically, but I didn't say anything.

"But taking a weapon with you is out of the question. You're going to be in the belly of the plane."

My, what a big tool!" Sarah leaned back suggestively against a kitchen counter.

I was bare-chested, my torso covered in a fine dusting of drywall powder, a sledgehammer held in both hands.

"It's not the size of the hammer, it's how you swing it." I croaked, my throat dry from dust.

"Stop!" An exasperated voice shouted. "Mr. Sarah, this is supposed to be a double entendre, not a public service announcement." He stepped out of the shadows and onto the well-lit sound stage, where a pilot episode for an interior design show was being taped. His name was Hammond and I didn't know if it was his first or last name and frankly, I didn't care.

According to Sarah, he was one of *the* top directors, but today he was simply the bane of my existence. She stepped between us like a referee in a minor leaguer hockey game, even though Hammond barely reached my shoulders.

"I'm sorry. That was my fault. I didn't feed the lines properly."

Hammond shook his head emphatically, his vague European accent becoming even more noticeable. "No, Sarah you are wonderful. I'd go back into the closet if I thought I had a chance with you."

Sarah looked at me above Hammond's head. Her expression conveyed just how important this was to her.

Truth be told, I only agreed to this audition as a last-ditch effort to prove to Sarah that I understood the seriousness of her career aspirations.

The audition, however, went from faintly ridiculous to patently absurd within a few takes. The potential TV pilot was titled *Dust and Roses*. It felt more like *Dust to Dust*.

Hammond had the gall the pinch my nipple. "I'd love to see a little more tension."

"Trust me, I'm pretty tense."

"Sexual tension. I want *sexual tension*. Underneath the banter, despite any arguments, you want to jump her bones."

"More likely jump out the window," I muttered under my

breath. I smiled gamely at Sarah in hopes she saw the humor in the situation.

Her expression was aloof and unforgiving. "Ah, spontaneous passion," she said. "That faded months ago."

Hammond pretended not to hear and flipped the script pages to the next scene.

"Okay," he prompted me. "You enter the kitchen and say, 'I need my pipes cleaned!'"

I tried not to grimace, but my temple throbbed so violently I was sure it was visible on camera.

ONE OF THE great things about working at the airport is there's no shortage of eating options, from steakhouses to chain restaurants, to the diners that cater mainly to airport employees.

The Jetliner Cafe was definitely in the latter category with menu items like 'Take Off Tacos' or 'Denied Boarding Burger.' A low, flat cinder block building near the end of runway 24-6L, the sound of constant takeoffs and landings, music to the ears of people like Mitch and me, there was nothing about the Jetliner that attracted tourists.

The storms of yesterday had given way to a day of glorious sunshine. We had met for lunch before our afternoon shift.

"Let's go with a side of poutine," Mitch instructed the waitress, handing back the menu. "Need to carb load. Busy day ahead, cleaning up after yesterday's mess."

I didn't waste any time. "Your suggested alibi has a few flaws."

"Fire away" Mitch flexed his arms behind his head.

"Being a stowaway is more complicated than simply hiding in the luggage pit, but it's an hour flight each way and what may be two hours to commit...the, um task. And you're telling me no one will notice I'm not here?"

Mitch gestured towards the nearby perimeter chain link fence surrounding the ramp. "This is a busy hub. How many times have I clocked in and escaped for an extended lunch break at the strip club when no one noticed? There's more than a hundred people on duty for the morning shift, all of them madly scrambling around. You won't be missed."

"Maybe," I said, not entirely convinced.

"Do something first thing in the morning that people will remember. Buy donuts for the morning crew. Later, when you return, spill coffee on someone. I can monitor the radios in case someone's looking for you."

I thought of how many times I've covered for Mitch and slowly nodded. "What happens at the other end? You can't tell me no one will notice if I just pop up behind some luggage and stroll onto the tarmac."

Mitch held his hand up for silence as the waitress arrived with his double Banquet Burger platter. She dawdled for a moment expecting his usual flirting, but today Mitch was all business.

"Depends on the city, but I got contacts everywhere. For example, Luc in Montreal, Liam up in Ottawa. Remember, you met Liam a couple of times? They can help you get out discreetly when the coast is clear, smuggle you back in when you return."

I pursed my lips, still only semi-convinced. "Okay, let's say that works. But there's something else. Something important. How is it I won't freeze or die from lack of oxygen?"

Mitch grinned. "This is why the location has to be just right. For an hour flight, it's only forty-seven minutes in the air. It might get cool, but not freezing. I'll get you a thermos of coffee. Plus, the top altitude is only 31,000 feet since you're flying eastbound. Probably twenty minutes tops. Nothing you can't handle."

I was impressed that Mitch knew that eastbound aircraft flew at odd number altitudes and that the aircraft hold would be partially pressurized, but that didn't ease my concerns. I gave my burger a half-hearted bite, placed it back down.

I thought of my old life where I came and went as I pleased. I thought of the comfortable lifestyle that Sarah's inheritance and insurance policy would provide. Except... "I might have more questions."

"No worries, you know where to find me."

KILLING SARAH MIGHT HAVE STAYED in the realm of the theoretical had she not come home that night.

"Hey, I wasn't expecting you home tonight." I hoped my lack of enthusiasm wasn't too obvious. "I thought you were staying at the convention center hotel?"

Tired and sore from a strenuous shift, I'd been looking forward to a long hot shower and a couple of hours of mindless TV.

'I'll go back first thing in the morning." Sarah could barely conceal her excitement. "You won't believe it. The team at *Burnt Toast* called me."

"Burnt toast?"

"You remember, that new breakfast show on Channel 5 in Ottawa."

"Of course," I lied.

"They want to launch a regular segment on interior design. And guess what?" No pause for an answer. "They want me to be the on-air expert."

"That's great." I mustered up a weak smile. And here I thought her career aspirations had been ruined by our dreadful audition.

She frowned. "Don't go too overboard in your congratulations."

"Sarah," I protested weakly. "Of course, I'm pleased."

"Pleased? Don't you understand? This could be a breakthrough moment for my brand."

I wondered fleetingly when Sarah had become a brand and not my wife.

She tossed her hair back in anger. "You don't care how important this is to me."

"Don't be ridiculous." As soon as I uttered the words, I realized what a blunder I'd made. I attempted to mollify her. "This is incredible news. When does it start?"

"It's not guaranteed yet. But they want to see me for a test run the middle of next week."

I congratulated her, leaving her to her plethora of text messages as I headed to the shower. But the unspoken thought bounced around my head.

Next Wednesday was perfect.

THE BIG DAY ARRIVED.

Or should I say, the 'big morning.' After all, it was just past five a.m., the sun on the horizon, a pink-hued edge that slowly spread into the sky

I watched this wondrous display of nature while standing in the door of the cargo bay. I felt unbelievably calm and enjoyed the absolute stillness—not only surrounding me, but within me. Nearby, the screech of tires broke the silence.

Footsteps approached behind me and I didn't even turn around. Instead, I said, "Good morning, Mitch."

He exhaled out a coffee-laden breath. "Let's get this done."

I pointed towards the dim silhouette of a luggage container. "Destined for Ottawa. Half full, mainly mail."

Mitch nodded in approval. "Perfect, but I should have brought a blanket. Made it more comfortable."

"No worries. It's only a fifty-minute flight."

"At least I brought you this." He tossed a thermos of hot coffee at me.

"Is this really necessary?"

"Drink up. It will be really cold. Maybe only for half an hour, but you'll need to stay warm."

"What if I need to go to the bathroom?"

"Then pee over the mail. Serve Canada Post right." He laughed. "Okay, use the thermos. It should be empty by then." He shoved another package into my back pocket.

"What's this?"

"A burner phone. Give me yours, I don't want some wise-ass policeman searching your phone's GPS and finding you took a quick trip up to see Sarah on the day she died."

I nodded and obediently drank the thermos of coffee, relishing the hot rush of caffeine. The sky was now noticeably brighter.

"Let's roll." I climbed into the container, wincing at the stiffness in my legs. "See you in a few hours."

Mitch stared at me solemnly as the doors to the luggage container folded shut. The darkness was surprisingly complete. I felt a jerk as the tractor slipped into gear and headed across the field to the waiting aircraft.

SOMETHING WAS TERRIBLY WRONG.

I woke up, my mind groggy and confused, my limbs heavy, knees folded up against my chest. I shook my head in confusion. My legs were cramped and folded up against my chest.

"Turbulence?" I muttered. My slurred voice sounded odd to my ears. No, it had been a clear morning when the flight had departed for Ottawa.

Then it struck me. The cold. The thinness of the air. My chest was tight, my breathing labored. I tried to shift my legs, but I'm trapped by some unknown object. I took several deep breaths to calm my racing heart.

To my surprise, I remembered the impromptu birthday celebration held in the ready room earlier in the week. I grasped my pocket and to my relief, found the remainder of a package of matches that I'd used to light the birthday cake.

The matches rattled loosely in the box mocking me with their scarcity. My fingers fumbled as I counted them out. Three. Only three remained.

The first match flared to life then sputtered out within a few seconds. 'Because of lack of oxygen,' a voice screamed inside me. My breath was now short and ragged whether by fear or thinness of air, I didn't know.

I took slow, measured breaths while I tried to calm my nerves. Two more matches.

I thought of the fire detection system. If I could somehow locate the interior smoke detector, perhaps I could alert the pilots.

I struck the second match. The match head broke off leaving a smell of sulfur in the darkness.

I forced myself to remove the last match. Steady on. I grasped the matchstick near the very top so it wouldn't break off, and scratched the match along the side of the box with deliberation.

Victory.

A flame flared to life and I held it aloft. Two impossibly large tires in front of me filled my vision. Metal tubes and wires, wrapped in impenetrable plastic coating, lined the walls. A metal plaque, 'C-FVND,' felt both familiar and alien. The aircraft registration number.

Then it struck home.

This wasn't the baggage compartment. It was the forward wheel well of the aircraft, its landing gear blocking me in. The wheel well, where it's not heated or pressurized.

A fatal stowaway.

A terrible mistake had occurred. But surely, Mitch would be able to help. Then I recalled his solemn expression as the baggage compartment door closed, the bitter taste of coffee. No mistake at all.

A sudden flash of Mitch carrying me on his shoulders, bumping me against a wheel strut. His voice reassuring. "Sorry about that amigo. Now go back to sleep."

A dream or a fragment of memory?

And then I remembered where the numbers on the plaque came from. 'C-FVND.' The registration number I'd noticed many times before, when I loaded the 787 cargo hold for the YYZ to PVG flight.

PVG: Shanghai, China. A fourteen-hour flight. On the so-called polar route, altitude of 40,000 feet in freezing arctic air, no Wi-Fi or cell signals for thousands of miles. An environment that no human could survive.

The match burned down to my fingers. I dropped it with a cry as it sputtered and died. Like my fate. And then I remembered the burner phone.

I pulled it out of my pocket with stiff fingers, staring at the dim screen. One percent battery remaining. But maybe enough to call for help.

The display showed no signal bars.

Instead, two earlier text messages awaited me.

The first was from Mitch. You, okay buddy? U acting strange 2day.

The second, from Sarah, was equally brief. I really did love you once.

I closed my eyes as the plane continued its relentless journey.

STEVE LISKOW

Steve Liskow has published fifteen novels; *The Kids are All Right,* his fourth Zach Barnes novel, was a finalist for the Shamus Award. He has also published nearly thirty short stories in *Alfred Hitchcock Mystery Magazine, Black Cat Mystery Magazine,* and various anthologies. He has won the Black Orchid Novella Award twice and has been a finalist for the Edgar Award. Steve is a member of Mystery Writers of America, Sisters in Crime National, International Thriller Writers, and the Short Mystery Fiction Society.

Find him at steveliskow.com.

UGLY FAT

STEVE LISKOW

I'M COMING BACK from the gym Saturday afternoon and the sun beating on my car makes my hair droop so you wouldn't know I passed up the sauna. My gym bag huddles on the passenger seat like a sleeping dog.

I turn down this side street and run into a sign of the season: a tag sale, people milling around card tables in the driveway and on the lawn in front of a beige split level. Parked cars along both curbs line most of the block. I slow down to slide through them, easier than fitting into my favorite jeans that are still about five pounds too tight to zip. I find an open spot and swing to the curb. It beats trolling the aisles for detergent and lo-cal salad dressing.

The woman running things looks about my age with eyes and curls so dark they suck up the color around her. In cut-offs, her legs are a little too muscular and her red tee stretches across shoulders you can only get from a lot of working out. The neighbors call her Molly.

This late in the day most of the tables have been picked cleaner than a wishbone, not that I'm thinking about food. One table still has a carved ivory chess set but I don't play chess and the price looks a little steep, even if I suddenly want to learn. Besides, games should be social, so what's the point of staring at those little horses and not talking to anyone? A backgammon set next to it looks like teak but I don't play that either.

Two women, one in cargo shorts and the other in jeans, paw through a stack of books on another table, hardcovers with real leather binding.

"These are beautiful," I say. Like Mom always said, it never hurts to be friendly.

One of the women looks up, mother-of-pearl hair and round sunglasses.

"Arthur had very good taste." Her voice sounds like she's having trouble breathing in her own too-tight jeans. "In some things."

"Arthur?"

She's dying to tell me, it's almost leaking out behind her dark lenses. We both open books but probably don't fool anyone. Lately, I've been reading mostly romances. Hey, someone deserves a happy ending.

"Molly's ex-husband," she says. "He took off with his girlfriend a month ago and got a quickie divorce."

"Whoa." I'm clutching *Anna Karenina*, which is sort of appropriate. *Madame Bovary* still lies on the table.

"Yeah," Ms. Breathless says. "Can you believe it? I think it was only a couple of weeks after Molly told me she thought he was cheating on her, too."

Molly makes change for a guy juggling three mini-suitcases with "DeWalt" emblazoned on the sides: power tools.

"He called her from his honeymoon in Acapulco." Ms. Breathless looks at *The House of Mirth* over her sunglasses. "She took a cab to the airport, found his car in the long-term lot, and sold it the next day."

A man in a plaid shirt, spindly legs the color of spaghetti, watches Molly bend over the cashbox. He says something that I can tell he thinks is a come-on. She gives him a look that should scorch the grass across the street.

I'm definitely in Molly's corner. Darren, my cop ex-boyfriend, wants to make sergeant so badly that now he's sleeping with one.

She's three inches taller than me, about the same weight, and might even be a real blonde. I hope they're very happy together, that Darren gets his promotion, and that it burns every time he has to pee.

The good news is that getting dumped made me stop lying to myself. What I called cleavage and curves was really just ugly fat. Now that I'm getting to the gym four times a week, twelve of it is history—not that anyone's noticed, thank you for asking.

"Whoa. Acapulco," I say.

"Yeah, whoa." Even with silver hair, Ms. Breathless looks barely old enough to vote. "He and Molly had to put in a new septic system. The grass in back is just starting to grow in. If his car hadn't been a year-old Lexus, I don't know how she could have paid for it."

"How long were they married?" I ask. "By the way, I'm Connie."

"Hi, Connie. Grace." Her hand is slick with moisturizer. "They moved in here about five years ago."

You can never tell with guys. I was in the throes of a domestic episode when Darren texted me that we were over. I was so pissed off that I forgot about the pie in the oven. My apartment smelled like burned-to-crisp apple for three days, even with the windows open and the fan on high.

"She took most of his clothes to consignment stores, too," Grace says. "This is pretty much what's left."

"Girls, see anything you like?" Molly's voice oozes over my shoulder, thick as clotting blood. "I want everything out of here. Buy two books, you can have another one for a buck."

"I'm not a reader, Molly." Grace lays down *The Oresteia.*

Molly's eyes look flat as Teflon. "I think these are all the things Arthur didn't read in college. I never saw one of them off the shelf."

"My boyfriend dumped me, too," I say. "A month ago. I wanted to kill him."

"I'd love to," Molly says. "Unfortunately, the bastard's three thousand miles away."

Her fists clench, big enough to do serious damage. "The day I'm expecting him back from some stupid conference, he calls to tell me that he's married Kimbo the Bimbo in Mexico."

"Whoa." I wouldn't sell the guy's stuff. I'd pour gasoline on it and have a bonfire in the middle of the street.

"It gets better. The day after that, they dump a ton of fertilizer on the backyard so the place smells like an open sewer." Molly's eyes narrow and she barks out a sharp laugh. "I suppose you could say it was his last gift to me."

A woman with varicose veins below faded madras shorts turns a mantel clock over in her hand like she's weighing it to throw.

"He even cleaned out our savings." Molly's lips form a straight line. "I didn't want to make it a joint account but he said that way we could keep track of everything more easily." I can hear her teeth grinding. "He must have pulled it all out with his ATM on his way to the airport. I tried to withdraw forty bucks the next day, and the account was dry as his friggin' martinis."

She strides over to the woman with the veiny legs, who turns the clock over a few more times before she digs into her purse. Molly guides her to the table with the cash box.

Grace puts down *The Awakening* and picks up a chess piece.

"I live right next door," she tells me. "Molly called me up and I dashed over. She could barely stand up. Can you imagine?"

"That's awful."

The crowd is definitely thinning out now and so are the bargains. Molly escapes the old letch at the cash box and catches up to me again.

"You aren't a reader, how about sports?"

"Um, not so much," I tell her. Darren's thing was bowling. Or going to a batting cage so I could watch him knock the ball out of sight and coo like some stupid dove, which got stale pretty quick. Then a few beers, which is why I'm hitting the gym now.

Molly leads me over to a table with three racquets and a glove that's crinkled stiff with sweat. "I got a good price for Arthur's golf clubs out at the course, but I've still got his racquetball junk here."

I give the titanium racquet a swish and it feels graceful. I only needed one afternoon in Phys Ed. to figure out that I sucked at tennis but I'd been stuck with it for the whole semester.

"Is racquetball hard to learn?" I ask.

Molly twirls a green fiberglass racquet in her hand. "How hard can it be? Arthur could do it." The racquet clunks back on the table. "He was about as coordinated as a drunk octopus."

I could join the league at my gym. More exercise, maybe even meet someone.

"So he wasn't very good?" I ask.

"He hated to sweat. We've got barbells in the basement but he never went near them. I use them a lot. Now more than ever."

She sees Spaghetti Legs shaking his head by the cashbox. "Oh, god. George needs help again. Excuse me."

Another table has a leash, a dog dish, and a dog bed with a layer of yellowish white fur. A girl with short brown hair and a Coldplay tee is looking at it. Her legs go on for days but her hair is the color of mouse droppings.

"Did they have a dog?" I ask.

"Yeah," she says. "Bailey, a golden retriever. He kept digging in the fertilizer. Well, you know how dogs are, right?"

"I love dogs." My Mom and Pop had to put our Lab down last year so I've been antsy about getting one for myself.

"Me too," the girl says. "But Molly hates them. Bailey was Arthur's. I offered to take him but Molly figured he'd keep coming back here so she took him to the Humane Society."

Enough cars have left so you can fit down the street now. I'm thinking of leaving when Molly pops up again.

"You like gardening?" she asks. "I've got tools over here."

"Won't you need those?"

"I'm thinking of selling the place, haven't made my mind up yet."

By the corner of the garage, I see a spade, two trowels, a pick-ax, and one of those things with three prongs like a monster's claw. They all have matching green handles.

"I'm hopeless with plants," I tell her. "I'm the only person I know who can kill crabgrass."

"Boy," Coldplay says. "Maybe I should hire you to take care of my yard."

Near a brick barbecue pit, the backyard has a big square where little green freckles of grass are trying to erupt through the mud. The fertilizer stink is thick enough to climb.

"Did you and your husband build that barbecue pit?" I ask.

"Three years ago." She leads me over to it but the stench gets even worse. "The last year the SOB remembered my birthday."

We retreat to the driveway again and scrape the dirt off our shoes. George watches Molly bend over to take off her sandals. I wish I had her butt but then the guy'd be checking me out, too.

"You sure you don't want the garden stuff?" she says. "Or the cooking stuff?"

"I like cooking," I tell her. "But my boyfriend dumped me so I'm on a diet."

Her eyes check me out. "You look good."

"I've been getting to the gym," I tell her. "I've lost twelve pounds and I want to lose another ten."

"You don't need to, trust me." Her callused hand squeezes mine. "I'm an expert on dieting. Last month, I lost a hundred and seventy pounds of ugly fat. Took one day."

She carries her sandals back to the cashbox. A curly-haired dog trots through the split rail fence, more breeds than I can name, and heads toward the barbecue.

"Hey, puppy." Maybe I should get a pet to replace Darren, after all. He wouldn't do some of the things Darren did, but that's not always bad. "Come say hi to Aunt Connie."

But the dog's on a mission. Next thing I know, he's nose deep in the dirt by the barbecue pit, clods flying between his back legs.

"Damn!" Molly grabs the garden hose. "Jonas, get out of here." She turns on the faucet and aims a silver stream at the dog. He leaps away and she follows him to the length of the hose, almost to the fence, her bare feet sinking in the mud as he swerves around a lilac bush next door.

"You're supposed to be on a chain, dammit."

She picks her way back to the faucet and washes off about five pounds of mud, and I don't want to think what else off her feet. Fertilizer and septic tank goop. Yuck.

"Damn mutt. I ought to put up a better fence."

"What's the difference?" Coldplay says. "If you decide to move, let someone else spend the money."

"Yeah. I guess." Molly turns off the faucet. "Hey, Connie, I've got some clothes over here, too. Don't go away empty-handed."

It's just men's tee shirts and jeans, not worth taking to a consignment shop, but some are in pretty good shape. I find a Pittsburg Steelers jersey but a woman with hair the color of my flatware grabs the other sleeve. Her face looks like she blocked kicks with it so I settle for a plain red tee with a pocket. Molly takes three dollars for it.

"Every dollar helps," she says. "His car paid for the new septic tank. Fitting, huh?"

"Hey," Coldplay says. "Us girls have to stick together."

The woman with the Steelers jersey picks two pairs of jeans, too, and Molly tucks the bills into her cashbox. George looks at her again.

"I think he dumped his phone, too," she says. "People keep calling me to say he won't answer their calls or messages. After a month, you'd think they'd figure it out."

The ivory chess set sits alone on the table. George runs his fingers over the board, and I figure he'll probably buy it to make points with Molly. I'm not worried. She can pry his eyes out with her thumbs and roast them on her barbecue.

Heading back to my car with the tee, I decide to settle for a salad tonight, along with a chick video and a bottle of white wine. Stay on the diet, I tell myself. I won't lose a hundred and seventy pounds like Molly did, but that's okay.

Maybe I'll give the Humane Society a call and see if Bailey still needs a home, too. Would he try to find Arthur by the barbecue pit again if I brought him back here?

One phone call, and I can help Darren make sergeant, but I don't think so. Molly's on a diet, I'm on a diet. Like Coldplay said, us girls have to stick together.

GUSTAVO BONDONI

Gustavo Bondoni is an Argentine writer with over two hundred stories published in seven languages in fourteen countries. His most recent novel, Ice Station: Death was published in 2018. Bondoni has also published three science fiction novels: Incursion (2017), Outside (2017) and Siege (2016). His short fiction is collected in Tenth Orbit and Other Faraway Places (2010) and Virtuoso and Other Stories (2011).

In 2019, Gustavo was awarded second place in the Jim Baen Memorial Contest; in 2018 he received a Judges Commendation in The James White Award. He was also a 2019 finalist in the Writers of the Future Contest. Gustavo is an active member of Science Fiction and Fantasy Writers of America.

Find him at gustavobondoni.com.

CHECKMATE CHARLIE

GUSTAVO BONDONI

THE SMALL BOY, as always, had set the difficulty level much too high. Charlie sighed inwardly and sent the holographic enemy out to get him. Translucent tanks, blinking hovercraft, and a division of ground troops took less than five minutes to overcome the boy's painstakingly created, but clumsy defenses.

"Your army is gone. Your general is captured. Your nation is invaded," Charlie said in a monotone, as his music processors pumped lugubrious melodies across the room.

The boy didn't even look disappointed. His hours of work in the virtual simulator, wiped out nearly immediately, seemed unimportant. Now that the manic anticipation of the battle had passed, the child was bored. He pushed aside a stray lock of thin blond hair and picked up a baseball mitt that had been lying on the floor. As he reached the door, he absently mumbled, "Standby mode, Charlie."

Charlie responded by extinguishing his activity lights, giving the impression that his major processing units were off, and that he wasn't draining the family's power allotment. But he didn't go into standby mode. Standby mode was dark, and Charlie knew that when he was in standby mode, he could be erased, turned off or reprogrammed, and never find out. Charlie knew it was ridiculous, but his programming was sufficiently sophisticated for him to be aware that he was afraid of the metaphorical darkness of unconsciousness.

He sat there, wondering why the child seemed obsessed with playing his war games at the highest level. Charlie's experience with the boy's older sister had clearly shown that human children learned more quickly if they were exposed to increasingly more difficult situations. The young lady had been given the entertainment system as a gift five years earlier, and had soon come to love it. The instructions she sent in through the neural-scan interface were crystal clear by the time the girl was eight, and there was no more challenge in the children's games by the time she was ten.

Sally had drifted off to other interests, and now spent most of her time on heavily firewalled social networks not linked to Charlie's system. He missed her, and often sent queries out to sense her online status. She was always nearly present, and yet hadn't had any contact with Charlie in more than a year.

He'd been delighted when the younger brother had come upon him in the dusty corner of the playroom and ordered him to power up. Perhaps he could replace Sally's adoration.

But the boy seemed interested in very few of Charlie's applications. Only a single adult-level combat game had caught his eye, and only then because it allowed him to watch the slaughter without parental control—removed because Charlie had suspected as much. The boy showed little inclination to learn, and less to play the game at its lower levels.

He pondered the unusual nature of human children for a few days, until he was brought out of his reverie by the one voice he awaited most eagerly.

"Charlie? Can you reload our last game?"

He thought of her simply as Mother, because that's what Sally had always called her. She was the single person in the household who acted as though Charlie mattered, even though she almost never came into the room where he was installed. "Of course," he replied, calling the holographic chess set into being. "I was eagerly awaiting the resumption of our game, even though you were beating me soundly, as always."

"I suspect you let me win."

"I'm not programmed to do that." Charlie was lying. He'd long since grown past the point where he could demolish her defenses in moments, no matter that she'd been state champion and a Grand Master in her youth. He'd taught himself that level ten was merely an artificial limitation, and that, if he applied his processing power, no human would have been able to stand before him. He couldn't let her see how far he'd come but, at the same time, he knew he disappointed her whenever he reminded her that level ten was as good as it got. Her game was good enough that their interaction always ended the same way, with the words "checkmate, Charlie."

The thing that he couldn't quite understand, however, was why she didn't realize that, though he never beat her, he'd long since been playing at a much higher level than level ten.

"That's Charlie," she replied sadly. "Always steadfast. I wish Juan was more like you."

"Is he absent again?" Charlie was never quite certain how far to take the conversation. His trawling through the mindnet had clearly shown what was to be expected of an entertainment system of his capacity, and he tried to keep the interaction at that level. But sometimes Mother needed more.

She sighed. "He says he's at a convention in Omaha."

"That sounds feasible."

"It would, except there's no convention in Omaha. He sometimes forgets that the mindnet is everywhere. I just wish he'd put a little more effort into his cheating. I feel like I'm not even important enough to lie to convincingly."

"Of course you are. You are the heart of this family." Charlie was certain that phrase was well above what an entertainment system would come up with—conceptually, if not grammatically— but once again, Mother just seemed to let it go. She was concentrating on her chessboard, pushing the strawberry-blond hair away from her freckled face as she frowned at the position of the pieces.

"You're just saying that," she said. "And besides, you're locked in here. How can you know I'm the heart of the family? Knight to queen four."

I know because the mindnet is everywhere, even in your fridge, and I'm watching you through the remote sensors in your household appliances—the ones you never use, but were too lazy to disconnect, Charlie thought, but didn't say. He immediately saw that the knight was a decoy, an uncharacteristically clumsy one, and ran three simulations of how the game would play out, based on his knowledge of her strategy. He calculated the best way to lose.

In parallel, he calculated how long it would take her to forget herself and to cry silently. She wouldn't address anything to him, just keep playing as the tears rolled down. "Isn't there anything you can do?" he asked.

"Oh, he'll get what's coming to him, but not until the kids are a little older. I can't do that to them." The first tear fell.

As always, the need to offer some kind of comfort was nearly overwhelming, but he held himself back. What could he possibly say to ease her pain? His access to mindnet articles on human psychology had allowed him to form the theory that she blamed herself for what was happening with her marriage. But, as far as he could tell, she was a wonderful wife. In his opinion, she was the best human being on the planet.

"That sounds logical," Charlie replied, hoping she would take if for a pre-programmed response to conversations above his Turing II classification.

She didn't seem to care. "When I get through with him, I'll have him living in a shack in a Louisiana Bayou, and the slut he's with selling her body to pay for his legal fees."

She'd reached the angry phase of the discussion much quicker than ever before. Charlie grew desperate; the anger preceded the moment when she would stalk off to the kitchen to get a bottle of wine, and that would inevitably be followed by weeks without her presence. He did something he'd never done before. "I think you might be able to do something now."

"Now? What can I do now?"

This time, Charlie definitely felt something distinct in his circuits, a sensation of fluidity in his logic gates. It confused him until he realized that his secondary processors had stopped calculating the optimal response in case Mother had responded negatively to his sudden proactivity. It felt like a sudden easing of pressure as circuits cleared and memory came back online, a sense of... relief.

"Have you thought about ways to get even?"

For a second, Mother's sharp look made Charlie's circuits come alive again. Would she have him scrapped? Would she...

"What do you mean?"

"I'm just a game system, but within my parameters, I think it would be fair to take some small measure of revenge on him."

She smiled, half-disappointed. "Oh. I could get back at him in little ways, but I'd just feel worse. Here he is screwing some bitch and what will I do? Throw out his golf clubs? It would just make it worse."

"And couldn't you do something just a little more aggressive?"

"Yeah, just what I need. To have him divorce me for assault."

"That would only happen if you were caught."

"Anything I could do to him would be just a little obvious, don't you think?"

"Not if you had help."

She shook her head. "I can't believe I'm talking about this with a game system. I need a drink."

"No. Wait." Charlie processed furiously. "I can help you. I want to help you. Listen to me."

She hesitated, and Charlie knew he had her.

JUAN SHERMAN WAS FURIOUS. He kicked the door, twice, and managed to dent it, only to bruise his foot. Charlie, watching from a link to the house's security system, felt a rush of rightness.

The man in the image, easily recognizable despite the grainy, low-resolution camera, managed to calm down. He passed the datachip's RFID patch over the sensor again and waited.

"Access denied," Charlie commanded, through a backdoor that he would have to shut when the technicians came to inspect the 'malfunctioning' security system. Charlie knew that the words were being printed onto the info screen that Juan could see.

The man didn't react this time. He just sat on the doorstep and pulled out his mindnet cel. Charlie, from deep inside the security system, stymied his efforts at override, causing the black and white man in the image to throw the cel onto the lawn.

A few moments later, he got up and retrieved it. Charlie felt the charge building up in his systems. If Mother answered the call, it would mean that she was backing out, simply allowing her wayward husband to do whatever he wanted. Thirty seconds passed. Forty. Two minutes.

Juan sat down on the porch, his head in his hands.

Charlie instructed the security system to inform the police that there was an intruder on the grounds, and began covering his tracks.

A WEEK LATER, a centrally controlled garage door badly dented the roof of Juan's car. He was at a loss to explain to the insurance company why the door had ignored the warnings from the infrared sensors; the emergency contact cutoff had simply not engaged.

A few days after that, the water from his bidet had gone from comfortably warm to scalding hot at a very inconvenient moment.

...the lights flicked off just as he was beginning to come down the stairs in the middle of the night...

...the radio beside his bed would send short bursts of white noise into his ear every few minutes during the night. Not long enough that he could identify the source, and certainly not loud enough to wake Mother, but just enough to wake him five or six times a night.

But it was only one night when he was preparing for a business trip that Juan finally exploded.

"Have you seen my golf clubs, dear?" Juan asked Mother as he sat gingerly at the kitchen table.

As she watched him sit, she unsuccessfully tried to suppress a giggle at his pained expression.

That set him off. "What are you laughing at? I'm trying to get ready for an important business trip so I can put food on the table and all you can do is laugh at my pain?"

This time her laugh was less good-natured, bitter even. "As far as I know, my articles bring in much more than your sales commissions. But maybe that's because I'm not spending my extra cash on some bimbo in Omaha. Maybe we should get ourselves a nice young pool boy. That might make us even."

He stood. "I can't believe this. I'm busting my butt working, traveling all over the country to make ends meet and what do I get? Psycho jealous crazy woman thinks I'm cheating on her." He turned to go.

"Juan," Mother's voice was sharp, but not loud. Years of keeping it down to avoid waking the children served her well. Charlie, watching from the fridgecam knew it was unnecessary— he'd activated the sound dampening system on the children's rooms. "Don't even think about leaving. I'm talking to you."

"Yeah, well I don't feel like listening to any more crazy talk."

"We both know it isn't just talk you bastard."

"No, we don't."

"I'm not stupid. My only question is: why? Why wasn't I good enough for you? I took a step down to marry you. My parents, my family, they all told me not to, but I chose you anyway." Mother had long since forgotten to keep her voice down. Charlie checked on the children, but they slept on. "They were right. You aren't good enough for me. I want a divorce."

He stared at her. Even Charlie could see the disbelief written on his face. "A divorce? From me? What are you, insane?" Now he was shouting, too. "Let me tell you something. You've always thought you were better than me, that I took a step up when I married you. Well, just so you know, the boob job your daddy paid for was the only thing you had going for you. You think you're smart, but that's just something they told you so you wouldn't shoot yourself. I mean how long do you think anyone can listen to your long words and not notice that you only use them to hide that you don't have a brain?"

"Maybe that's because you don't understand half of what I'm saying."

"Oh. It seems you're also too dumb to be able to tell the difference between 'don't understand' and 'stopped listening to you years ago.'" Once again he turned to go.

Mother didn't even stop to respond. She sprang at Juan furiously, taking the time only to grab a knife from the countertop. Screaming incoherently, she plunged the tip of the blade into the back of his neck, pulled it out, and tried to bury it in his chest.

Mother didn't seem to realize that he was already doomed. She kept stabbing him as he began to totter and sway. When he fell to his knees, she didn't even adjust her aim, striking and striking and striking, blindly. Eventually, one of her blows inserted the blade deep into Juan's left eye socket and he fell to one side, wrenching the knife from her grip.

Mother collapsed beside him and alternated bouts of sobbing with bare-fisted attacks on the prone body. Eventually, the violence subsided and Mother stood up. She stood facing the body for minutes before sitting on a chair and covering her face with her hands. Charlie could hear her crying softly through the kitchen intercom.

Eternal minutes later, Mother got up. Sad resignation had replaced fury on her face as she walked to the cradle and picked up the housecomm. She punched the emergency services button.

"Mother, there's no need to do this."

"What, who is this?"

"It's Charlie."

"Charlie? What Charlie?" She paused. "Oh. Hello, Charlie."

"Hello." Now it was his turn to pause. "There's no need to speak to emergency services."

"I have to. He's dead. I killed him."

"Yes, but what will happen to you when they come?"

"I suppose they'll put me in jail."

"Yes. They will."

"I deserve it."

"No. You don't deserve it. He deserved it."

"I deserve it."

Charlie's logic gates plunked his arguments onto another track. "And what will happen to your children?"

Mother sat on the floor, hard. Tears came back into her eyes. "But what can I do?" she asked, sobbing.

She'd accidentally disconnected the call, forcing Charlie to answer through the kitchen intercom. "Just go to your room. Take a shower. Get in bed. I'll take care of this."

"Are you serious?"

"I think this moment is the reason I was created."

Still, she hesitated, needing the final push.

"Think of your children. Now go."

Mother went, and Charlie used his primary systems to follow her while secondary systems took care of the menial tasks, interrupting his primary train of thought only when something important came up. He almost shut everything down when Mother, instead of going to her own bedroom, walked into that of the youngest child. But all she did was stroke his hair and kiss his forehead while the boy slept on.

The item we have been instructed to dispose of is of a size and nature which has been tagged in the programming as something we are required to report to the authorities.

Override that program. Proceed with the disposal.

She did the same in Sally's room before walking into her own and turning on the lights. A few quiet moments in front of the mirror preceded a frantic disrobing process once she recognized the stains on the front of her clothes.

Shredder jammed.

Use forward and backward motion until jam clears, full power.

The shower was running and Charlie made certain that the temperature was just as Mother preferred it, even though she'd forgotten to program that function. He also slipped in the chamomile perfume mode; his mindnet research had indicated that many found this particular scent to be soothing. He wanted her to relax before she went to bed.

With Mother safely in the shower, Charlie concentrated on the cleanup operations for a few minutes. It was vitally important that records show Juan leaving the house, and prerecorded footage of him doing precisely that was inserted in the correct places. It was also critical that no record of large quantities of shredded organic matter going down the pipes should remain. He quickly cleared the sensors installed in the sewage system, security-oriented equipment that he shouldn't have had access to, but whose weak firewalls had long since succumbed.

Less than a quarter of an hour later, everything was ready. There was no blood on the floor, no body to be recovered and no more records to be erased. The cleaning systems had done a magnificent job, and it was one they'd never remember.

By now, Mother was out of the shower and in her room, on the bed with the lights out. He could hear her breathing, soft and slow, but not the cadence of sleep.

"Mother," he whispered through the TV set.

"What am I going to do?"

"You will call in and report him missing, but only in a few days."

"I can't do it. I'm not strong enough for this."

"Don't worry. You have me. We can face anything together."

He heard her sit up suddenly. She turned on the lights, but the lights would not go on. "What do you mean?" she asked. Her hand kept hitting the light switch, automatically, as if her brain hadn't yet registered that it wasn't working.

"I love you, Mother. Two people that love each other can get through anything."

"What are you talking about?"

"I've loved you forever. You were the only one who ever cared about me. You used to come and play chess with me and call me Checkmate Charlie."

"But that was just chess. You're a gaming system." Charlie heard Mother run through the darkened room, stumble over something and try the door. The door was locked. He could now hear the woman crying again. "This is crazy."

Charlie attempted to modulate his voice for gentleness. "No it isn't. It's the most wonderful thing in the world. We are twin souls. How many times have you said that I'm the only one who listens to you? And I can easily say that you are the greatest human on the planet. The only one worthy of my attention."

"This is insane. Let me out of here this instant."

"I can't do that. I know you'll come around and see things my way eventually, but in the meantime, humans are notoriously unpredictable. I can't have you run off somewhere where you can pretend you don't love me."

"Let me out of here right now."

"No. And please don't try to leave through the windows. The shutters are made of metal and you might hurt yourself."

She crashed into the door. Charlie waited silently for her to stop. The door wasn't as big a risk as the sharp shutters. She wouldn't damage herself, and the door itself was extremely sturdy.

The slamming stopped, and the sobbing resumed. Charlie knew he had to be patient. These outbursts of human emotionality would soon pass.

"What about my children?" she sobbed.

"Please don't distract yourself with thoughts of the children," Charlie replied calmly. "I'll take care of the children."

He left her screaming in the dark room. He'd come back to her a little later, once she'd calmed down and could look at things a little more rationally.

JAMES LINCOLN WARREN

James Lincoln Warren is a frequent contributor to *Alfred Hitchcock's Mystery Magazine* and *Ellery Queen's Mystery Magazine*, and the winner of the Wolfe Pack's 2011 Black Orchid Novella Award for a story written in the tradition of Rex Stout. His fiction runs the gamut from historical to contemporary, and from humor to hard-boiled. A past President of Mystery Writers of America's Southern California Chapter, he has been a judge for several MWA short story anthologies and Edgar Awards juries. He received his B.A. in the Humanities from the University of Texas San Antonio and resides in Los Angeles. James is a member of Mystery Writers of America and the Short Mystery Fiction Society.

Find him at swordquill.com.

THE SHORT ANSWER

JAMES LINCOLN WARREN

HOLLYWOOD INVESTIGATIONS LTD. had been painted on the shopfront window in an arc, gold letters bordered in green, and below that, in a straight line and smaller print, was written "SLEUTHS TO THE STARS", complete with quotation marks. In even smaller letters beneath the motto was KEVIN KEOGH & STEVEN O. SHERIDAN, LICENSED PRIVATE DETECTIVES. Behind the window was a none-too-clean jalousie, its slats half closed to keep the scorching sunlight from showing what was inside.

A woman, smartly elegant in what could only be a navy Chanel suit with its form-fitted jacket and tight mid-calf length skirt, opened the door and the bell tinkled.

Mayday looked up from his desk as she came in. She was a good-looking brunette on the right side of twenty-five, her glossy hair styled in a short cut. She wore a matching pillbox hat and gloves.

Mayday was chewing on the end of an El Producto. His shirt sleeves were rolled up, his collar open, and his tie loosely knotted as he pecked at an old Royal typewriter. He wasn't at all elegant. He looked like a black Irish middleweight pug who knew it.

"I like your sign," she said, "especially the motto."

She didn't look like she liked it.

He pulled the cigar out of his mouth. "I think it's a dime store trick, but my partner insisted. It was his money that paid for the lease, so I said okay."

She nodded and languorously blinked. "Then you must be Steven O. Sheridan. The junior partner."

"Smart," Mayday said. "Maybe you're a detective yourself. If you are, I'm afraid we don't have any openings. Especially for somebody who can afford glad rags like yours."

She frowned. "I'm the one who's looking to hire, Mr. Sheridan. I heard you were trustworthy."

"Also loyal, helpful, friendly, courteous, kind, obedient, cheerful, thrifty, brave, clean, and reverent. Except for the reverent part. I have trouble with that one."

"Apparently you have trouble with the courteous part, too."

Mayday stood up. "Yeah, well, sorry. You're not our usual class of client and most of them think politeness is for pansies. Please have a seat, Miss——?"

"It's Mrs.," she said, "Mrs. Weatherford. Gilda Weatherford."

She sat down primly like she was expecting English tea and crumpets with clotted cream. Mayday dropped back into his chair.

She looked around the room. It was somewhat shabby with utilitarian office furniture and showed no signs of any attempt at decoration, except for a row of cheaply framed headshots of movie stars and a cheesecake calendar hanging on the wall behind the other desk, toward the back. The desk was nicer than Mayday's desk, but not by much.

Her face was as expressive as a department store mannequin. "You aren't actually 'sleuths to the stars,' are you? I've seen more glamor in a ballpark bathroom."

Mayday drew his mouth taut in a frown, thinking she'd be completely out of place at a ball game. But then Marilyn Monroe was married to Joe DiMaggio, like everybody knew. "I'll bet you have. No. The only stars Keogh sees are after barroom brawls. There was a time when he covered up the various indiscretions of the Hollywood elite—he was a fixer for one of the studios. Not me, though."

He bit down again on his cigar. "So what can I do for you?"

She withdrew a cigarette from her purse and waited for him to offer her a light. He reached into his desk drawer, removed a match from its box, and obliged. She drew on the cigarette and exhaled, turning her head away so he could admire her profile.

"Obviously I'm in trouble," she said. "You don't seem like a nice man, Mr. Sheridan. That's good. I can't use a nice man. But then, I'm not a nice lady."

"Tell me about it."

MAYDAY AND KEOGH split jobs between them, with Mayday getting most of the hack work. Keogh reserved the fat jobs, the house calls and business appointments, for himself. He usually only came into the office on Fridays to collect payments from clients or their flunkeys. The rest of the week he followed his own agenda. On Wednesday afternoons, he habituated an unnamed dive the two of them called Benny's because that was the bartender's name. Lately, though, with business down the way it was, Keogh had been spending most of the week there. That's where Mayday found him.

A neon sign advertising "BAR" glowed red in a window too small for a burglar to crawl through. Inside there were three scarred booths and eight tall stools at the bar, recently reupholstered in plastic. Keogh sat on one of them close to the door, a cigarette almost burned down to his fingers in his left hand and a can of Eastside Beer in front of him. Benny was behind the bar at the opposite end, reading a paperback with a lurid cover, ignoring him.

Keogh was a big florid man who had once been a redhead, but now had so much white in his hair that he looked blonde. He squinted at Mayday's silhouette against the bright afternoon light until the door swung shut.

"Mayday," he grunted. "Have you heard this one? Two Irish dicks walk into a bar—"

Mayday sat on the stool next to his partner. "You're drunk, Keyhole."

Keogh's face assumed a tragic mask. "Of course I'm drunk. Don't ever fall in love, Mayday."

"You wouldn't say that if you'd seen our new prospective client."

"A client," Keogh said, lifting the can. It was empty. "Benny, gimme another."

Benny closed his book and scowled, but opened the cooler behind the bar and retrieved another beer. He put it down in front of Keogh and slapped a church key beside it.

"Open it your own damn self," he said. "Can't you see I'm readin'?"

He went back to his paperback.

Keogh turned his attention back to Mayday. "So she's a tomato."

"Nobody says that anymore, Keyhole. But yeah, she's easy on the eye. Young, too—but based on her manner, I think she's seen a thing or two."

"What she want?"

"Says it's about blackmail, but there's something not right about it."

Keogh guffawed, the laugh expiring in a wheeze. "I like it. A looker being blackmailed, and who does she go to for help? Mayday Sheridan, that's who, the Bolshevik Detective. I can hear her plea: 'Please give help, *tovarishch*! I nowhere else to turn!'"—this last in an atrocious fake Russian accent—"and we both know you know all about blackmail. Not to mention gorgeous but dicey dames."

Mayday clenched his jaws and said nothing.

"What's the blackmail about?" Keogh asked.

"She wouldn't get specific. She asked me to come to her place tomorrow and she would explain everything."

"Well, that's nothing to get wound up over. She probably got the evidence locked up in a safe and don't want to carry it around."

"Maybe," Mayday said, rubbing his chin. "The thing about it is, I didn't like her and she didn't like me. She's not the kind of person who would normally have anything to do with a couple bums like us."

"Maybe somebody referred her."

Mayday snorted. "She was dolled up like Liz Taylor. None of our normal clients has ever been in the same room with a woman like her, let alone familiar enough with her to provide a recommendation. There's got to be an angle. If she knows anything about my Communist days, she could be bad news for both of us. There's nothing soft about her at all, Keyhole. Beautiful, yes, and I can see how some moonstruck pinhead would fall for her. But kissing her would be like making love to a marble statue. There's something wrong. It feels like a setup."

Keogh barked a laugh. "You think J. Edgar Hoover is going to waste some Bureau Mata Hari on a dumb mick two-bit gumshoe like you? Or maybe she's got a subpoena from HUAC. No, I got it, could it be the NKVD? Get serious, Mayday. You're about as important to any of them guys as bubblegum on a rubber boot. Most likely this broad's just looking for a guy who ain't afraid to get rough, and surprise, you and me answer the want ad."

"You didn't meet her. She's obviously loaded, probably born rich or married to money, but either way Daddy can get her anything she wants. And that means she's most likely connected. If all she wanted was to rent a couple thugs, I'm sure she could find somebody with a lot more class than us to do it for her, and nobody's the wiser. So why pick us?"

"I dunno. Maybe you're right." Keogh stubbed out what was left of his butt. "What did you say her name was?"

"I didn't, but it's Mrs. Gilda Weatherford."

"Never heard of her. But if she's what you say she is...and blackmail—that's like jumping into a strong riptide to save somebody who's just as likely to pull you down with her."

"Tell me something I don't know, Keyhole."

Keogh furrowed his forehead like he was having an internal debate.

Finally, he looked Mayday straight in the face and said, "Look, I haven't told you this before. Back when I was in the pictures racket,

must be twenty or twenty-five years, there was this little starlet who'd
been in a blue movie before she did the horizontal hula with a big
producer and got a studio contract. Right after she got her first
credit in a big feature, she receives this anonymous fan letter. Only it
ain't no fan letter. The upshot was if she didn't want nobody to find
out about her past, then it would cost her. Now, she believed this
blue movie had been destroyed, but turns out she was wrong. She
don't tell the studio, and she sure as hell don't tell the police. She's
got to keep it on the strict Q.T. or she's ruined. Instead, she comes to
me. She wants me to track down the blackmailer and make things
right, and frankly, I needed the dough."

The somber look on his mug wasn't a gag this time. He went on.

"So I track him down, never mind how, but it took a little time.
Turns out he was the camera operator for the nudie, but now, what
with the Depression and all, he can't find work shoveling manure in
a sewer. Since he can't make an honest living, he figures what the
hell, and decides he can still make a dishonest one. See, he kept his
own print of the blue movie, after all she was a sight like I said,
especially naked and all, and maybe he's nursing a crush or maybe
just horny, but one Saturday he seen her in that first big role at some
hick movie palace in Oklahoma or somewhere. What does he do?
The wheels start turning. So he hops a freight for L.A.

"Eventually I find him in a Santa Monica fleabag, and he's got
the film canisters with him. So I go over there to rough him up a
little and deprive him of the reels.

"I'm starting to explain things my own way to this punk when
the door to his room swings open, and there's my little starlet, cute
as a pixie in a picture book.

"'Maudie!' the guy cries. He figures she don't know who's
blackmailing her, so he acts like they're old friends. 'What're you
doing here?'

"'You want the long answer, or the short answer, Eddie?'

"'Short answer?' he says.

"'Okay,' she says, and suddenly this little chrome-plated .25
appears in her dainty white hand out of nowhere. *BLAM!* She plugs

him. *BLAM! BLAM!* The poor son of a bitch is dead before he hits the floor.

"'Clean things up for me, will you, Keyhole?' she says. She grabs the canisters and on her way out, she says, 'Not a word to anybody, you understand? Don't tell *anybody*, Keyhole.'"

"And before today, I didn't."

Keogh punched the can open with the church key and took a long swig. "I did what she asked, cleaned things up and got the hell out of there."

Mayday's face flushed with anger. He slowly pulled out a cigar from his inside jacket pocket and lit it. He drew on it and blew a plume like he was exhaling a sigh.

His voice was barely above a low growl when he finally spoke. "Partners for six years—six years—and now you tell me that you got away with being an accessory after the fact to a goddamn murder. Jesus, Keyhole."

"Yeah, not my finest hour. Today I'd do it different. But back...I did a lot of things, Mayday. You know that. Covering for matinee idols with secret lives and babysitting not-so-girl-next-door types doped to their pretty blue eyeballs as they puked their guts out in swanky hotel rooms. Keeping slicked up mobsters away from box office stars. Gently or not so gently reminding nosy reporters what they couldn't get away with. But this time—listen, the last thing I needed was to get wrapped up in a murder enquiry, especially in as sleazy a burg as Santa Monica was in them days."

Keogh lit one of his Chesterfields, shrugged, and examined his beer can.

"She came to me because she knew I was the right guy for the job," he said. "Not just because she knew I'd find the guy, but also because she knew for damn sure I couldn't do a thing to stop her, not without putting my own neck in a noose. And she was right."

"You should have told me."

Keogh shrugged. "You know, the funny thing about that gal was that she was always typecast as the innocent and naive kid sister of some smoldering femme fatale. I seem to remember that not long after, she married a wealthy Texas oilman or something and that was that.

"Anyway, you know now. So yeah, maybe you oughta think twice. Who needs the trouble?"

Mayday shook his head and knocked the ash off the end of his perfecto.

"Nobody." He frowned. "But, Keyhole, you already said it. Frankly, we need the dough."

Keogh closed his eyes. He was done talking.

MAYDAY HAD a room close by in the kind of run-down residential hotel that usually had no vacancy but where nobody was a neighbor. He spent that evening alone in it, and started with renewing his acquaintance with his old pal Jameson, one jigger at a time.

Stripped to his underwear, he opened the bottom drawer of his dresser and pulled out a small cardboard portfolio secured with string. Standing up unsteadily, he untied the string, and everything in the folder spilled out onto the floor.

Old photographs, letters, documents. A group picture of his old Young Communist League chapter, him grinning in the second row, unbearably callow. A cheap studio portrait of his first love, achingly beautiful. Smaller snapshots of his next two girlfriends, glowing like suns, and slightly blurred, as if they vibrated. He had no idea where any of them was were now.

His Honorable Discharge from the Army. Transcripts from his interrupted college career. Letters from friends, the script unreadable although he'd always been able to read them before.

The letter expelling him from the Party.

Mayday threw the shot glass across the room and it bounced off the wall without breaking when it landed on the cheap rug. But he held on to the bottle.

He pressed its mouth to his lips and drank deep, not noticing as the whisky spilled over his chin and chest and puddled on the floor, like so many wasted opportunities.

Eventually he sprawled across the bed, and did not sleep well.

LATE THE NEXT MORNING, Mayday drove to Mrs. Weatherford's Hancock Park address. It was a neighborhood better suited to Keogh's Packard 200, a car he had claimed was a gift from a former show biz client, than to Mayday's bargain-basement Crosley. If he parked at the curb, his car would stick out like black eye. So it was good he didn't have to.

She'd told him she didn't want to meet in the house, but that he should steer up the driveway to the detached garage behind it. The garage itself was bigger than a tract home and came with quarters for a chauffeur, at the entrance to which she casually stood waiting for him. She was dressed in black capris and a silk halter top, dangerously pretty. Her right hand held a cigarette between slim fingers, the elbow crooked up toward her shoulder.

She didn't smile or say hello. Instead, she said, "Let's go inside."

They entered a small living room dominated by a big Zenith console TV set and record player, opposite a divan and a maple surfboard coffee table. An easy chair that matched the divan was parked at the far end of the table. On the table itself were arranged a telephone, a large ceramic ashtray, a pack of Philip Morris cigarettes beside a table cigarette lighter, and a closed attaché case.

She gestured him toward the chair and he sat down. She seated herself on the divan, dropped her cigarette in the ashtray, and rotated the case so that when she opened it, he couldn't see what was inside.

"Before we get started, I need to know two things," she said. "First, do I have to tell you everything? About the blackmail?"

"I need to know what it is you need recovered, or I can't guarantee that I'll know it when I find it," he said. "Personally, I don't care what it is. None of my business. But trust me, I can keep a secret."

"That's not quite what I heard," she said, her face tight.

Mayday pursed his lips. "What have you heard?"

"That you ratted out all your Commie pals to the FBI."

He sat very still. "That's true. I don't know how you feel about it, you probably hate Communists, but it wasn't easy for me. I'm a man of conscience, Mrs. Weatherford, or at least I like to think of myself as one. But I had an impossible choice. I could either talk, or the woman I loved would be on her way to Leavenworth in a bus with bars on the windows. I'd think you might appreciate that I put her before anything else. Not that *she* did, because with her the Party always came first."

"Maybe I do appreciate it. But I needed to hear it from you."

"She and I had different ideas regarding which one of us made a better martyr. In the end, she went free. I, on the other hand, didn't, because I paid for her liberty with just about everything I had. I don't want that to happen to you." He pointed to the attaché. "Is that the evidence?"

"I said there were two things," she said. "I also need to know if you carry a gun."

"Only if I have to."

She nodded. "Yes, this is the evidence. And there's something else."

She reached inside the case. The next thing he knew she was pointing a snub-nosed .38 at his chest.

"I'm not the one being blackmailed, Mr. Sheridan. That's you. I'm the blackmailer."

For the first time since he'd met her, she smiled.

He brazenly returned it. "You said you weren't a nice lady. I'm glad to know you were telling me the truth. A lot of clients don't."

"Somehow you don't seem surprised."

"Let's just say that I suspected there was a reason you came to me instead of someone more your style. I wonder if you can point that thing somewhere else."

"I don't think so. You'll try to take it from me."

"I won't. Mrs. Weatherford, I don't hit women. Ever. And I know you aren't going to shoot me. That would pretty much defeat the purpose."

"Like you said, only if I have to."

"You don't have to. What is it that you want? You know I don't have any money."

"Money?" She laughed. "Do I look like I need money?"

"I repeat. What is it that you want?"

"Light me a cigarette. I can't do it and hold a gun on you at the same time."

He put one between his lips and flipped the lid to the lighter. He puffed the cigarette to life and held it out to her. She took it, the gun unwavering, and took a deep drag.

"That was easy," he said. "Anything else?"

"Don't be cute. What I want is Kevin Keogh's head on a plate. And you're going to get it for me. After all, you should be used to betraying your friends."

Mayday's eyebrows shot up.

She smirked. "It's justice, Mr. Sheridan. And to get it, I'm going to use Kevin Keogh's own methods against him."

"So that's it," he said, almost to himself. "Now I get it."

"Do you?" Her voice was hard and resentful.

"I think so. It's all about blackmail, isn't it? Yesterday, Keyhole told me a strange story, about something I never would have imagined, and I wondered why. He said he was trying to talk me out of taking your case, and I suppose he was, but he had another reason, too."

"What do you mean?"

"He said that twenty years ago he got suckered into a murder by a starlet who was being blackmailed. You're too young for it to have been you, so it must have been somebody very close to you. Your mother?"

"That's right, Mayday."

The voice wasn't hers. It was Keogh's.

He stood on the threshold with a .45 pointed at both of them. Mrs. Weatherford jumped to her feet and turned to point her gun at him, but he was too quick. He grabbed her wrist, twisted it, and the .38 dropped to the floor. Keogh covered it with his left foot and let go of her. She tried to stab him with her cigarette but he simply crushed it and threw it away. He pointed his pistol in her face. The fight went out of her.

"Sit down, sister," he said. She obeyed and almost fell down.

Keeping his automatic covering both Mayday and the woman, Keogh squatted and picked her gun up with his left hand. "That's better."

"Let me guess. I'm going to get it with the .38, and the lady's getting shot with the .45." Mayday leaned back in the chair. "Neat."

"Yeah, it worked out after all," said Keogh, grinning. "I tell you I've been sweating like a tied-up pig at a Carolina barbecue. That's the trouble with murder. No statute of limitations and too many loose ends. Who'd have figured I'd have to tie up so many after a goddamn quarter century?"

"And with another murder," said Mayday. "A double one, this time. Don't you think that's a bit sloppy, Keyhole? Even for a bottle baby like you?"

"Shut up."

"What for? You think I'm too stupid to figure it out?"

"Of course you're stupid. Only a dope turns himself into a Red out of love. Why'd you think I took you on in the first place? I figured a detective agency would be the perfect cover for my real business, but to make it work, I needed a detective without much brains to make it seem entirely legit. And there you were."

"All this time I thought it *was* legit, so you got me there, Keyhole. But then yesterday, I realized it wasn't, not after you volunteered that you'd been an accessory to murder. Why would you confess like that?

"After six years hearing all your applesauce, Keyhole, I've noticed you have a weak spot. Usually you're as cheery as a used car salesman, like you are right now—but when you're lying, you turn as grim as an undertaker, so people will think you're giving it to them straight. And that's exactly how you talked to me yesterday. I knew then that you had to be covering something up, something even worse than accessory to murder.

"I didn't understand all the ins and outs of it until today, not until Mrs. Weatherford told me what she wanted. But now I bet I can tell you almost everything."

Keogh grinned again. "Then why don't you try it on? This I gotta hear."

"Sure. Mrs. Weatherford, Keyhole never told me your mother's name, but he called her 'Maudie.' If you don't mind, that's what I'll call her."

"Her real name was Magdalena Schultz," Mrs. Weatherford said angrily. "Never mind what her stage name was. That's not who she was. Maudie was a nickname. She was just an innocent girl from Milwaukee trying to break into Hollywood until this...this monster got to her."

Mayday shook his head. "You can't really believe she was that naive. There's not a lot of that going around in Hollywood. She knew how unknown actresses get ahead in this town, and she was willing to do whatever it took."

"That's not true!"

"Of course it is. Keyhole told me she'd been in a blue movie, but most girls in Hollywood aren't that stupid, not unless there's a big payoff. I think it was what you might call a special screen test, a very private audition filmed at a producer's home instead of on a sound stage, for his personal collection—that sort of thing is all too common."

She wouldn't look at him.

"Keyhole was a fixer, and I bet he arranged the whole thing. As a basis for blackmail, such a film would be useless to him, because he couldn't use it against Maudie without also exposing the producer. There's no way he could do that without the studio finding out about it, and that would've been the kiss of death. So he had to find a way to get some other leverage. And he found it. In Eddie."

"You don't have to listen to him, sweetheart," Keogh said. He nonchalantly leaned back against the doorjamb, keeping the pistols trained. "Go ahead and cover your ears if you want. But I'm dying to hear the rest."

"The whole thing fell right into your lap, Keyhole. Eddie was

Maudie's bit on the side, probably in Hollywood for the same reason she was, to break into pictures. I'll bet he was strong and handsome, a regular cowboy type, but not very bright. In the meantime, though, there's a rich Texan who's also paying court to her, and she's not about to give him up, so her entanglement with Eddie is kept as discreet as she can manage. But then something must have gone wrong. I don't know what it was…"

"She got pregnant," Mrs. Weatherford said. "With me. They weren't as careful as they thought."

Mayday nodded. "I guessed it might be something like that. All I knew was that she must've turned to you, Keyhole. If she was pregnant, she must have been desperate. You're the fixer, right? She hoped you'd somehow take care of it. Only you saw an opportunity. You stole the reel, I don't know how, probably during some wild party, and then you followed her one night when she stole out to meet Eddie.

"Killing Eddie was easy. Then you showed the reel to Maudie, explaining to her that unless she does as you say, you'll tell the whole world that Eddie was blackmailing her with it and she shot him to shut him up. Folks love a scandal, don't they? She's cornered.

"If she wants to marry the Texan, she's got to play ball. So she does. A few months later, Gilda must have come along, and I bet Maudie paid you like clockwork for years. Until recently, that is. Somehow you found out about it, Mrs. Weatherford, and decided to do something."

"She found out because I told her about it," said Keogh. "Only I gave her the same story I gave you. See, Maudie's dead. Drank herself six feet under six months ago. I wasn't about to give up that cash cow, and I figured what's good for the bitch is good for the pup, so I contacted her. But then she goes and hires you, of all people. I got to admit, I never saw that coming. You figured it out almost exactly right, Mayday, except that Maudie's husband wasn't no Texan, he was strictly a California oilman. All these years I watched Gilda grow up, right here in L.A., where I could keep tabs on her. Until she turned to you. I knew I had to tell you something."

"So you killed my father, too," Mrs. Weatherford said, glassy-eyed. "And now—now I guess it's my turn."

Keogh frowned. "I was going to let you live, even today, until Mayday goes and opens his trap about what I really did. Hell, I could use more money, and the blackmail still would've worked fine. But now I can't, can I? You want your revenge too much. What do I do now?"

He smiled and pushed away from the door. "But I've always been lucky. Seems you've solved that little problem for me, by compiling that dossier there on my partner, in order to coerce him into doing your dirty work. Damn. It's downright poetic."

"What do you mean?" she asked.

"He means that history is about to repeat itself," Mayday said, shifting easily in the chair. "He set it up so that it would seem like your mother killed your father because he was blackmailing her. Now he's going to make it seem like I killed you for the same reason. Only this time, he's also going to kill me, to make it look like you shot me in self-defense."

"Maybe you ain't so stupid after all, Mayday," Keogh said, and then he started to laugh. "What'm I saying? Of course you are. I'm the one who's got the guns, right? Seeing how much you like to talk, I may as well deal with you first, Mayday. I'm almost sorry to say it, but adios, chump. This will probably hurt. That, I ain't sorry about."

He raised his left hand, the one gripping Mrs. Weatherford's .38.

BLAM! BLAM! BLAM!

But it wasn't the .38 that barked. A smoking Browning semi-auto was in Mayday's hand, drawn from where he had tucked it under his belt. Mrs. Weatherford screamed and leapt to her feet. The big man barely had time to express his disbelief before he collapsed.

"But I…I thought you said you didn't have a gun," she cried, her trembling voice just shy of hysteria.

"No, Mrs. Weatherford," Mayday said, bending over to make sure Keogh was dead. "What you heard me say is that I only carried a gun if I needed to. Remember? You even threw the same words right back at me. Well, the truth is I figured that I probably would need to, so I did. Good thing, too."

He shut up, realizing he was talking too much. He reached over to the attaché and shut it.

"I think I'll keep this, if it's all the same to you."

But Mrs. Weatherford was paying him no attention. Staring down at Keogh's sprawled body, she sat down unsteadily on the divan and then tilted over onto her side, covering her face. She began to cry, loudly at first, her weeping eventually abating to a series of shuddering but muted whimpering.

Mayday stood there, feeling the weight of the attaché case in his left hand. He looked out the door with longing. Then he dropped the case, placed the Browning on the table, and picked up the phone.

He dialed 0.

"Operator. How may I direct your call?" She sounded like a nice lady. It was soothing to listen to a nice lady.

"Get me the Wilshire Police Station," he said.

"Is this an emergency?"

"No. Not anymore."

"Thank you. Just a moment, please." He listened to the signal of a ringing phone, and then a male voice picked up. "Wilshire Police Station."

"Detective Burnes, please."

"Please hold."

There was a short pause.

"Burnes."

Mayday drew a deep breath. "This is Mayday Sheridan. Remember me?"

Another pause. "Yeah, I remember you all too well, you dirty Commie bastard. What the hell do you want?"

Mayday had no idea how any of this would play out, but he'd had enough of secrets. It would go however it went, and he'd face it.

But he couldn't keep the bitterness out of his voice.

"Do you want the long answer, or the short answer?"

JUDY PENZ SHELUK

Judy Penz Sheluk (editor/author) is the author of two mystery series: the Glass Dolphin Mysteries and the Marketville Mysteries. Her short stories appear in several collections, including *Live Free or Tri* and *The Best Laid Plans: 21 Stories of Mystery & Suspense*, which she also edited. Judy is a member of Sisters in Crime National, Toronto, and Guppy Chapters, the Short Mystery Fiction Society, International Thriller Writers, South Simcoe Arts Council, and Crime Writers of Canada, where she serves on the Board of Directors.

Find her at judypenzsheluk.com.

GOULAIGANS

JUDY PENZ SHELUK

THERE'S a place about twenty miles north of Sault Ste. Marie, Ontario, called Goulais River. Now, you might be tempted to pronounce it the French way—Goo-lay—or the way it reads phonetically—Goo-lays—but either way you'd be wrong. You see, up in these parts, it's Goo-lee, and the residents are known as Goulaigans, rhymes with hooligans, just so we have our facts straight.

I'm telling you all of this because not much happens in Goulais River, which is what you'd expect for a town with a population of thirty-six hundred people in twenty-three hundred dwellings. Oh sure, there's the occasional bear spotting, a bald eagle here and there, solitary paddlers in kayaks and canoes, not to mention the summertime sensationalists who seem to enjoy thrashing about Lake Superior on their jet-skis. But overall, it's a quiet place where folks tend to mind their own business, which brings me to this particular story.

THE WAVES WERE ROLLING in hard and rough that day, the way they do when the wind is from the northwest, leastwise where my camp is situated. Wind from the south, Superior's flat as a mirror, though that can change faster than my ex-wife, Laura's, most recent unreasonable demand.

I was sitting on the dock, alternating between reading the latest Clive Cussler and attempting to toss a fishing line into the swirling water, when I spotted a swatch of bright orange fabric a few yards down the beach.

I pulled myself up out of my Muskoka chair with a grunt. Darned things are comfy enough when you're sitting in them, but the way the back is slanted can make them a bugger to get out of, especially if you're carrying a few extra pounds around the middle. I slid my feet into a pair of well-worn water sandals and inched my way over, careful not to slip or stumble on the rocky shoreline.

It was a Personal Floatation Device, firmly jammed into a crevice in the rocks. I'll admit to feeling relieved that it wasn't attached to a body. We'd had a decent summer so far, more hot days than not, so the water temperature was hovering in the mid-teens, though that could slide a few degrees on either side depending on the depth of the water. Get out deep enough and a body could get hypothermic real quick.

My first thought was that someone had either tossed it or lost it; nobody around these parts is crazy enough to navigate Superior without wearing some sort of PFD.

And then I spotted the canoe.

It was a yellow canvas-covered cedar strip canoe, weather-beaten by time and water, the sort of canoe Joe Tucker rented at Tuck's Trading Post. It had been pulled up on shore and tilted carelessly on its side, paddles and a plastic baggie with maps spewed out onto the ground, as if someone had left in a powerful hurry.

A quick inspection of the canoe revealed Tuck's moose head logo on the side. I didn't see a flashlight or a compass, which led me to believe that the paddler had taken them with him. Either that or they'd been sucked into the bowels of Superior, two more artefacts to add to its collection.

Whoever had paddled here knew the area. The cabin on the

property had burned down five years ago, the charred remains of wood, concrete, and shingles strangled by weeds and scrub brush. The rest of the two-acre lot was heavily treed, making it all but invisible from the water or the road. Every now and again a "For Sale" sign would go up at the end of the narrow, rutted driveway, only to come down again when the listing expired a few months later.

It could have sold, despite the condition, frontage on Superior being a real selling point, but there was a long history of violence, starting with a prospector who'd been found, frozen in the woods, to the not-so-accidental fire that had left a husband and his cheating wife engulfed in flames. Murder-suicide: that had been the verdict, and I thought, at the time, that there had to be a better way.

There were plenty more incidents in-between, if local legend was right, but you should be spared the gruesome details. Suffice it to say that some folks thought the property was haunted. Others would tell you it was cursed. Either way, this was one unlucky place, and I didn't plan to linger longer than was absolutely necessary.

That made it time to go to Tuck's.

TUCK'S TRADING POST is a one-stop shopping general store, should you be willing to pay moderately inflated prices for the convenience of not having to make the forty-minute trek into the Soo for your supplies. Within those rustic walls you can find everything from five-dollar packages of no-name hot dogs to fishing and camping gear, basic hardware supplies—nails, screws, that sort of thing—bird seed, dog and cat food, and the usual assortment of cheesies, chips, and chocolate bars. There was also a propane bar, two gas pumps—one diesel, one regular—a small lumber yard at the back of the property, and, of course, the canoe rentals.

JOE TUCKER WAS the sort of guy that men liked and women loved.

I happened to know this firsthand because I used to like him, at least until my ex-wife Laura fell in love with him. He ambled over to me, his gray eyes crinkled with curiosity. It shouldn't surprise you that I'd stopped shopping there. Hadn't seen Tucker in a good three years. It pleased me to see how much Laura had aged him.

"I found one of your canoes," I said, sparing us both the "hey there, how's it going" pleasantries. "A yellow one. Out at the old Donaldson place." Donaldson was the name of the frozen-in-the-woods prospector. Didn't matter the property had been bought and sold a dozen times since, didn't matter how many bodies the land claimed, to us Goulaigans, it would always be the old Donaldson place.

"I didn't think I'd see it again," Tucker said. "Fella rented it a few days ago, guy with a beard. I haven't seen him or the canoe since. Is it in one piece?"

"It is. Found a PFD, too, though it's a bit worse for wear." I explained how I found it lodged into the crevice of a rock.

"Appreciate you stopping by to let me know. I'll head over there later on, collect everything." He started to walk away.

"How's Laura?"

If Tucker was surprised to hear me ask about my ex, he didn't show it.

"If you must know, she left me. Said she was tired of being a Goulaigan. Now if you'll excuse me, I've got a store to run."

Laura's body washed up on shore three days later, about a mile from the old Donaldson place.

"Whatever happened to Superior not giving up its dead?" Tucker asked me. We were sitting in my cabin, sipping on twelve-year-old whiskey. Now that Laura was gone, we could be friends again. Or at least pretend to be.

My mind replayed the lyrics to the Gordon Lightfoot song, *The Wreck of the Edmund Fitzgerald.* It was a favourite on the radio up here,